She remembered the pain... Not the type of pain that you feel when you stub your toe, or slice your hand open with a kitchen knife. No, this pain was more than any she had ever experienced before in her life. It was as if someone had peeled away her flesh, strip by agonizing strip, and for good measure decided to replace the blood in her veins with acid. Each beat of her own heart brought on a new bout of agony that she could only imagine would end with her death. The room was filled with the sounds of screams that she didn't realize came from her until she could scream no more. Instead of the cries of anguish, she let out hoarse whimpers. The feeling of pins and needles in her throat was like a balm in comparison to the rest of her body. Fun times...

Chapter One

A few days earlier...

Leena couldn't believe that she had let herself be talked into going to a freaking night club...again. Most people would assume that at her age of twenty-five she would enjoy the party scene, but really she had no interest. Her repulsion didn't even stem from a lack of dancing abilities. Sometime around her tenth birthday, when she started spending a lot of time with her brother and father becoming more familiar with the underside of a car than the layout of a dollhouse, her mother had insisted on starting her in dance classes. Much to everyone's surprise, she has been dancing ever since. To this day Leena participated in dance competitions as well as owning a dance studio where she teaches dance to others. This, however, she could hardly call dancing. In most cases, it looked as if the men were using the thump of the music, and the alcohol that they likely had consumed in order to excuse themselves for their hands wandering up the skirts of the women that they were dancing with. And the women were using it as an excuse to let them. In one instance, a couple that Leena passed was actually having sex in the shadowed corner of the club.

Shaking her head as she passed, she continued on in her pursuit. With each step she rose up even further on her tip-toes than the four inch heels already forced her to be. Gaze sweeping the crowd, her vision caught just a moment on a couple "dancing." The woman was standing in front of the man, bent over at the waist, grinding her rear into his crotch. What was actually impressive to Leena was that she was able to keep time to the beat of the song with both of her hands and feet touching the ground. That required some skill, she supposed.

Moving on, she scanned the sea of gyrating bodies, rewarded in her attempts with a few blinding flashes of the blue and red spotlights that hung from the ceiling, swiveling about for some sort of effect—what kind, she really wasn't sure. They had so many decorations from different eras and themes that Leena couldn't help but wonder if the decorator had known what he was doing, or if he was drunk at the time. There was a disco ball over the middle of the dance floor, the aforementioned swiveling spotlights, and cages and poles where half naked women danced. The bar lining the room had an old diner feel to it; mostly aluminum, with red vinyl covering the stools in front of the counter top. A hip-hop song that Leena was unfamiliar with was blaring over the sound system, offering just enough contradictions to have one wondering just what kind of club this was supposed to be.

On her third sweep of the club Leena finally spotted her sister, Amy—the crazy woman that had dragged her to this ridiculous place—dancing with two men near the bar, where Leena had been sitting before nature called. You would think that after having lived together for most of their lives Amy would know her well enough to realize that this is not something Leena would consider fun. And to think that she came all the way to South Carolina for this. If this was Amy's idea of fun, she would have been better off traveling up to Pittsburgh to see her. Living within a fifteen minute drive of the town of South Side, there would have been far more options to choose from. Ones that had more of a coherent motif.

Shouldering her way through the cluster of people, Leena made her way to her sister as swiftly as the dense crowd would allow, using the balance that her dance training required just to keep herself on her feet. When she finally reached them, the men turned to face her and she noticed that neither of them was the same man that she had seen Amy with last. *What is that now, numbers six and seven?* Frowning, Leena shook her head in disapproval.

Although, she probably shouldn't be too disappointed in her sister…yes, she had a husband, and even a baby now, but she was just dancing. She also couldn't blame her because she knew that Amy did not seek these men out, they flocked to her. They always had.

In school, just about every boy had tried to get his hands on Amy. Not that Leena minded. Much better Amy than her. She did always wonder though, what she must have been projecting for men to decide not to bother with her, even then. She assumed that it wasn't because of her looks, mainly because she and Amy looked so similar that they had been mistaken for twins on more than one occasion. Both had naturally tanned skin that came from a combination of their Native American great-grandmother and the ivory skin of their European father. They even had the same body type, if you take away the fact that dancing gave Leena thicker muscles in her thighs and rear. What set them apart was the thick ebony hair and matching dark brown eyes that Amy had inherited from their Native background, while Leena got the auburn hair and dark blue eyes from their father. If she were being honest, though, Leena knew that the main thing that set them apart was Amy's *joie de vivre*. She enjoyed every moment of her life, while Leena had always been more of a "nose to the grindstone" kind of girl.

Working, whether it had been at her schoolwork, her dancing, in her father's garage, or her hobby of throwing knives, Leena always put all of herself into everything she did. When it came to the opposite sex, however, Leena had always shied away. Each and every time a man had made the attempt to get close to her—the rare occasion that it was—Leena had always kept them at an arm's length; a part of her knowing right off the bat that he wasn't the man for her. Of course, a woman had needs—even if they were never completely satisfied—which was where her live-in boyfriend had come in. She was beginning to see though, that she was driving him away as she had everyone else, his frustration evident each time he tried to get close to her.

No, don't think about that right now, she chastised herself. This was not the time or the place to reflect on her personal issues. Instead, she reached out to Amy and grabbed her hand to get her attention. Amy whipped her head in Leena's direction, and when she saw who it was, she threw her arms around her neck and screamed.

"Leena! Where've you been?"

Fantastic…she was *trashed.* The alcohol on her breath was strong enough that as she spoke Leena was getting light-headed just from the smell of it. With the small steps that Amy had taken she barely stayed upright, and after releasing her hold on Leena's neck, she went back to clutching the bar stool next to her for support, somehow managing to make her drunken swagger move in time with the music.

"I was in the bathroom," Leena answered.

"Oh, okay." Amy responded, and Leena doubted that she actually heard what she had said, or even remembered that she had asked.

Amy continued to move and sway, while Leena shifted uncomfortably next to her, torn between the desire to ask her if they could leave and the need to keep her sister happy. It was a compulsion that Leena was so used to that she hardly registered when she was doing it anymore. As strong and forceful as she could be in certain aspects of her life, she could never be that way with Amy. When it came to Amy, Leena felt like a five year old girl looking for the approval of her big sister all over again.

Amy brought her attention back to Leena, looking rather contrite as she said, "Oh, I'm being rude…"

Perhaps it was her uncontrollable urge to grab her sister by the arm and haul her out to the car, but part of Leena thought that Amy had seen her distress and decided that it was time to leave. She should have known that her luck wasn't that good. What Amy ended up doing was tap each of the men hovering over her and say, "Guys, this is my sister, Leena."

Actually, "Leena" was not the name she had been given at birth, but rather a nickname that had been instilled by her father when she was little. Kalina was her name. Kalina Abrams. Her mother was the only person that actually called her Kalina, though. Her father had started calling her Leena because he thought that the name Kalina was far too feminine for his wild daughter that would rather play with a carburetor than a Barbie doll, and everyone she met seemed to agree.

Growing up, people assumed that Leena hung around her father's garage in an attempt to win his affections, and that's why she had turned out the way that she had. In actuality, her father had treated each of his children equally. It just so happened that Leena enjoyed getting dirty and greasy. The satisfaction that came with fixing or building something with your bare hands was not comparable to anything Leena had felt while combing a doll's hair three hundred times a day. Her father had been shocked the day that Leena had decided to open up a dance studio, but he was ready to be as supportive as he always had been. She loved him for that. His astonishment quickly turned to amusement when she told him that she was using the second half of the building as a metal shop. She fondly remembered his booming laughter ringing throughout the house while her mother's smile faded to a glare.

Out of habit, Leena placed her hand just over her left breast as tears stung her eyes. God, she missed that man. He was always so tough and imposing on the outside, but he was a big softy when it came to his children.

Determined not to cry, Leena blinked back the tears that threatened to fall.

Leena turned away from her sister and the men dancing with her to deal with her grief privately. As she turned though, her arm was snatched up by the man that had been dancing in front of Amy. He gave one good tug, pulling Leena between his body and Amy's before she could do anything to stop him. He placed his meaty paws on her hips, digging his fingers into her, and forcing her to sway her hips back and forth, rubbing her ass across his pelvis. She tried pushing him away and asking him to let her go, but instead his grip on her tightened—enough that she would be bruised come morning—and he pressed her even closer to him, if that were at all possible.

Frustration boiled within her. She realized that he was trying to get her to lighten up and have a good time, but the brutality that he was using to get his way was unacceptable to Leena. Without thinking, she reacted, doing something that her father had taught her a long time ago. She wrapped her small hands around his beefy ones, and rather than try to pry herself from his grip again, she squeezed his hands, grinding the bones to his fingers together. The curse he let out was so satisfying that Leena couldn't hold back a grin; especially since it caused him to release his hold on her. Served the bastard right.

That episode pushed Leena toward her boiling point. She didn't care how much fun Amy was having, or how much she wanted to please her sister, she wanted to leave. Now. As she shoved the idiot's hands away, she leaned in close to Amy and yelled over the music so that she could be heard. "Can we go now?"

Amy glanced at the clock that hung behind the bar and frowned. "But it's only one o'clock. We've only been here for a few hours."

Pssh. That was a few hours too many if you asked Leena. Rather than blurt that out, though, she frowned at her sister. Making sure to add just the right amount of pitiful, but not overdoing it, she pleaded, "Please, Aim?"

She must have conjured the perfect amount of forlornness, because Amy sighed and then nodded. Leena tried to hide her triumphant smile, but it was unnecessary. Amy had already turned away from her to say goodbye to the two men that she had been dancing with. Leena supposed she should feel sorry for cutting her sister's night short. It's not often that Amy gets to go out and have a good time, but at that moment she couldn't muster the remorse. She had already indulged Amy enough by agreeing to come to this place.

Leena allowed herself to relax and smile for the first time that night. The smile didn't last long though. As she waited for Amy, Leena felt a shiver run down her spine, and she tensed. She knew that feeling. It only ever happened when she was being watched. Trying not to show her reaction, Leena turned slowly and looked about the dance floor as casually as she could manage. It should have been easy to track down the person that caused her unease. Most of the people in the vicinity had their heads either bowed or thrown back as they danced. But, after a few sweeps of the crowd she came up with nothing. *Weird…*

"Okay, ready." Amy shouted at her ear. The words were enough to shake Leena's unease, and, without delay, she grabbed Amy's hand and began shepherding her to the exit.

It seemed to take forever to reach the front door. This time, as Leena pushed through the crowd, she had to try to hold on to her sister, so that she could both support her, and so that they wouldn't get separated. With every few steps her heels stuck to the floor in what she kept telling herself was spilled alcohol. If it was anything else, she had no desire to know the truth.

She was pushed and shoved. Elbowed and stepped on. Did people not understand the words "excuse me" anymore? She felt as if she were on the television show that her brother enjoyed watching, where the contestant had to make their way across a seemingly impossible obstacle course. As the door loomed in front of her, she couldn't help but remember that most of the contestants were in the home stretch, end in sight, when they were thrown from the course and disqualified.

Finally they reached the front door, but before they could leave, a bouncer began interrogating Leena about being designated driver and waving a flashlight in front of her eyes. He studied her reactions, both voluntary and involuntary, before he deemed her fit to drive. Briefly, she wondered what he would have done if she had been drinking, but thought she'd rather not ask.

As all of this was going on Amy — not quite the patient one — began dancing around to the music that was spilling out from the open door of the club. She jumped around, throwing her hands in the air and bumping her hip against Leena's, and anyone else's that walked past her. Despite Leena's previous reservations, she let out a chuckle at how little inhibition her sister had while she was drunk.

She reached out to Amy, in an attempt to guide her to the car. Before her hand clasped Amy's, however, a foreign hand grabbed Leena on her ass, and gave a rough squeeze. Pain shot through Leena as the drunken douche bag squeezed her even tighter. That was *enough!* She was so sick of this group of patrons pushing her about, and grabbing at her. She was so far beyond her breaking point that she couldn't see past the red in her vision.

Acting entirely on instinct, and before she even realized what she was doing, Leena grabbed the hand from her ass, spun around, and twisted it behind the culprit's back, giving his elbow and extra thrust upward for good measure. The hiss of pain she earned gave her immense satisfaction.

"Jeez, bitch. Chill out." The younger man yelled. "It was just a joke." He couldn't have been more than twenty-one years old. He was probably out drinking with his friends for the first time in his life. Already, he was pretty toasted, which is the only reason that Leena let him keep the hand that had more likely than not bruised her tender flesh.

"It was a funny one too," she spat back at him. "Learn some respect, asshole." She placed her free hand between the guy's shoulder blades and shoved him away from her. He stumbled at first, but quickly regained his footing, turning quickly to glare daggers at her. Normally, Leena would feel bad after doing something like that, but right now, the only thing that she could do was meet him scowl-for-scowl.

Sure, he was upset at having been humiliated in front of his friends, who were currently laughing at him, but Leena couldn't muster the compassion for his bruised ego. She had been disrespected enough for one day. She couldn't believe that this boy—for that's what he seemed to be acting like—was so close in age to her. He may be in his twenties, but his maturity level was on par with a fifteen year old. The insults that he started calling out to her were proof enough of that. Instead of feeling regret for the way he had treated her, he lashed out at her as if she were the one that went after him at random.

A trip from Amy brought Leena's attention back from the idiot boy to her sister, who was now sprawled out on the pavement. She didn't seem to have any scrapes from her fall, but Leena doubted she would have noticed even if she had. She was giggling like a schoolgirl as Leena peeled her off of the cement and set her back on her feet, this time keeping a good grip on her hand to be ready for the next time.

The moment her feet hit the ground, Amy had started dancing again. Even without music she danced the entire walk to the car, while Leena dug for the car keys in her handbag, and while she tried to stuff Amy into the car. Finally she seemed to calm once Leena settled her into the passenger seat, replacing her incessant movement with incessant talking.

As she drove Amy's little Ford back to her house, Leena missed her own vehicle. Her Jeep would have had her sitting higher from the ground, and, while the ride would have been bumpier, it would have made her feel safer with its custom roll cage and brush guard, instead of the plastic bumpers and fenders of the Ford.

It was about fifteen minutes later when Leena was pulling the sedan into the driveway of Amy's two story red-brick house, putting the car into park, and then turning off the engine. She stepped out of the car, and being away from the crowd of people she was finally able to relax. She titled her head back and inhaled deeply, reveling in the smells of the outdoors. The wind lifted her hair from her shoulders as it carried the crisp saltiness of the nearby ocean. The humidity in the air was palpable and, surprisingly, soothing. The night was beautiful. Hardly a cloud in the sky, and this far from downtown Charleston, you could see the thousands of stars twinkling above.

Hearing the passenger door open brought Leena back to the moment at hand, and she quickly walked around the car to help Amy climb out of it. Apparently inebriation caused one to forget exactly how to get out of a vehicle, because Amy was attempting to crawl out, head first when Leena made it around the car to set her right. After dragging her to her feet, they walked side by side to the front door, Leena using every ounce of strength she could muster to keep her sister standing.

As she fumbled with the keys in front of the main door, Leena again experienced the creeping feeling that someone was watching her. She snapped her head around quickly, attempting to catch the person before they saw any movements from her. Again, there was nothing out of the ordinary.

Hmm, perhaps one of the neighbors had just glanced out of their window to see what the noise was about.

Dismissing the tingling sensation, she shoved the key into the lock of the door and turned it, all-the-while trying to support her sister. Before she had the chance to push the door open, someone else pulled it from the inside, the unexpectedness of it making her lose her footing and stumble.

Standing in the doorway, with his arms crossed over his chest, was Amy's husband, Matthew. Whereas most husbands would probably be pretty pissed to have his wife come home at about 1:30 in the morning, completely hammered, Matt just stood there grinning while Leena struggled to support his wife.

"Rough night?" He asked, his voice dripping with barely contained laughter.

"You could say that," Leena gritted out, which seemed to entertain him even more because his grin turned to a soft chuckle.

He let her struggle a bit longer, watching in amusement as Leena tried to get Amy moving again, before he stepped forward, taking Amy's arm and pulling it over his shoulder, supporting all of her weight. He was at the perfect height to pull that off. At about 5'11 he was only about an inch taller than her with her heels on. Whispering loving words in her ear, he turned with her and half-carried her back into the kitchen.

Closing the front door, Leena followed him and squinted as the light reflected off of the white tile surfaces and hit her eyes. The room was brighter than a room had any right to be after she had been surrounded by darkness for the last five hours. She blinked rapidly to try to rid herself of the burning sensation that came with the harsh lighting as she blindly made her way to the island in the middle of the kitchen and dropped herself onto one of the bar stools.

Matt hoisted Amy into the bar stool next to her and then walked over to the sink as Amy draped herself across the island and put her head on her arm. He pulled out a bottle of aspirin and a glass, filling it with water, and placed it in front of Amy. As Matt attempted to nip Amy's hangover in the bud by coaxing her to consume aspirin and water, Leena felt her chest tighten with a pang of jealousy. Jason would never be as sweet with her as Matt was being toward Amy. While she was extremely happy that her sister had found someone to love, and care for her, Leena couldn't help but wonder if she would ever find the same. Real life never seemed to be like the books that she found herself reading, or the films that she watched. She didn't have someone that she couldn't stand to be without, someone that she thought about at every moment of every day. In fact, as she considered this, she just realized that she hadn't even called Jason yet that day to let him know that she had arrived safely. She should probably be concerned by that fact.

With an inward shrug, she pulled her phone from her clutch, and flipped through the call history, making note of the fact that she had to scroll quite a bit to find Jason's name.

"Who are you calling?" Amy demanded after she gulped down another drink of water. She tried to reach for the phone but decided it was too much of an effort and dropped her arm hard enough that the smack of skin on granite reverberated throughout the room.

Leena smiled at her sister's drunken stupor, and then answered, "Jason," at the same time touching the screen where his name was, connecting the call.

Amy mumbled something unintelligible, of which, Leena only caught the words "ugh" and "douche." She had always known that Amy didn't care for Jason, and the fact that she was drunk eliminated what little filter her sister normally possessed. In all that time, though, Amy had never given Leena a reason as to why she didn't like him. Granted, he wasn't without his faults, but he had his good points. It had been about two years since they met. Leena had been closing up her studio for the night, when she turned and walked into Jason, knocking them both to the ground. After jumping to her feet, and apologizing to him profusely, Leena had turned to walk away, but he had stopped her, asking her for her number. She politely declined, but he was persistent. He came back to her studio over and over for the next few days until she had finally agreed to go out with him.

She had secretly wondered if staying with him so long was due to cowardice, but she never admitted that to anyone before. She was supposed to be the strong one. How could she admit to her family that the she was afraid of something, let alone something that they never would have expected of her? She had always been independent, even as a young girl. How could she tell her family that she was afraid of never finding someone to love her as unconditionally has her father had loved her mother?

After several rings, Jason answered her call, breaking her from her musings. "Hey, babe," he said, sounding breathless, presumably having to run to answer the phone. "How's your trip?"

"Good." Leena answered, trying to sound convincing. "I got in around six, and then Amy and I went out dancing."

"That's great, babe."

She could tell that he wasn't really listening to her, and that he was on auto-response, but she didn't comment on it. Especially since Amy seemed to be listening intently to their conversation. She was saved from having to think of a response when she heard an unfamiliar voice in the background, and instead she asked, "Who was that?" curious as to who would be over at this time of night.

He hesitated for a moment then said, "Oh, no one. That was the TV. I just walked past it."

"It didn't sound like a TV."

"It was," he said flatly.

Leena had always been good at reading people. The tone of their voices, their body language, their ticks and tells. Even over the phone, she could tell that Jason was lying to her. She should have called him on it, and at any other point in time, she may have, but just then, in Amy's over-exaggerated mocking of Jason, she had fallen off of her stool.

"Oh, shit!" Leena shouted. "Amy, are you alright?" Her sister turned on the floor to face her, giggling like crazy. Matt picked her up off of the floor, as Leena said into her phone, "Jason, I have to go. I need to help Amy."

"Alright, 'bye babe."

"'Bye."

She ended the call and set her phone on the island in front of her. "'*Bye, babe.*'" Amy mocked, as Leena took her from Matt to help her to bed. "What a douche... Why do you date that asshole? '*Babe, babe, babe...*' He doesn't even call you by your name...ever."

"Amy, stop," Leena said in a firm voice. Amy pressed her thumb and finger to her lips and made the motion to zip her lips, though that didn't stop her from making faces and mouthing the word "babe" repeatedly. Stubbornness kept Leena from admitting to her sister that she also hated when he called her "babe" all the time. Mostly because it was a name that he used for almost every woman he came into contact with. Instead, she kept her mouth shut as she half-carried Amy to her bedroom.

Thankfully Amy's bedroom was just around the corner from the kitchen. The stairs would not have been fun, especially since even in the short trip down the hall Amy had almost fallen a few more times. When they got to Amy's bedroom, Leena helped her wash the make-up from her face, and dress into sleep pants and a tank top. By the time she had her dressed Matt had finished cleaning up in the kitchen and helped her put Amy into their bed. He followed Leena to the door as she left, closing the door behind her and murmuring, "Goodnight."

She went up the stairs to the guest bedroom, stopping on the way to peer into the nursery, to check on her nephew Aiden. He was fast asleep, lying on his side, facing the wall with his back to the doorway, clutching the face of the teddy bear that her Nana had made for him when he was born. He was the most adorable thing Leena had ever seen in her life.

He was a week away from turning five months old, and it felt like he was born just last week. She was disappointed that Amy lived so far away, and that, as a result, she didn't get to see them more often, but she knew that was the way that Amy preferred it. She liked the feeling that she had started her own family and no one was around to tell her how to raise her son.

Leena partially closed the door to the nursery, letting a little light flood in from the hall, before she proceeded down the hall toward the guest room.

⊰⊱

Reed was sitting in his home office with the plans for his next project spread before him. On the corner of his desk also sat his laptop with tabs upon tabs of news websites that he needed to scan for his "other job." The plans were coming along great. He had thought of a few different scenarios for the house that his company was commissioned to build just in case the client didn't like the first plan he showed them.

After rolling up his paperwork, he pulled the laptop to the center of his desk, and did searches for key words. "Dog" "Animal" "Wolf" "Attack"…anything that would help him find something out of the ordinary. As if he didn't work hard enough running his business, and leading the small crew of fighters for his father, he also had to go through numerous amounts of news articles, per day, to try to make sure none of their kind had made it into the limelight. That was the last thing that they needed. He went through each article, bookmarking the questionable ones that would need to be investigated—which would also be done by him and his crew. There weren't many, which was always a good thing. Halfway through the articles he had come up with two attacks that looked to be caused by one of their kind. Not bad, considering that accounted for all of North America.

When his vision began to blur, and his eyes to burn, he decided to go to the kitchen and make himself a sandwich to give his eyes a break. It had been several hours since he ate last, definitely time for a snack. One of the worst things to do is to starve the beast within. That never ended well.

As he bit into the sandwich—one that was the size of his hand in diameter, and at least three inches thick—the sound of a familiar car coming up the drive carried to his ears. Odd, he wasn't expecting anyone today, least of all her. Devouring the sandwich as he went, he made his way to the front door and opened it. He crossed his arms over his chest and leaned against the door frame, waiting while the Dodge crossover pulled in front of his house.

A beautiful blond-haired woman emerged from the vehicle, flipping her hair out of her face, the wind all too eager to assist her, giving Reed the impression of a Baywatch lifeguard. The image was accentuated when she closed the door to the car, and her attire was revealed. She was dressed in the tightest black dress he had ever seen in all his life— which was an extremely long time. It hugged each of her curves as if it were painted onto her skin. The neckline was so low that it was a wonder that she was able to keep her breasts in the dress at all.

"Annabelle," Reed called out in greeting.

"Reed! How are you?" She called back.

Her tone was surprisingly sweet; with a hint of what he could only presume was an attempt at being sultry. When she came within range, Reed was able to get a reading on her emotions, which completely belied her tone. She was trying to project an uncaring, flirtatious vibe, when in actuality, she was anxious, determined, and he could even sense a hint of frustration.

Curious by her emotions, he decided not to answer her question, and instead asked one of his own. "What are you doing here?"

She climbed the stairs of the porch and walked toward him, shoulders back, breasts out, until she stopped directly in front of him. With a sultry look, she ran her finger down his chest, making him cringe at the contact. If there is one thing that Reed cannot stand, it is being touched. The physical contact had his body absorbing her emotions, and converging with his own, making it nearly impossible to distinguish between the two. His heart rate sped up from the myriad emotions, the only tell that he was unable to control when it came to his ability.

Annabelle smiled, misinterpreting his accelerated heartbeat. "You haven't been to your father's lately. I've missed you," She said on a pout.

Again, her words and the tone of her voice were endearing, but her emotion hadn't changed. Reed learned a long time ago never to trust the words with this female, always read her emotions. They are harder to falsify.

She trailed her finger down his abdomen, and as she got closer to the waistband of his jeans his muscles clenched protectively. She took the response as a sign of pleasure, if her sense of triumph was anything to go by, but really she had only succeeded in pissing him off. He shoved her hand away from him, but spoke to her as level-headedly as he could manage. He wasn't stupid. He knew that pissing this woman off wasn't a smart move to make.

"Annabelle, we've been through this," he started. "I'm not interested. I'm sorry. It's not just you, though. I have no interest in being with any woman." After he said the words, he knew that they weren't exactly the truth. He had no interest in being with any woman that he had met up to this point. He did, however, hold out hope that one day there would be a woman that he could love enough to withstand being with. His ability, while it came in handy in some situations, for the most part had him craving solitude.

His ability didn't just work on women, but their emotions had always seemed to be stronger than any of his male friends. Especially Annabelle's. Her emotions are the strongest that he has ever encountered, and they are never happy or content. She is the angriest, most bitter woman Reed has ever been around, and when she touches him, those emotions flow through him, and he starts to feel the same. Granted, he wasn't known for his cheerful disposition, but he did know how to enjoy himself, which was more than he could say for her.

She reached out to him again, as if to test him, but rather than put himself through that again, he took a step back, letting her hand drop between them. "Just leave, Annabelle. I know what you're doing and it won't work. You're a beautiful woman, and I'm certain that you will find your mate someday, but it is not me."

In the next instant, Reed was certain that he had made the right decision. Normally when he turns a woman down because of his abilities, he feels her hurt and disappointment at being rejected, but with Annabelle he felt anger. It lashed out at him like a slap in the face, and in case that wasn't enough, he could see it burning in her icy blue eyes. That reaction was enough to tell him that her advance had nothing to do with feelings that she may or may not have had for him.

"You'll regret this one day, Reed. I promise you that." With that, she turned on her heel and stomped back to her car, making sure to shake her arse as she went in an attempt to show Reed what he'll be missing. Women…. He just didn't understand them. Even knowing exactly how they are feeling at any given moment wasn't enough for him to understand the way they think. As she peeled out of his driveway, he turned back into the house and slammed the door behind him.

He sat back down at his desk trying over and over to read the news articles in front of him, but as the frustration and anger began to boil in him, he could not focus on what he was reading.

She has a lot of fecking nerve coming here and doing this to me again.

Several years back, Reed had actually given in to her attempts to draw him into her bed. It gave little satisfaction, for either of them, and the entire time he could feel that she was not actually interested in him. The fact that she continued to pursue him after their interlude confused him. She knew of his ability, and she had to know that he could read her like an open book, yet each time they were thrown together, she pretended as if he hadn't discovered that the only thing that she wanted from him was a guarantee that she would remain in power amongst their people.

As the second in command, and the leader of the *Lyca Laochra*—a unit that polices the activities of their kind, and enforces their laws—the woman that he chose as a mate, would become the female monarch of the North American territory. Annabelle currently occupied that role, since she was considered the most dominant female. Reed had a hard time believing that she was the most dominant, but none had stepped forward to challenge her, so she remained in that position, and would until she lost it in a challenge, or until Reed found a mate.

In actuality, any mate of Reed's wouldn't be secure in that position either. His da, the true sovereign of North America, could take a mate, and she would automatically, and without contestation take that role. Unfortunately, the likelihood of either of them taking a mate was extraordinarily slim; surprisingly, more so for his da than for Reed. Reed at least had hope that one day he would find a mate, his da on the other hand had no interest in ever finding someone to stand by his side again. Annabelle really didn't have much to worry about at all, so Reed had never understood her persistence.

It wasn't for a lack of effort that Reed hadn't found a woman. It was his damn "gift." His ability threw him into the deepest parts of someone's emotions, forcing him to become intimately familiar with someone he would have just met.

There was once a time that he thought that his ability would help him with women. He should be able to feel if they were enjoying themselves or not, and adjust if needed. Whereas that certainly was the case, it didn't help that he also felt every other emotion that woman was feeling, and that they all overshadowed his own. It wasn't worth it to him to lose himself just to feel the touch of their skin. Thankfully, each of those women had been as disposable to Reed as he was to them. Though, he couldn't help but think of what it would be like to finally find a woman that he *did* want to get close to, enough to allow her emotions to meld with his own. It was both his greatest wish and his deepest fear to finally find such a woman. His mate. He had all but given up on trying to find her, and now he only hoped that she would find him before the emotions of those around him started to consume his sanity.

Slamming his laptop closed, Reed shot to his feet, needing to clear his head. He stripped out of his clothes and padded down the hallway toward the back door. His hand outstretched toward the door knob, Reed heard his cell phone ring. He froze, debating between ignoring the phone, pretending he hadn't heard it and running out into the night, or answering it. Something drew him back to his office. He picked up his phone and looked at the screen, to see his brother's name.

"What?" he barked into the receiver, after touching the screen to answer the call.

"Reed. We need to go. Now."

⚜︎⚜︎

Leena was absolutely amazed. The next morning, instead of nursing the mother of all hangovers, as most would, Amy was back to her usual perky self. She bounced around, talking a million miles per second and wiping down the kitchen counters as Leena brushed her feet along the floor and reached for the coffee pot. The sun reflecting off of all of the white, shiny surfaces, as well as Amy's incessant babbling, crashed into her fatigued senses as efficiently as a freight train. As she poured herself a cup of coffee, she held up her hand to

Amy to silence her for a moment. She took a sip of her coffee, the hot, bitter liquid trickling down her throat, and bitch-slapping her senses into awareness. It was heaven. Leena nodded and flourished her hand to indicate that Amy could proceed, although, even with the coffee, she barely registered the words coming out of her sister's mouth.

Amazing really. The woman was incoherently drunk mere hours ago, and now she was the freaking energizer bunny. Hell, she would probably put the damn bunny to shame right about now. As Amy spoke, Leena gave her usual non-committal "uh-huh" response that she used when not really paying attention. Or rather, what she had thought was non-committal before she said the words "uh-huh" and Amy replied with a squeal and the word "Great!" screamed loud enough that Leena almost fell off of her seat in surprise.

Aw, crap. I've got to start paying attention to her when she talks. Trying to rack her brain to see if she could recall what she had agreed to, Leena came up with nothing. Damn. At this point there was nothing left to do but ask. "What's great?"

"I love taking Aiden for walks, but Matt never wants to go. It will be wonderful having you there with me so that I have someone to talk to."

Yep. She really had to start paying attention to her sister. Whereas she loved walking, and even running, she was exhausted and miserable after their outing the night before. Looking at her sister's face though, Leena couldn't bring herself to back out, especially since it would require admitting that she hadn't been listening to Amy.

Instead, she reluctantly pushed herself up from the stool that she was perched on and, after downing the remains of her coffee, she went upstairs to change into a pair of spandex capri pants and a tank top. Who knows, a walk could even do her some good. Getting the blood flowing could help break her out of her morning-after funk.

Then again, probably not.

As much as she was trying to convince herself that this funk was from their night out, Leena knew that it was more than that. For a few weeks now, she had been feeling this sense of *ennui*. Like something wasn't right. That she was meant to do more with her life, but she just hadn't figured out what that was yet. *That* was what was frustrating, not knowing.

As Leena emerged from the guest bedroom, she could hear Amy in Aiden's room, getting him ready for their walk. Making herself useful, she went downstairs and retrieved his stroller, filling the basket in the back with a few bottles of water. With the scorching heat, and Amy's love for ridiculously long walks, they were going to need them.

By the time she had the stroller set up, Amy and Aiden were ready to go. The moment they stepped outside, Leena could feel the sun caressing her skin, deepening her color, and causing beads of sweat to form instantaneously. The wind blew gently across her skin, doing absolutely nothing to battle the heat, but it did bring the scent of dew and freshly mown grass to her nose. Leena loved the smells of the outdoors. It brought back memories of both camping with her father when she was young, and her Nana's teachings.

With a prod in the back from Amy, Leena made her way down the path, and waited on the sidewalk for Amy to lead the way. Following next to her, they conversed about life back in Pittsburgh—which had nothing new to report on— and how Amy liked being in South Carolina. She had only recently moved here, having grown up in the suburbs of the Greater Pittsburgh area with Leena and their brother Scott.

It wasn't long before the conversation turned to Jason; if you called a lecture from your sister a "conversation." Amy had just started getting into her usual rant of finding a *worthy* man and settling down to have babies, like she had, when Leena stopped dead in her tracks.

"Leena, are you listening to me?"

Leena held up her finger to quiet her. Again, she got the tingling sensation that comes when she is being watched. She turned a full 360 degrees to get her bearings, squinting into the distance to see why she kept getting this feeling, and again getting frustrated when she came up with nothing. Amy stopped and furrowed her brows as she saw the look of concern on Leena's face.

"What is it?" She asked.

"I feel like we're being watched." Leena responded. "I felt it yesterday too, but when I look, I come up with nothing."

Amy took a look around and shook her head before saying, "I don't understand how you and Nana can tell when someone is watching you. I have never been able to feel anything like that."

Leena's hypersensitive senses were just one of a few things that their nana had helped her to develop, but she refrained from saying so to Amy. The woman was descendant from a long line of Native American shamans, as she tells it. Of course, she never used the term "shaman." She used to say that "giving a name to something gives people a reason to fear it. Just like the witches."

According to her nana, their family began losing their abilities when one of her ancestors left the tribe to integrate into society. Each generation letting go of their heritage a bit more than the last. Nana's goal had always been to try to revive the talents of her ancestors, and while she hadn't quite managed to pull it off just yet, some of the things that Leena had seen Nana do gave her chills.

Leena had always been the one to hang around Nana's work space, watching intently, while Amy and Scott preferred to play outside. She didn't know if she believed that what her nana did was called "magic," but she did know that she wanted to learn as much of it as she could. She had always been that way, with everything, craving knowledge as if it were a form of drug. Her mother used to call her a sponge, absorbing ever bit of information that she could.

Now, Leena gave another sweep of the vicinity, shrugging to indicate that she couldn't find anyone watching them. Amy took that as incentive to continue walking.

"Perhaps you are losing your touch," she said, and Leena could have sworn she detected a hint of pleasure that her sister derived from that thought. She doubted that Amy was right, mainly because if she were, it would be more likely for Leena to feel nothing than to get the sensation and have it be nothing.

As they walked, Leena continued to look around as discretely as possible, trying to see if she could catch anyone following them.

After only a few short minutes, when Leena had just started to let her guard back down, a clicking noise sounded on the pavement from somewhere behind them. She turned to see what had made the noise, and at the end of the street she saw the most enormous dog she had ever seen in her life. It must have weighed close to two hundred pounds, and reached her chest in height while all four paws were on the ground. It was primarily gray with a white face and tail. It actually looked wolf-like, but seeing as they were in the land of sun and sand, she doubted that's what it was.

Leena grabbed Amy's arm to still her and she turned just in time to see the dog's lips pull back to show a mouth full of long, sharp fangs. Amy drew a sharp intake of air, and Leena couldn't help but hold her breath. She had never seen such a thing in all her life. Dogs normally only attacked when provoked, but there they were, staring into the snarling muzzle of the biggest, most ferocious looking dog she had ever seen. They held their ground for a long moment, waiting for the dog to realize that they meant it no harm, but it never backed down. Instead, the dog took a few steps closer. When she noticed that it had no intention of backing down, Leena leaned down to pull Aiden out of the stroller, moving as slowly as possible so that she didn't spook the dog into attacking.

"Amy..." Leena whispered, trying not to move her mouth too much. "When I say so, we need to run." Aiden started fussing in her arms, so Leena clutched him a little closer to her chest, making soft hushing noises to calm him. "Grab your keys, leave the stroller."

Amy gave a short nod and pulled her keys out of the cup holder on the handle of the stroller and pocketed them. The dog took another step toward them and stopped, snarling and snapping its jaws.

If Leena didn't know any better, she'd say the dog was playing with them; trying to judge how frightened they were. They held their ground still, waiting for it to make a move. It cocked its head to one side, and raised its gaze to meet Leena's. She didn't look away. Instead, she tried to pretend that she was not afraid by staring back into its eyes. She had read somewhere that canines used staring as a dominance game, and the last thing that she wanted was for this dog to think that they would be easy prey.

Neither of them backed down, and Leena could feel Amy getting antsy next to her. Finally the dog dropped his gaze from hers, and relief flooded through her. Her relief didn't last long though. The dog must not have been happy with the results of their staring contest, because the moment he looked away Leena heard a growl reverberate through his chest. In the next instant, he kicked his back feet off of the pavement and launched himself into the air toward them.

"Go!" Leena yelled at Amy the moment his paws left the ground. They turned in unison, and Leena ran as fast as she could without hurting Aiden, or jostling him too much. Amy trailed closely behind. Leena glanced back over her shoulder to see that the dog was gaining on them. With each moment he drew closer and closer. Leena looked around frantically for anything that could help them widen the gap between them and the dog.

Ahead, Leena saw a fenced-in marsh and turned toward it. She bent forward slightly trying to pick up speed as she ran, and made a B-line straight for the fence. As Leena approached it, she jumped as high as she could and grabbed onto it one-handed so that there was less of it to climb. That jostled both her and Aiden, but she couldn't let that stop her. She scaled the fence as quickly as she could with the baby in her arms, digging her feet into the links for support so that she could move her hand up further, and pull herself up and over the fence. Amy made it over first—seeing as she had two free hands to climb with—and she stood in the muck, griping rather than running. Leena jumped down from the fence, and the moment her feet hit the ground on the other side, she continued running, yelling over her shoulder for Amy to step where she stepped. Still keeping pace with a brisk jog, Leena jumped from one patch of solid land to the next, weaving through the marsh lands and making her way to the fence on the other side.

About half-way through the marsh, Leena heard a splash and turned in time to see the dog recovering from his landing and jumping back into action, pursuing them even more fervently. *Jeez. Was this thing on some kind of steroids?* No way a dog that bulky should have been able to run that fast. She expected that the dog would sink in all of that mud, and it did, but it didn't hinder it as much as she had hoped.

Leena picked up the pace. Her throat burned with the need to breath, but she did not stop. Instead, she crouched over a bit further, still cradling Aiden close to her and ran even harder. They reached the other end of the marsh and began climbing the fence again. Once they were at the top, Leena glanced back to see the gap between them and the dog was closing. Her hopes to put enough distance between them to make it up a neighbor's walkway and ask for help diminished. The dog was too close. *He just won't give up, will he?*

At the top of the fence, she grabbed Amy's arm to still her.

"Take Aiden and go!" Leena said, handing Aiden over to her sister. "We aren't going to lose it. I'll stall it so that you can get Aiden somewhere safe."

Leena dared to look back to see the dog charging toward them and she could tell that it was running at a steady lope instead of a full out run. No way would they out-run this thing.

"Go!" She yelled, giving her sister a light shove.

"No." Amy said. "I am the older sister, I should be protecting you."

"Don't be stupid! That boy needs his mother." Giving her a swift kiss on her cheek, Leena pushed her sister down off the fence—thankful that she landed on her feet—before jumping down on the marsh side of the fence. She turned back to look into her sister's face, and it was almost her undoing. It was full of sorrow, and while she wanted to comfort her, and tell her that she would be okay, she knew that she could never lie to her like that. The truth was, Leena didn't think she would ever see her sister again, but she knew that thought wouldn't sway her decision. She would do anything within her power to protect her family.

Instead of giving her sister false hope, she said the one thing that she knew to be true. "I love you, Aim. So much. Now go!"

A tear rolled down Amy's cheek and she whispered, "I love you too, Lee." Her voice caught as she held back a sob.

Leena turned away from her sister to face down the damn dog that was hell-bent on ruining her life. She allowed herself one last glimpse of her sister, and saw that she had turned and run as fast as she could. *Good girl.*

Leena planted her feet into the mushy ground and braced herself as the dog came almost close enough to touch.

Shockingly, the dog started to move past her, and toward the fence. Amy still wasn't out of sight, and for some reason, instead of going for the easier target, it seemed to want to continue its chase and follow Amy. Leena didn't stop to think about her next move. She lunged for the dog and grabbed it around the waist, wrestling it to the ground. It struggled to try to get away but she tightened her grip around its waist. It thrashed, and squirmed, trying to break free of her hold.

She held on for dear life, trying not to think about the creatures that were crawling around in the disgusting marsh that she was now rolling in. Finally, the dog managed to wriggle free and it looked in the direction Amy had run with Aiden. She was nowhere in sight.

Leena heaved a sigh of relief, and dropped to her back in the water. While she knew that any canine would be able to easily track her sister's scent, she also knew that no dog would be able to catch up to her at this point. *Safe...*

A low rumble brought Leena back to the situation at hand, and she realized the dog was snarling again. Its chocolate brown eyes were glowing with a hatred she had never seen before, let alone in an animal. She started to scramble to her feet, but before she found purchase, the dog lunged, knocking her back to the ground. It bit into her right shoulder, and she let out a shriek. Where the fangs pierced her skin, a searing pain shot through her, and it was more intense than any pain she had ever felt before. It felt as if its fangs were branding irons as they sunk into her muscle.

Leena balled her left hand into a fist and punched the dog as hard as she could in the jowls. Thank goodness she was left-handed otherwise she would have had no effect on it. As it was, she only had time to lift her hands to cover her face and throat before the dog was back on her.

It tore into her flesh, over and over, wrenching a wail of agony from her. Tears streamed down her face and black spots danced in her vision. Just when she thought that she would certainly die, right then and there, she heard another snarl, and a black-as-night blur plowed into the dog, knocking him from her. The dog recovered quickly, and rather than stay and fight, it leapt the fence in a single jump.

Sweet relief. At least she would be able to die without an angry canine feasting on her flesh.

The world around her turned to hazy images that she could barely make out. The one thing that she was able to distinguish was the pair of muscular arms that scooped her up off of the ground and cradled her close to a bared chest. Even half-dead, she couldn't help but admire his flawless skin and perfectly sculpted muscles. She nuzzled closer to his chest, and her last thought was that if there was a better way to die, she couldn't think of one, and then she fell into oblivion.

Chapter Two

Reed paced in one of the small rooms in his father's basement that they used for medical emergencies. They didn't get very many of them, but these reinforced rooms are certainly required for such things. In this particular room a beautiful young woman lay on the hospital bed that dominated the room. She had been there for the better part of three days, mostly unconscious, but every now and then she would thrash and scream from the pain of the venom coursing through her veins.

Reed had been worried when he first brought her here. His father wasn't sure that she was going to survive, but he had faith that if anyone could keep her alive, it would be Shaun, their doctor. The man was a complete *eejit,* but the one thing that he excelled at was medicine. Add that to the woman's apparent strong will, and here she was; heart rate steady and face serene.

He had seen her face contorted in agony, filthy and sweaty from the marsh they found her in, and clean and peaceful such as it was now. No matter the state of her, Reed thought that she was the most beautiful woman he had ever seen in all his life. He barely took his eyes off of her. He told himself that it was to make sure that her condition didn't worsen, but he knew that was only part of the reason.

For some reason, he felt drawn to this woman, which made him uneasy. It wasn't just her tanned skin—that he couldn't tell if it had been kissed by the sun, or if the color was all natural—or her long, dark eyelashes that brushed across her cheeks, her thick brown hair that splayed across the pillow and cascaded over the sides of the bed. It wasn't even her full red lips that were swollen from her biting them to keep from screaming out in pain. He found an odd sense of…peace when he was near her.

For as long as he could remember, he had been bombarded by the emotions of others. Only ever finding relief when he was alone. And not just in a room by himself, he normally needed to be at least twenty feet from a person to be certain that he wasn't absorbing their emotions. But here, in this room, he felt relief.

Not that he couldn't sense what her emotions were— pain, fatigue, worry—but they didn't consume him as they normally would. In fact, to get a reading on her at all, he had to project his ability and concentrate on her. Even then, he sensed her emotions, but they did not muddle his own in any way. It was…addictive.

He couldn't begin to imagine how she had such an effect on him, the only thing that he knew was that he wanted her to pull through more than he'd wanted almost anything else in his extremely long life. Another thing that he didn't understand. He had never spoken to this woman before in his life. He didn't know if she was kind or rude, humble or conceited. The only thing that he knew of her personality was that she was fiercely protective, which in itself was enough for him to know that he would like her. She had sacrificed herself to save her sister and her nephew, knowing that she had little chance of survival. That act alone was enough to convince Reed that this woman was perfect for him.

He also knew that he wasn't worthy of her. For him, a physical relationship would be something that he had to work at every day. She deserved more than that. She deserved a man that would worship every perfect curve of her body. A man that would rain kisses along her smooth, tanned skin.

If only he could be that man.

He pinched the bridge of his nose with his thumb and forefinger and resumed his pacing. *Why am I doing this to myself? I must be out of my fecking mind.*

As he paced, Reed tried to decide if he would be better off leaving this room to clear his head. He needed to distance himself from this sleeping beauty. He needed to get back to his life and quit daydreaming about what he would never have. Above all, he needed to grow his balls back and stop acting as if the woman in front of him was some sort of gift from the gods. He was acting like a swooning maiden.

Resolved in his decision, he turned toward the door. As he reached for the handle a rustling noise came from the bed behind him. He turned back to see that the woman had shifted slightly and her eyelids started to flutter. He leaned over her, ready to tell her that she should relax, and that she was safe, when he was hit in the forehead…hard.

⸎

In the distance, Leena could hear people having a conversation, but she couldn't interpret what they were saying, or even how far away they were. Slowly other noises and scents bombarded her senses. She was relieved that the feeling of being burned from the inside out was absent this time.

She didn't remember much after blacking out in that damn marsh, but she remembered the pain… Not the type of pain that you feel when you stub your toe, or slice your hand open with a kitchen knife. No, this pain was more than any she had ever experienced before in her life. It was as if someone had peeled away her flesh, strip by agonizing strip, and for good measure decided to replace the blood in her veins with acid. Each beat of her own heart brought on a new bout of agony that she could only imagine would end with her death. The room was filled with the sounds of screams that she didn't realize came from her until she could scream no more. Instead of the cries of anguish, she let out hoarse whimpers. The feeling of pins and needles in her throat was like a balm in comparison to the rest of her body. Fun times…

Each time Leena woke over the last few days the only thing that she was able to comprehend was that pain. More than once she begged for someone to just kill her and release her from her own personal hell, but the faceless blurs hadn't given in to her request. In fact, they had strapped her to a bed to keep her from hurting herself as she writhed in anguish. Hurt herself? How ironic.

The only thing that had kept Leena sane over the past few days was a scent. It had been there the whole time, and she had used it as an anchor when everything felt hopeless. It was a combination of sandalwood and peppermint and an underlying musky scent that she realized belonged to a man. He didn't know it, but that man saved her life just by standing nearby.

She could smell that scent again now, and it drew closer and closer as she seeped into consciousness. She could track the man that it belonged to as he moved about the room, until he was right next to her. She stiffened, waiting to see what he would do. She waited for what seemed like an eternity—but in actuality ended up being mere seconds—before she shot straight up, and smacked her head against his.

She opened her eyes to see an unfamiliar man standing next to the hospital bed that she had been laid out on. He was rubbing a hand against his forehead, and she knew that this was the man that had been by her side non-stop since her attack. He was as handsome as the scent led her to believe he'd be. He stood at about six and a half feet tall, with short dark brown—almost black—hair, and green eyes that were slightly flecked with gold. A plain white T-shirt was stretched taught against his muscular chest and abs, while a pair of blue jeans hugged his strong thighs and hung low on his waist. He had a squared jaw speckled with a light dusting of a beard. At the moment that jaw had muscles rippling from his clenched teeth. At the sight of him, the pain in Leena's forehead was forgotten.

"Da," he gritted out, not really loud enough that anyone outside of the room that they were in should have been able to hear him. "She's awake."

His voice was deep with a rich Irish accent that seemed to sooth Leena just as effectively as his scent had.

Movement out of the corner of her eye drew her attention away from the mouthwatering feast of a man in front of her to an almost equally handsome man. In fact, they looked as if they could be brothers. They had the same green eyes, dark hair, and ridiculous amount of muscles. The newcomer was slightly shorter, probably about six-foot-three, his face was clear of a beard, and his expression was softer, more welcoming. Even with their similarities, He didn't compare to the first man, if you asked Leena.

"Ah, you are awake. Finally." He, too, had an Irish accent, but his voice was softer, and somehow more commanding at the same time.

"Where am I?" Leena asked. It came out more of a croak. Her voice was hoarse, her tongue was dry, and she craved water like an addict craves their next hit. Seeming to know exactly what she wanted, the newcomer handed her a glass of water, and she downed it without delay.

"You're in Pennsylvania." The newcomer—man-two she'd call him—said, giving her a warm smile that touched his eyes.

"Pennsylvania?" Leena squeaked, dribbling water down her front. "Where in Pennsylvania? And how did I get back here?"

"Technically, you are in Carnegie. You're here, because my men found you and they brought you here to save your life."

"Carnegie? Did I need to be life-flighted?" Leena asked, knowing exactly where Carnegie was in conjunction to her home. However, looking around her, Leena knew that she was not in a normal hospital room, and their location sparked a question in her. "And why Carnegie? I live not far from here, and the best hospitals are in the city."

"Indeed," man-two said. "But there is no hospital that could treat you as effectively as we can here. Especially considering the nature of your attack."

At the mention of the attack, bile rose in Leena's throat and she shuddered. She could only imagine what she looked like, and wondered if she would have permanent damage from the injuries she sustained. She braced herself, preparing for a gruesome sight, before slowly looking down at her arms and seeing...nothing. Not a bandage, not a scar, not a scratch. Just beige flesh with a few brown freckles.

"How did you do it?" She whispered in awe. "I had chunks ripped out of my skin."

Man-two smiled again, and said, "That explanation is one that will have to wait a moment. First, I need to ask you to explain everything that happened to you?"

Still staring at her arms, completely shell-shocked, she thought back to her walk with Amy and Aiden. "Amy!" She yelled. Leena had done all she could to ensure her sister's safety, but was it enough? She hoped so. She moved to get off of the hospital bed, but a strong hand held her in place.

"Relax, my dear. Your sister is safe. I am certain of it. If you would like to call her in a moment, you may do so, but first, I need for you to tell me about your encounter with the wolf."

Leena shot man-two her most intense glare. *Insensitive prick. Amy, and her well-being, are far more important than recounting what that stupid wolf—.*

Her jaw dropped as she registered the rest of what he had said. "It was a wolf? I didn't think it would have been since we were in a highly populated suburban area, not to mention the lack of wooded areas where wolves could run in the Charleston area. Wait," she said, as something else dawned on her, "how did you know that Amy is my sister?"

"Another explanation that will have to wait." He said calmly, but firmly. "Please, the attack? I swear to you that it is important."

She studied him for a moment, before giving a sigh of resignation. She had little desire to relive what had happened to her, but if man-two thought that it was important, she believed it was. There was something about him that Leena couldn't quite understand, but it made her trust him—something that she normally had a hard time doing.

She took a deep breath and played the events over in her head. The words spilled from her mouth, but the images had her full attention. They played behind her closed eyelids like a film on a screen. As she replayed the final events—the actual attack—she not only saw each flay of her flesh, but she felt it, as if it were happening all over again. Her voice began to crack, but she didn't stop until she got to the point where she had blacked out.

When she was done, she opened her eyes to see that man-two had closed his eyes during her story as well, while man-one had moved to prop himself against the wall. The expression on his face was slightly pained and his breathing had increased, as if he felt each bite, scratch, and tear on his own skin. He was also staring at her intently. She didn't have to look at him to see that, she could feel his gaze on her. It didn't give her the tingling sensation down her spine as usual, but rather a hot caress wherever his gaze landed. It was comforting, and surprisingly arousing at the same time.

Man-two brought her attention back to him when he said, "And now, you may call your sister, if you would like. We have a lot to talk about, but first, you should check to make sure that your sister is well."

Finally. She gave a relieved sigh, and then nodded. Man-two reached out his hand to man-one, and without a word, he dug into his pocket, and withdrew a cell phone, placing it on man-two's palm. He passed the phone to Leena, and she accepted it graciously.

She hesitated for only a moment, before she turned on the screen, and dialed her sister's phone number from memory. It rang only once before Amy's subdued voice came across the line. "Hello?"

"Amy?" Leena asked, which sounded stupid to her after-the-fact. She knew damn well it was her sister on the other end of the line, but the moment she heard her sister's voice, Leena fell dumb-struck.

"Leena!?" Her sister yelled. "Is that really you?"

She could hear the disbelief in Amy's voice, and it was almost her undoing. Tears began stinging her eyes, but she refused to let them fall. She just barely managed to whisper her reply into the receiver. "It is."

"Oh thank God! Where are you? I'm coming to get you."

Leena looked to man-two for guidance, and he whispered the word, "hospital." The weird thing about his whisper was that Leena could hear it quite clearly, as if he had spoken in a casual tone.

"I am in a hospital," she replied to her sister. "But I am not in South Carolina anymore. I was life-flighted to a hospital back in Pittsburgh."

She looked back to man-two and he nodded his approval. Strangely, that approval affected her. She yearned for it as a neglected child yearns for her mother's affection.

Amy hesitated for a moment and then said, "Leena, please just tell me that you're okay."

Again, tears stung at her eyes, but she blinked them back. "I'm okay. I really am." She looked to man-one, who was still staring at her, before she said, "I was saved before the w — dog did much damage."

Amy was breathing heavily into the phone, and the raspy breaths soothed Leena like nothing else could have. She was alive, her sister was safe, and that was all that mattered.

"Amy, I am a bit tired. Would you mind if I called you back after I got some rest?"

For some reason, she directed the question to man-two, just as much as her sister. He nodded his head at the same time that Amy rasped, "Of course."

"Alright," Leena said. "I love you, Aim."

Amy sniffled and then said, "I love you too, Lee."

Leena pressed the *end* button on the screen of the phone and then held it out to man-one. He moved from the wall and, without taking his eyes off of her, slid the phone from her hand, careful not to touch her, and stuffed it back into his pocket.

"Thank you," she said to both of them, putting as much emotion into the words as she could to show them how grateful she was.

"You're welcome," man-two said. "Leena, was it?"

She nodded. "Kalina, actually. Kalina Abrams, but everyone just calls me Leena."

"Lovely to meet you Kalina," he said, reaching out a hand to her, and she shook it. "My name is Declan McAndrews, and this is my son, Reed."

He indicated man-one when he said it, and Leena couldn't help thinking that the man was crazy. He barely looked thirty years old. No way was he old enough to be man-one's — Reed's — father.

Man-two, Declan, smiled at her. "I know it may be hard to believe, but truly, he is my son. I will tell you more about that in just a moment, but I will start by telling you why you are here." He paused, waiting for her to respond, but all she could do was nod. "Reed and my younger son were able to find you during your attack," he continued. "Normally Reed would have given chase to the wolf and disposed of him, but he sensed the life fading from you and stayed to help save your life instead. My other son is too young, and too inexperienced to either give chase to the wolf, or to aid your healing, without assistance.

"You may have noticed that the wolf was quite large, yes?"

Leena remembered thinking that very thing the moment she saw the monstrous creature standing at the end of the road, and again when she had wrapped her arms around its middle and she wasn't able to clasp her hands together.

She nodded her head, and Declan continued. "What would you say if I told you that the wolf that you encountered was actually a man?"

She sat and stared at him, waiting for a sly grin to show that he was joking with her, but one never came. Still, she replied with a hint of snark, figuring that this had to be a joke. "I would say that you were crazy, and that your *son* should have you checked into a different type of hospital."

He grinned and at the same time a growl — yes, a growl — reverberated from his son's chest. She looked over to see Reed scowling at her. She thought that she heard him mumble the words "Fecking bint," but had no idea what that meant, so she figured that she must have heard him wrong.

Whatever he said, it must have been something unpleasant, because the instant the words were mumbled, the smile was wiped from Declan's face and it was replaced by an intense scowl. Without a word, Declan smacked Reed in the back of the head, which in turn caused Reed to scowl back at him. The sight was almost enough to make Leena laugh, but she decided against it. She preferred those intense glares directed at each other rather than at her.

After a long moment of silence, Declan spoke to Reed in a foreign language. It was a beautiful language that Leena had never heard before. Of course, that piqued her interest. The side of her that loved to absorb knowledge hoped that one of them would teach the beautiful language to her, while the intelligent side of her kept her from asking. She became even more intrigued when the color drained from Reed's face and then he looked back and forth between Leena and Declan. He looked as if he wanted to argue with Declan, but before he opened his mouth to say anything, Declan gave him a short nod that stopped Reed from arguing any further.

Without a word, Reed grabbed his shirt by the collar and pulled it up over his head. He could have stopped right then and Leena could have died a happy woman. Her blood heated instantly, and her jaw *may* have dropped. A little. Okay…a lot. His ivory skin was flawless, and those muscles…. She was tempted to grab his shirt and see if she could wash it on his abs. If his previous reaction to her hadn't shown her that he had no sense of humor, she probably would have asked him if she could do so.

Reed's head snapped in her direction then, and Declan laughed heartily. Their reactions made Leena question whether she had said that out loud. She slapped her hand over her mouth and looked away from Reed, her cheeks flaming in embarrassment.

The slightest hint of a chuckle brought her attention back to Reed, just in time for her to catch his smile. That smile…. It completely transformed his features. If she thought that he was handsome before, right now he would put angels to shame with his beauty.

With a continued tug at the corner of his mouth, Reed unbuttoned his jeans and slid the zipper down with deliberate slowness. The act drew Leena's attention as effectively as if he would have lit fireworks and had an illuminated arrow pointed at the front of his jeans. He slid the jeans down his legs, which were as strong and muscular as his chest. He was any woman's wet dream, standing in black boxer shorts and nothing else. A light dusting of black hair coated his legs, arms, and a small trail extending from his belly button to the waistband of his boxers, and disappearing.

She barely registered when Reed crouched down to the floor, she was so distracted by his strip show. She waited, trying to figure out what he was doing, when she felt a pulsing energy in the room. She had never felt anything like it before, and wondered what was causing it. Suddenly she heard a snap, and saw that it had come from Reed's back. The bones were cracking and moving under his skin. Leena let out a gasp and slapped her hand over her mouth, but she couldn't tear her gaze away from him. His ribs popped next, followed by his legs and arms. Bile rose in her throat as she watched him, and she had to squeeze her hand even tighter to her mouth to keep from vomiting. It looked as if he were being beaten by someone with an invisible baseball bat.

The last of it happened quickly. The muscles and bones in his face started shifting, and black hairs shot out of his skin. Only, they didn't look like hairs. It looked more like... fur. Then, in the next instant, standing where Reed had just been was an enormous black wolf, even larger than the one that had attacked Leena.

The room spun around her before everything went black.

❧❦

Reed didn't know what his father was thinking when he told him to show Kalina what they were without giving her any kind of warning, and now, he was certain that they had made the wrong decision. She hit the hospital bed with such force when she fainted that Reed thought that she would certainly have a knot on the back of her head for the next few hours, minimum.

Did he agree with his father that "seeing is believing?" Yes. But he also believed that it helps to be prepared for what you are about to see. It's one thing to show someone proof when they are skeptical about what you are telling them, it's another completely when you drop the bomb on them without explaining what is about to happen. He had tried to avoid looking at Kalina's face when he was shifting, but it was no use. His face sought hers for comfort through the pain of the shift, and what he saw there caused him equal the amount of pain. She had been horrified. On the verge of emptying the contents of her stomach, if there were anything left in it.

Reed knew that the terror in her eyes was for his well-being, which made it all the worse. For one thing she shouldn't care about his well-being; she hardly knew him. And secondly the fact that she *was* worried about the pain he was in nearly felled him in a different way entirely. No one ever worries about the pain that befell him. That was probably due to the fact that he was the leader of a band of warriors that slayed immortals on a daily basis, or it could be because they know that he doesn't need or want their sympathy when he is injured.

With her, it was different. He not only liked the fact that she was concerned for him, but for some absurd reason, he wanted to show her that he could endure that pain, and much more. He wanted to show her that he was a warrior, and that he would stop at nothing when it came to protecting those close to him. In fact, that's how he spent most of his days. He eliminated threats to his family—actual family and extended—on a daily basis and he would protect her just as ferociously.

He shook himself. He had no right thinking this way. He may be able to protect her, but she would seek more than that, and he didn't know how much of himself he could ever give her.

Hell, she didn't even seem to need the protection that he could offer her. The way she took on that werewolf without any regard for how badly he could have destroyed her was both admirable, and ridiculously insane. And slightly arousing....

He could already tell that she would make one of the greatest alpha bitches their pack had ever seen. The hard part will be getting her to see her potential, not to mention getting her acclimated to their world. He knew that it wasn't an exaggeration that her life was about to change on every level. She would feel things differently, see things differently, and she would crave things she never imagined craving. He just wished that he could have prepared her for the life that she was about to lead. That he could have helped her in some way.

Reed had faith in his father to find someone to help her with the changes. Of that, he had no doubts. His father was the best of them all. He was more clever, more cunning, and a better fighter than every single one of them. Not that he needed to fight much anymore. While the men of the pack still fought each other regularly for position, they had all given up hope of ever dethroning Reed's da, and Reed would have it no other way. He would follow no other man. Even less did he relish one day taking the position for himself.

He looked at the man in question and chuffed at the sight of him. He had never seen his father so shell-shocked before. He was still staring at Kalina, playing through the events in his head, wondering where he had gone wrong. Reed could sense his father's confusion. He truly hadn't expected her to pass out from the knowledge that they had just thrust upon her, but Reed had expected worse. Her body was weakened from clawing its way back from death's doorway, the bouts of searing pain and being restrained, and going three days without real food. She had been nourished by an IV, but it wasn't the same as biting into a rare steak and having the blood-soaked meat slide down your throat. Weak didn't begin to describe the state that she should be in. And yet, she seemed to be regaining strength by the minute. She was a resilient little thing. Definitely the makings of a great alpha bitch.

Reed looked back to his father, wondering if he would snap himself out of his musings and fetch a cold, wet cloth to dab on her face to wake her. He didn't seem to be moving any time soon.

Without thinking, Reed took a few steps toward her, and before he processed what he was about to do, he slid his tongue from his muzzle and ran it the length of her face. He was certain that if he would have thought about what he was doing beforehand, he would have stopped himself. Certain...

Chapter Three

Something wet pressed against Leena's face and stroked her cheek, over and over. It felt coarse, yet it seemed to be dripping with some warm liquid. She opened her eyes to slits and saw a large pink tongue start at her chin and work its way up to her eye.

"Ugh..." she grumbled as she swatted at the muzzle housing the gross tongue. "That is disgusting."

The black wolf backed away from her, and as she wiped the slobber from her face she could hear a wheezing sound coming from its throat. She slowly pushed herself back to a seated position and looked at Declan, who had a look of bemusement plastered on his face. "Is it laughing at me?"

He looked down at the wolf, and his confusion slowly turned to amusement. "*He* is laughing at you Kalina, not *it*. That is Reed."

The memories began flooding back to her. Reed, bent over with his bones shifting and popping, until an overgrown wolf stood in his place. The sickening sounds reverberated in her head, making her feel nauseous all over again. The whole process of his transformation had taken about two minutes, but it felt like hour after agonizing hour to Leena. She could only imagine what it felt like to Reed.

A part of Leena kept whispering "this is just a dream, this is just a dream," a man should not be able to transform into an animal. Period. But, on the other hand, Leena had seen things in her life that she couldn't have possibly explained to a rational person. She had seen the extraordinary things that her grandmother was able to do, not to mention what she was able to do herself. But, never in her wildest dreams had she thought to ever see something like this. She wanted to pinch herself...or to call her Nana and tell her what she had just seen. Her Nana would be the only person in the world to believe her without question. The question was, could she believe it herself?

Leena looked up to see that both Declan and the wolf, Reed, were looking at her expectantly. What they were looking for, she had no idea. How should she proceed from here? There were questions that she wanted to ask, certainly, but they were questions of how their existence came to be, and why they were willing to show her that they did exist. They obviously didn't go around showing everyone that they came into contact with that a man could transform into a wolf. If they did, she knew that they would be hunted until each and every one of them was eradicated. She was not disillusioned enough to believe that the human population could handle something like this. People fear what they do not understand, and that's how fanatics are made. That's also how she learned early on in her life not to share with anyone what she could do. So why were they showing this to her?

These were the questions that she wanted to ask, but she couldn't get the words to form. A part of Leena wanted to share with them what she herself could do, since they had trusted her enough to show her their secret, but it had been engrained in her all her life not to trust people so swiftly. She needed to remember that she didn't know these people, and that even though they had saved her life, and apparently trusted her, she needed to keep some anonymity. So, instead of asking the questions that she wanted to ask, she asked the question that she thought they would expect her to ask, adding as much incredulity to her voice as possible.

"What are you people?" Leena almost cringed at the words, but knew that they were necessary. The question itself, she was pretty certain she already knew the answer to, but she still wanted to hear him say it. She couldn't be crazy enough to have made up what she had seen, but she still needed his validation. His confirmation that she hadn't been hallucinating after all she had been through.

Declan gave her a knowing smile, rather than the outrage that she half-expected at her insulting words.

"Kalina, I will appease you in this one instance. From here on, you will say what you mean to say. Am I understood?"

Her jaw dropped. It was one thing for him to have guessed that she had other questions that she wanted answers to more so than this, but he didn't question her at all. He spoke as if he knew, without a doubt, that she was holding back. *That* frightened her more than anything that Reed had shown her.

She tried to answer him, but the words just wouldn't come out of her mouth. She was completely dumbstruck. The only thing that she could do was nod her head and wait for him to continue talking.

"Good girl. Now, I know that you have an idea of what we are, but I will say it. We are lycanthropes, or werewolves, if you prefer."

He paused long enough to let her absorb his words. Werewolves… Hearing the word just seemed so surreal. As if she had stepped into a dream. She pinched herself, and looked back down at Reed, remembering his gruesome transformation.

Werewolves. Not just myths and legend, but living creatures. And she was in the presence of two of them. Reed looked nothing like the monsters that mythology portrayed werewolves to be. There was nothing humanoid about him after his transformation, aside from his intelligent green eyes staring up at Leena. If she saw him in the woods, she would assume that he was just an oversized wolf.

Again, question after question flooded into Leena's head. There was so much that she wanted to know, and the side of her that craved knowledge wanted to know everything, right here and now. She knew, however, that she would only get so much information at one time, so she asked the questions that plagued her the most. "Why am I here, and why are you showing this to me?"

"Ah. Finally we get to the good stuff," Declan said with a wry smile. That grin irritated Leena almost as much as his pretentiousness. It was grating enough that Leena didn't know, or understand, anything that was happening, but the fact that he was taking pleasure in her ignorance was enough to piss her off.

Declan frowned. The immediate change from his cocky grin to his grimace had Leena wondering if she had called him pretentious out loud, but he didn't comment on it either way.

"There are two ways for a werewolf to come into existence," he began. "The first is to be born. To guarantee that a child would be a werewolf, both parents would have to possess the genes, but an interbred child could still be born a werewolf. The child has a fifty percent chance of being born lycanthrope with only one parent possessing the genes." He paused for a moment, checking her face to see if she was keeping up. "The alternative way to become a werewolf, is to be bitten by one of us. We carry a venom in our fangs that weakens your body to the brink of death. If the venom doesn't cause your death, it will continue to course through your body, not only healing the wounds that were inflicted, but giving back so much more. Giving us a magic that allows us to change to and from wolf form, to regenerate, and to enhance not only our senses, but strength, speed, and, in some of us, abilities that we never knew that we possessed."

Leena barely registered the last of what he had said. She was stuck on the ominous words, "bitten by one of us." That is why they were showing her all of this. She had been bitten, and now he thought that she was one of them. The only thing she could do was shake her head back and forth vehemently, chanting the word "no, no, no..." over and over, as if saying the word would make what he had said untrue.

"You are one of us, Kalina," Declan gently assured her. "The proof is in your wounds. The injuries you sustained from your attack would have required an innumerable amount of stitches in a human, if they hadn't killed you first. As it were, you only required bandages on the plane, and by the time you touched down in Pittsburgh, your wounds were already stitching themselves back together."

She looked down at her arms, and knew he was right about her wounds. If she wasn't killed from the attack, she should have at least had scratches, bite marks, and a great deal of stitches. Still...a werewolf? No. He had to be wrong. She couldn't become a ravenous beast, she wouldn't. As awestruck as she had become by Reed and his transformation, did not mean that she had the desire to join him in sprouting fur and a tail. Perhaps her healing was another ability passed to her from her grandmother that she had been able to tap into in order to save her life. That was it. It had to be. She was *not* a werewolf.

She opened her mouth to tell Declan how wrong he was, but before she could say a word, he cut her off.

"Kalina." He didn't raise his voice as he said her name, but the tone in which he said it matched with the look in his eyes had her rethinking her words, and she snapped her mouth shut. When she first saw him, she wouldn't have believed that he could ever look so fearsome, but just then, he was the last man on earth that she wanted to cross. "What would I gain from terrifying you, and telling this to you if it were untrue? Absolutely nothing. Choose to believe it, or don't. You will find out soon enough."

With that, he turned on his heels to leave, not so much as sparing another look at Leena.

"Wait! Please!" She called after him. He turned back to her, but his face no longer held the welcoming smile, or the pretentious grin. His mouth was set in a thin line, and his jaw was turning white from clenching his teeth together. "I'm really sorry." She whispered. "This is all just too much."

She pulled her knees up to her chest and wrapped her arms around her legs. A few minutes ago, she had been so curious about werewolves. She had wanted Declan to tell her absolutely everything about them. Now, having discovered that she was possibly one of them, she felt sick to her stomach. She had a life that she needed to get back to. One that didn't involve transforming into an animal periodically. She wondered if she would be able to go about living her life without ever having to turn into a wolf, except perhaps once a month, if mythology had *that* part right. Perhaps nothing would have to change at all. Except for all of that stuff that he mentioned about heightened senses and increased strength and speed, but she could get past that.

"Kalina..." Declan breathed out. She glanced up at him, and his expression was somber now. Sympathetic. "The changes to your life will be vast, this I know. I was turned myself, many years ago. Not only will you be forced to change during the full moon, but if you do not change in between the moon cycles you will start to get temperamental. The wolf in you will get restless. I know that you did not choose this life, but, if it is any consolation, I think that you will adapt tremendously. You have already reacted far better than most would. Not to mention the power that I can feel coming off of you. You will be strong. You just have to learn to harness it."

Strong. Pft. She didn't feel strong. She felt like a child on the brink of weeping. She pulled her heels closer to her butt and put her face between her knees, closing in on herself. She had just started thinking that if she stayed that way, there was a possibility of the world around her fading away, when something heavy plopped onto her feet. Perhaps not. She peeked over her knee to see Reed's oversized muzzle resting across her feet. Her heart swelled at the act of comfort she was receiving from a virtual stranger.

"You know," she said to Declan, as she gently stroked Reed's head, never taking her eyes off of the gorgeous black wolf. "He's actually quite beautiful."

She could hear the smile in Declan's voice when he replied, "Not quite the man-beast mythology depicts us to be, yeah?"

The corner of her mouth lifted in a slight smile. She wrapped her fingers around Reed's massive ear and burrowed them into his fur, which was surprisingly soft. Softer, even, than the finest velvets that her Grandma Abrams used to love. She scratched behind his ear, using her thumb to massage the front of it. He turned his head into her hand, a low grunt sounding in his throat as the line of his mouth pulled up into a canine smile. Just like her dog, Wraith, would do, Reed pressed into her palm, a silent command to continue.

For the first time in days, she laughed. Well, it was more of a wheezing chuckle, but it was a step in the right direction at least. They stayed that way for a few minutes. Her hand buried into his fur bringing her the most comfort she felt in…well, years, if she were being honest with herself.

Declan cleared his throat, and Leena nearly fell off the small hospital bed when she gave a startled jump. She had been so engulfed with the wolf at her feet, that she completely forgotten that Declan was watching them. "I will warn you, that you may not want to do that to anyone else." He glanced down at Reed, brows furrowed in confusion. "In fact, I am surprised that Reed is letting you pet him. Most of us feel slightly degraded when treated like a house pet, not to mention that Reed in particular has an aversion to being touched in general."

She snatched her hand back as if she had just been burned and hastily mumbled her apologies to Reed. He didn't look at her, and his expression was unreadable, but she took it as a good sign that he didn't look ready to bite her hand off. She just hoped that she could get the whole werewolf-etiquette down before she did something to insult someone that was less understanding than Reed had been.

"Don't worry," Declan said. "You will get the hang of things. We will see to it. Reed, why don't you go into the hall and change back, and then you can escort Miss Abrams upstairs while I try to figure out how we will proceed from here. I will send someone to sit with her shortly so that we can talk."

With a slight hesitation, Reed slid his head off of Leena's feet and gave Declan a short nod. He walked over to his clothes, and shot Leena one last wolfish grin before scooping his clothes up with his teeth and trotting out into the hallway, causing her to giggle. *Giggle,* as if she were a pre-teen that had just been asked to the dance by the cutest boy in school. Embarrassing much?

❦

The moment that Reed stepped out into the hallway his head seemed to clear all of a sudden. The sounds and smells of the basement came flooding back to him, along with the emotions of everyone else in the house. He hadn't even noticed that while he was in the room with Kalina and his da, his gift seemed to have been honed in on her, blocking out everyone else. Even his da, now that he thought about it. That had never happened to him before.

Under normal circumstances, he could sense anyone within the house, their emotions an unwelcome intrusion. He briefly wondered why it had been different this time. Was it Kalina? If so, he had every intention of making sure that she was close by whenever he was around the others.

Having all of those emotions back would have turned Reed's mood sour if he hadn't still had her addictive scent in his nostrils. She smelled so sweetly of jasmine with just a hint of citrus. It was…hypnotic. Why else would he have rested his head on her and allowed her to scratch his ear as if he were a house pet?

Although, if he were telling the truth, the moment that her fingers had plunged into his fur, he was lost to anything but her touch. Her emotions had faded from apprehensive and afraid to contemplative and content, which, in turn, soothed him. The world around him had faded away, but for her beautiful scent, the low thrumming of her heart beat, and her soft hands caressing him.

His reaction to her was actually somewhat startling. Never in all his years had he been so drawn to a woman. Yes, she was beautiful. She was one of the most beautiful women that he had ever seen, but he had been around beautiful women before, and never had every single one of his senses — including his ability — honed in on one person.

Distance. He needed to distance himself from this woman, if only emotionally, while he figured out what was going on. The last thing that he needed was to be playing the cuddly little house pet for this woman when he should be figuring out a way to stop this rogue wolf.

Reed closed his eyes and concentrated on pulling his human half to the fore, when her voice drifted out to him. He listened over the sounds of his bones cracking and his flesh tearing to hear her talk to his da in a way that no one else ever had. Even newly turned wolves could feel the power emanating from his da. When it came to Declan McAndrews even the most dominant wolves turned submissive, but not her. She spoke to him as if he were exasperating her. It both annoyed Reed and entertained him.

Declan wasn't just his da, he was Reed's king. Declan McAndrews was the single-most important werewolf in all of North America, and as such should be spoken to with respect. Granted, he was aware that she had no idea to whom she spoke, and that was likely the only reason she still lived. Or, at least one of the reasons. For a brief moment Reed wondered if his da even remembered the last time someone spoke to him in such a manner.

"You know," she snapped. "I don't need a babysitter. I am more than capable of sitting in a room by myself."

Surprisingly, her ire had no effect on his da. If anything, he seemed to be entertained by it as well. It must be refreshing to have someone express their pique toward you when no one else would dare.

"I don't question your ability to take care of yourself, Kalina." Declan responded. "But I need to make sure that someone is keeping an eye on you at all times. Your first few changes may be violent, not to mention unexpected, and we need to make sure that someone is there to see you through them."

"Violent?" She asked, her anxiety increasing. "As in, I will become violent like the wolf that attacked me, or violent as in it will look like I'm being beaten to a pulp with a baseball bat like it did to Reed?"

His da hesitated to answer for a moment, and Reed couldn't do much but chant in his head; *Don't tell her, Da. Don't tell her.*

Up until this point, she had handled everything better than most people would have, but everyone had a breaking point, and Reed worried that they were fast approaching hers. He wondered just how much more information she could take before she ran from the house screaming without a backward glance.

Against his thoughts, his father answered Kalina truthfully.

"Both," he said. "Werewolves are hot-tempered and capricious. Even more so during the first stages of a transition."

Reed knew better than to think his da would lie, even if it was to spare someone from an anxiety attack. His da was never successfully lied to, due to his ability, so in return, he never lied to others. Some would even say he was brutally honest.

Quickly, Reed shoved his legs into his jeans and threw his T-shirt over his head. He half expected Kalina to turn hysterical after his da's proclamation, but again, she surprised him. Instead, he was hit with a bitter resignation, followed quickly by her mumbled, "Great...."

Tough little female. Would she ever cease to surprise him? A part of him hoped not.

⊷⊶

Leena could sense the moment that Reed reentered the room. She also knew, without looking, that he was staring at her again. Once again, the usual prickling sensation was replaced by a burning heat wherever his gaze fell. She glanced over at him to see that he was leaning against the doorjamb with his arms crossed over his chest, and his gaze on hers. The intensity of it had her returning her eyes to Declan, but not before she noticed that the seams of his T-shirt were perilously close to tearing from the stress of his bulging muscles.

Can you say, 'Yum!?' she thought as a rush of heat coursed through her.

Again, both men had reacted as if she had spoken out loud. Declan gave a soft chuckle, trying to hide it with an unconvincing cough, while Reed furrowed his brows in confusion.

That wasn't the first time that they had reacted to something that Leena had thought, and this time she knew for certain that she had not said it out loud. She was afraid to ask about it, but she knew her inquisitive side would not easily let it go.

Declan watched her expectantly for a moment, but when she managed to keep her mouth shut, he said, "Ask it Kalina. Ask your question."

Son-of-a-bitch! "How do you keep doing that?" She practically squealed.

Again he chortled, but this time he made no move to cover it up. Her anxiety kicked up a notch, and her heart slammed against her rib cage so hard, that she half expected it to leap out of her chest.

"Da," Reed began. "I don't think you should—"

Declan cut him off before Leena could find out what he didn't want his father to tell her, and she couldn't help but to be grateful for Declan's interruption. She wanted to know everything. It was like taking off a Band-Aid…the quicker the better. Pulling it off slowly just prolongs the pain.

"Earlier you asked me how I knew that Amy was your sister." Declan said. "The reason I knew that is the same reason that I knew that you could handle knowing that our species is volatile, and that I know you want as much information as possible right away…. I am telepathic."

Leena opened her mouth to speak, but Declan raised a hand to halt her. "Before your inquisitiveness takes over, let me finish."

She snapped her mouth shut. That statement, more than anything else, opened Leena's mind to the possibility of him actually having telepathy. Most people would have assumed that she was about to refute his claim, but she was more intrigued than disbelieving at this point. Especially after she just watched a man sprout fur and a tail. She wanted to ask Declan a million questions, starting with a sarcastic, "What number am I thinking of?"

"Three thousand, five hundred, and forty-three."

Oh. My. God. Leena's jaw dropped, and the only thing that she could do was gape at him. He gave another of his pretentious grins before he recommenced. "Not all werewolves, but a large number of us, develop gifts during our transition. Abilities. Mine is telepathy. We have yet to figure out the actual cause of it, but from what we have discovered, it looks as if dormant abilities that we would not have been able to tap into if we were human get kick-started with the first stages of the transition. For example," he said as he began pacing in front of Leena, the passion of the subject evident on his face, "my younger son, at sixteen, just developed his ability when his first transition began about a week ago. The interesting thing, that still confounds me, is that even though the three of us have the same lineage, our abilities are all rather different."

He stopped pacing and turned to face Leena, measuring her reaction. This was all so...surreal. Magic was real. She had always known that had been, but she had assumed that it had faded to practically non-existent. Werewolves were real too. Not only that, but now she *was one!* She still had a hard time processing that bit of information. The man in front of her had telepathy. There was no use trying to refute it, the evidence of it was incontrovertible.

Her life had pretty much flipped upside down in the course of about twenty minutes. She could handle this. She had to.

Leena took a deep breath and gave a short nod of her head. She really just needed to go somewhere quiet and wrap her head around all of this, without having someone with the ability to pry into her mind next to her.

She reached for the edge of the blanket that was draped over her and threw it off, revealing her bared legs. Thankfully she wasn't particularly modest, after spending the majority of her life in a leotard. In fact, the first thought that came to her mind was, *Thank goodness for laser hair removal.* She swung her legs over the side of the bed and slid down, grateful that her legs held her weight, however unsteadily. She made sure to hold the hem of the T-shirt that she was wearing so that she didn't flash these two men her private areas, as a second thought hit her. *Oh no...will my wolf have bald spots?*

The images that popped into her head were rather comical, if Declan's grin was anything to go by. Oh well. She supposed she'd find out sooner or later.

Extending her hand out to Declan, she said, "Thank you, for saving my life."

"I'm not the one to thank," he replied. "But I'm glad that we were able to save your life. I have a feeling that you're going to be a breath of fresh air around here."

Leena smiled, and then followed Reed out of the room. When she stepped out into the hall, she stopped dead in her tracks. She could tell that she was in a basement, primarily due to the stone walls, and the small, high, windows, but this was the basement of all basements. The floor plan was open, and seemed to be shaped like the tip of an arrow. She was in the middle giving her full view of both wings. Down toward the left, at the far end, was an open doorway that showed a full theatre, decked out with loveseats and recliners rather than those tiny, stiff seats that you find yourself squirming in when you go out to the theatre. There were a few doors between her and the theatre that looked exactly like the room that she had just come out of. Hospital beds in the middle of the room, and state of the art medical equipment lining the walls. The right wing was an entertainment area that could have put Dave & Buster's out of business. It had video games from Pac Man and Duck Hunt, to Time Crisis. Skee ball, Pinball, multi-player racing games and a pool table. All of that, and that end of basement still wasn't cramped. *That's* how big the place was.

Directly across the hall was a long bar, lined with glasses, and so many brands of liquor that Leena hadn't even heard of most of them. She walked in that direction to reach the staircase that led to the next floor. When she reached the top of the stairs, she was met by Reed's glowering face. Even with a scowl the man was more beautiful than any man had a right to be, but the beauty of him wasn't enough to distract Leena from the house around her.

The walls and floor were all wood, as well as the support posts, giving it the look of a high-end log cabin, if cabins were the size of mansions. Everything was open on this floor as well, except for a few rooms at the back of the house, where they currently stood. Down one wing of the house, she could see into a kitchen that would give any chef a mini-orgasm. There were *two* restaurant-sized stovetops and ovens, a walk-in refrigerator, and even a convection oven. The appliances were all a shiny, stainless steel that reflected the light, much like a beacon that beckoned Leena to them.

The dining room was separated from the kitchen by a granite-top peninsula extending from the wall. The cherry wood bar stools surrounding it matched the dining set that had to have been custom made. The table was long enough to have about twenty chairs on either side of it, spaced far enough apart that each occupant would have plenty of elbow room.

Down the other wing of the house was a very large sitting room, with several sofas and recliners gathered around a beautiful stone fireplace, the wood floor left open and bare in the middle of the room. At least forty people could have sat around the room comfortably, not to mention that she could tell that the room was shorter than that wing of the basement, leading her to believe that there was another room behind the sitting room. The sheer size of the place had Leena wondering how many people actually lived in this house.

"Come," Reed beckoned, and the sound of his voice had Leena jumping out of her skin. She had almost forgotten that she was supposed to be following him. He was already at the top of the next set of stairs, glowering down at her as she took in her surroundings. She took the stairs two at a time, mumbling her apologies for falling behind. She couldn't figure out what had gotten into him, he had seemed so sweet as a wolf, comforting her through Declan's revelations.

Rather than comment on his mood, she decided to keep her mouth shut and follow, just barely holding back a sarcastic, "yes, master."

Of course, keeping her mouth shut only lasted until she got to the top of the stairs. There were closed doors lining the walls on either side of the staircase, with another staircase at the far right leading to yet *another* floor. Reed headed in the direction of those stairs with Leena hot on his heels.

"Jeez," she said, in awe. "This place is freaking enormous!"

Reed continued walking, not so much as cracking a smile.

"You know," Leena started, trying to get him to lighten up a little, "you talk too much."

Reed stopped abruptly, turning on his heels to face Leena. He moved so quickly that Leena didn't even notice that he moved until she walked right into him. It was like walking into a brick wall. He was so muscular and solid that while Leena stumbled backward, and almost fell onto her rump, Reed stood unmoved, and unfazed, arms crossed over his chest scowling at her once again.

"Ever hear of brake lights?" Leena said, fixing him with a scowl of her own. "You should invest in some."

Alright, probably not her best quip, but it should have at least earned a somewhat less intense scowl. As it was, he continued to glare at her as if she'd just thoroughly insulted him. Apparently mister tall-gorgeous-and-menacing doesn't have a sense of humor.

"You know, the brooding look doesn't really work for you," Leena said, which she knew was an utter lie. No matter how he arranged his features, he was still the most mouth-watering man she had ever seen.

She looked up into his eyes and wanted to melt from the intensity in his gaze. Her knees weakened, and her breath hitched. Her reaction to him scared her, so rather than let him know that he had such an effect on her, she continued with the safe route, snarkiness. "You should at least try for impassive, rather than 'I've-got-a-stick-up-my-ass.'"

As anticipated, his scowl deepened with such intensity that if Leena hadn't known that he did find her at least somewhat entertaining, then she might have actually been afraid of him. A predator stared back at her, and she knew that she would have to keep that in mind for future instances.

Reed backed away from her, swiftly turning on his heel and continuing down the hall. The moment their eye contact was broken, Leena's heart skipped a beat, as if she had actually been a little worried by what his reaction might have been.

She tried to shake the feeling of apprehension as she followed Reed to the door at the end of the hall. He turned the knob of the door and stepped aside, letting Leena precede him into the room. She squeezed awkwardly past him, trying her damnedest not to touch him. He raised his eyebrow at her giving her a quizzical look, which Leena decided to ignore. If he wasn't going to use words, she didn't have to either.

The room that she entered was a large bedroom. It was rustic, yet beautiful. The bed looked like it was made from hand-carved wood, with a bright white comforter that looked to be made of fur. The small sitting area had two black leather loveseats arranged around a flat screen television. There were faux fur rugs on the floor in front of the sofas and next to the bed. The armoire and dresser were antiques that were in pristine condition.

As Leena admired the room, Reed brushed past her and sat on one of the loveseats. He flipped the television on, but he wasn't watching it. His eyes followed every step Leena took, never saying a word.

The constant scrutiny and the lack of communication had Leena already getting annoyed with this situation.

She spotted a doorway at the far end of the wall that had the TV mounted on it and decided to go through it to get away from Reed for however long she could manage. As she walked toward it she caught a glimpse of a shower and realized that it was a bathroom. All the better. She picked up the pace, but by the time she got to the doorway and tried to close the door, Reed had stood and followed her, preventing the door from closing with his foot.

Really? She whipped around to face him, fist slamming onto her cocked hip in frustration. "What are you doing?" She snapped.

Again the scowl returned to his face. "What are *you* doing? I'm supposed to keep an eye on you at all times." His Irish accent was thicker with his irritation, but even that sexy voice didn't tamper Leena's frustration.

"Well, as good as you are at doing that, I'd rather you didn't while I go to the bathroom."

"The door stays open," he said before turning away from her and returning to the bedroom. He sat on the far loveseat, so that he could see very little past the door jamb into the bathroom.

Apparently that was the most privacy she would be getting. She threw up her hands in resignation and turned away from the frustrating male. She used the facilities, washed her hands and face, and then just stood there, looking at her reflection in the mirror.

She didn't look much different. Although, she didn't really know what she was expecting, for her face to be more wolf-like? She did notice that everything seemed clearer to her. She could make out the dark streaks of her irises that gave them the look of sapphires, every tiny freckly that spattered her nose and cheeks. She could even see the reddish hue to her brown hair that was usually only seen in the sun.

Leena closed her eyes and leaned her forehead against the cool mirror. Just as her vision had seemed even sharper than normal, she also noticed that now she could hear *everything*. She could hear the drip-splat of the of the water droplets making their way from the faucet to the basin, the low hum of the electronics in the next room, even past the voices that came from the television. Above all, she could hear the beat of Reed's heart. It was as if her senses sought him out, just to make sure that he was real, and that he was still there.

Of everything that she noticed, her sense of smell seemed to be the most affected. She could smell the cleaning products that were used in the bathroom, the laundry detergent that had been used on the T-shirt that she donned, but above all, she caught the peppermint and sandalwood that had been her only source of comfort over these past few days.

For a long time, her senses had been more acute than anyone else around her, but this was just insane. She shouldn't be able to pick out a man's personal scent from ten feet away.

She stayed that way for several moments, forehead absorbing the chill from the mirror. With each minute, she could hear Reed getting restless, shifting from side to side on the sofa, and expelling exaggerated breaths of frustration.

With a roll of her eyes, she sent up a silent prayer to help her endure the infuriating man in the next room. She backed away from the mirror, and went back into the bedroom. Reed sat staring at her with his arms crossed over his chest as she moved to the opposite sofa, somehow managing to keep the T-shirt covering her as she sat.

"You know, I didn't ask for you to be my babysitter. You don't need to take your irritations out on me. If you don't want to be here, then leave!"

"How are you taking this all so well?" Reed asked without acknowledging her outburst.

"Excuse me?"

"Even the werewolves that ask to be changed have a hard time adapting after they wake. They have a hard time controlling the wolf in them, or they're frustrated because being a werewolf isn't as awesome as they thought it would be. Why are you so calm?"

"Let me get this straight," Leena said, "you *want* me to be upset and rail at the fact that I'm a werewolf?" Reed didn't answer, he just stared at her expectantly, eyes narrowed. Again, Leena considered telling him about her family. She couldn't decide why she shouldn't tell him anymore. Reed and Declan had been nothing but forthcoming about all things werewolf, so instead of trying to lie, she answered.

"I don't know…probably because of my Nana."

Reed still didn't say anything, he just quirked his eyebrow at her, so she elaborated. "My great-grandmother, who was an Iroquois Indian, had certain magical talents. You might call her a shaman, but you would never have called her that to her face. I don't know what the full extent of her talents were, and neither does my Nana, but I know that they were real. None of my great-grandmother's children seemed to have inherited all of her gifts, but my Nana has a few special talents, and I have also learned some of my own. They are so miniscule, though, that my Nana fears that I will be the last of our line to exhibit any extraordinary abilities."

Reed just stared at her for a few moments. She squirmed under his scrutiny, before he finally said, "I wonder if any new abilities will surface now that you've gone through the transition."

Leena opened her mouth to ask him what he was talking about when she recalled Declan's earlier words. *Not all werewolves, but a large number of us, develop gifts during our transition. Abilities…from what we have discovered, it looks as if dormant abilities that we would not have been able to tap into if we were human get kick-started with the first stages of the transition.* "I guess we'll find out," she murmured. "What is your ability?"

Reed studied her face before answering, "Empathy."

This time it was Leena's turn to quirk her eyebrow. "Empathy? That's an ability? A lot of people have empathy for others. Though, I suppose in your case empathy would be considered an ability."

If looks could kill, Leena had a feeling that she would have just died a slow and painful death, accelerated healing or not. "You don't know anything about it…about me."

"Really? You mean that you didn't just get mad because I was able to cope with something that most people can't?"

"Not exactly," he said, turning somewhat somber. "To be honest, I don't know why I was angry. My Empathy is not simply recognizing someone else's emotions, I actually feel them. Most of the time, I cannot differentiate another's emotions from my own. It could have been that any person in this house was feeling angry and I absorbed it. It is worse if I'm already feeling the emotion on some level. If I became irritated, and someone else was angry, I would absorb it and become enraged over something small. It's even worse with physical contact. That's why my da told you that I don't like to be touched, because it magnifies the connection."

Wow. And Leena thought that things were going bad for her. Not only did he have to go through the whole claw-and fur-thing, but to have a single touch cause you to lose control of your emotions...that would be terrible. Of course, as she was speculating all that his ability would hinder, she became curious about something. She probably shouldn't have asked, but if she didn't, the curiosity would have plagued her.

"Can I ask you a personal question?" Reed shrugged, so she took that as an affirmation. "If you don't like to be touched, then how do you—how are you intimate with women?"

Reed averted his gaze, and silence followed her question. She waited a few moments, wondering if he would actually answer. Just when she was about to tell him that he didn't have to answer, he whispered, "I usually don't. When the urges become overwhelming I give in to them, but for the most part I try not to."

Leena's heart tightened in her chest. She didn't particularly care for sex, but she knew how much men liked it, and she couldn't help but feel sorry for him. At least she had the option to have sex, even if she decided not to utilize it. For him, the only way for him to experience it would be to lose control of his own emotions. Leena couldn't help but wonder if he could even enjoy the experience when he did give in to his urges.

As she debated asking him, she heard footsteps approach, and then a knock sounded at the door.

"Come in, Corrick." Reed called.

The door inched open and a teenage boy with flaming red hair walked through. He was wearing a Three Days Grace T-shirt and jeans that hugged his slender hips. He couldn't have been more than sixteen, with a sweet, boy-next-door look about him. All of this, however, was overshadowed by what he held in his hands.

"Pants!" Leena shouted as she leapt up from the loveseat and practically ran toward the boy. She snatched the sweatpants out of his hand and slipped them on, without bothering to go into the bathroom.

As she stabbed her legs through the opening, she looked up just in time to catch the boy watching her before he averted his gaze, his cheeks turning a darkening to match the color of his hair. At that moment, Reed stepped up behind her and said, "Corrick, this is Kalina. Kalina, this is my brother, Corrick."

Leena couldn't help but gape at him as she held her hand out for him to shake. He didn't look anything like Reed. While Reed was all muscle and hard lines, Corrick was soft and lean. He was built like a runner. The only similar feature that they had was their eyes. Both green, although you could hardly see Corrick's due to his long mussed hair that half-covered his eyes as it swept across his forehead.

"Please, call me Leena," she said.

As he placed his hand in hers, a few things happened all at once. The air around them shifted, causing Leena's hair to lift up from her shoulders, Corrick's entire body tensed, and his grip tightened on her hand as if she were his lifeline. He squeezed tighter and tighter, causing a bone in her hand to snap. She cried out, and distantly she could hear Reed calling Corrick's name as her hand was wrenched from his.

Corrick fell to his knees in front of her, eyes glazed over, fists balled tightly. Leena clutched her right hand to her chest as Reed dropped in front of Corrick and shook him vigorously, calling out his name. Slowly he came to.

Reed cupped him on the back of the neck, directing Corrick's gaze to his own. "Corrick, look at me!" When his little brother finally focused on him, he said, "What did you see?"

Chapter Four

Reed clutched the back of his brother's neck a little harder than he had intended, but the kid had scared the feck out of him. Corrick had never reacted to a vision so forcefully. Reed's heart was beating against his chest so hard that he could barely hear his brother whisper, "Too much," over the pounding.

Too much? Exactly how much had he seen for it to be so all-consuming? Had it all been future events? Were there some past events? These were all questions that he wanted to ask, but he knew that he needed to give his brother a moment to recover.

In an attempt to stand, Corrick grasped the back of Reed's shirt and used it to pull himself to his feet. When his legs wobbled, Reed had the urge to pick him up and carry him to the sofa, but he knew that his brother would not appreciate it. Since he started the first part of his transition, Corrick would be seen as a man. A man who just happened to be the ruler's son and any weakness he would show would put him in a position to be challenged for rank. But, no matter his age, he would always be Reed's baby brother.

None-the-less, Reed walked one step behind his brother and followed him to the loveseat that Kalina had been sitting on previously. He tried to ignore her scent as his brother began to speak again.

"It was the strangest thing, Reed. I got one glimpse of a future event, and at the same time more started flooding in. I couldn't even keep track of them all. They were so jumbled."

Reed had never heard of anyone with precognitive abilities ever experiencing something like this before. Was there something special about Kalina? Or were Corrick's abilities growing beyond the capacity of the precognitive wolves that have preceded him? His visions had been coming more and more frequently, and Reed had even thought that he had begun to gain some control over having one. He supposed that now they would have to focus him on learning to *not* have them, if possible.

"What were the visions that you could make out? Are there any that we need to act on?" he asked Corrick, remembering back to the last vision that he had of Kalina.

He looked from Reed to Kalina, who had moved to stand next to the sofa, and was still holding the hand the Corrick had broken. Reed could feel that her pain had decreased as it began to heal, but the fact that she was in such pain at all caused Reed's protective instincts to stir within him to make it right. The anger that had sparked the moment it had happened increased now that Corrick seemed to be alright. He tamped it down, wanting to make sure that everything was in the clear before he clobbered his brother.

Corrick must have sensed the change in Reed's mood, because he quickly answered Reed's questions, not waiting for Kalina's approval. "I don't think that we need to act on any of them. The first one that I saw looked as if—" he looked to Kalina once more, her face contorted with confusion, before he whispered, "—she was having sex with a blond man." The rage that had hit Reed when he saw Kalina holding her broken hand increased ten-fold. He had known that he shouldn't even attempt to pursue her, but to have his brother confirm it killed him inside.

Hastily, Corrick moved on to the next vision that he had seen, which didn't do anything to sooth the intense anger that had overcome him. "That vision was cut off quickly by one of her walking down the aisle in a wedding dress, which was then replaced with one of her fighting back-to-back with Tresize—and she was kicking major ass—and that's when it got jumbled, and I couldn't keep track of them, but it ended with Shaun handing her a babe."

Reed tried his damnedest to keep his expression impassive. He knew that Corrick would sense his anger, but he also knew that the kid wouldn't understand it. Hell, Reed barely understood it himself. The only thing that he knew was that he felt like a kid who had a toy dangled in front of his face and watched as the holder smashed it to pieces. The gods were cruel to dangle the idea of a mate in front of him only to let him know that she could never be his.

"I'm going to go talk to Da. Stay here with her." That was all Reed could manage to say through the haze of his fury. He strode toward the door and ripped it open, but before he left Kalina called his name and ran to catch up to him, stopping him by putting her hand on his shoulder. The hand that had been broken. The gesture, along with the feeling of concern he felt from her, calmed him slightly, but not enough for him to trust himself to speak without snapping at her. Instead, he took her hand in his, and laid a kiss on her palm before he stormed out.

At least he refrained from slamming the door behind him…too hard.

❧❧

Leena stood there, staring at the door that Reed had receded from, wondering what had upset him so much. If anyone should have been upset, it should have been her. The content of her private life was discussed as if they were talking about a movie or a book.

Instead of interrupting Corrick in an outrage at the mention of her sex life, she let him continue in hopes that he could calm the wild look that sparked in Reed's eyes. A lot of good that did her. The man was even more incensed when he left, that she feared for anyone who happened to cross his path.

One thing that had surprised her was that even though he was stomping around, practically tearing the door from its hinges, and slamming it hard enough to crack the frame, he had been so gentle with her. She still felt the warmth of his lips on her palm, and the feeling sent another wave of delicious shivers through her core. No one had ever elicited such a response from her, and that fact terrified her. The last thing that she needed was to develop an attraction for a man as unpredictable as Reed, even if she hadn't been dating Jason.

Holding her hand to her chest, she returned to the sitting area where Corrick sat scrutinizing her. She sunk into the loveseat that Reed had occupied earlier, and tried to ignore the comforting feel of being enveloped in his rich scent.

"How's your hand?" Corrick said.

Focusing on him, she held up her hand and flexed her fingers. The pain was gone entirely now. Amazing... She knew about the regeneration, but she had no idea it would work so quickly. "Good as new," she replied.

She contemplated using the opening of conversation to ask about the visions that he had seen of her, but she didn't know how much more information she could handle before her brain threatened to explode.

Then again, she had already learned so much today, what was a little more? Especially since it had to do with her and her future.

"So, you have visions? What kind of visions?"

He hesitated for just a moment before answering vaguely, "All types." She raised her eyebrow hoping that he would elaborate, and he did. "I see past, present and future events. Mainly future. I haven't been having them long, but when I do, they're normally future events, and I have just enough time to try to prevent the bad ones from happening, like with you and the rogue."

His cheeks reddened, as if he were embarrassed about bringing attention to the fact that he was the one who had pretty much saved her life. She remembered now that Declan had said that Reed and his other son were the ones that had saved her, but she hadn't put the two together until now.

"You had a vision of my attack?"

The flush on his cheeks deepened as he nodded his head.

She stood from the loveseat, and strode toward him, bending down to fling her arms around his neck. "Thank you, for saving my life."

Corrick wrapped his arms around her somewhat reluctantly, so she pulled away from him to avoid making him uncomfortable. As she stood, her head spun, and her stomach clenched, making an audible growling sound.

"You need to eat," Corrick said, as he jumped to his feet and took her hand, leading her toward the door. "You should never go very long without eating now. You are going to burn through food three times as fast, and if you're hungry, you're likely to change involuntarily. You don't want that…trust me."

She followed him back down the staircase to the main floor, and as she turned to go toward the kitchen she stopped. She had just heard someone mention her name from one of the doors at the back of the house. She fell back as Corrick walked on, into the kitchen, and tried to listen to what was being said about her.

"Can't you get someone else to do it?" she heard Reed shout.

"There is no one else right now, Reed," Declan's voice replied levelly. "The twins just touched down in San Diego, Shaun isn't an option, Leo either, for obvious reasons. I need Lucan here to train Corrick, and Milo and Spencer are on their way back from Toronto. We will have a meeting tomorrow night, once the boys get back, and we'll decide how to proceed then. For now, she is your responsibility."

"I could train Corrick."

"No. As much as I could use your experience with him, he needs someone who will be able to set their emotions aside. Even at one-hundred and ninety-two years old, you still don't have control over your ability. He is going to get angry and frustrated, and I would need for you to not absorb those emotions and try to stay level-headed."

Leena never heard Reed's response to his father. Her head swam and everything around her faded. One-hundred and ninety-two years old... How...how was it possible? She knew that the regeneration was what kept Declan looking so young, but she never imagined that it would keep him looking that way for around two-hundred years. That made him....eight times her age. Holy. Crap.

"Leena?"

She practically jumped out of her skin at Corrick's interruption of her internal musings. She hadn't even heard him approach her, but now he stood less than two feet in front of her, a questioning look on his face.

"I was just—" she stumbled over her words trying to come up with a good enough excuse for lingering. "—looking for the bathroom."

"Oh. It's that door right there," he said, pointing to the farthest door from where she heard Reed's voice. "I'll meet you in the kitchen when you're done."

She went into the bathroom and closed the door behind her. Since she had no need of the facility, she ran her fingers through her hair a bit to try to tame it as she let what she had just heard sink in. Reed had been alive for almost two whole centuries. When her city had become a land of steel, he had been alive for that. It was absolutely mind-boggling.

Deciding that she had been in the bathroom for long enough, she made the trek to the kitchen thinking of other milestones in history that this man who appeared to be about thirty years old had been alive for. *The gift of the Statue of Liberty!*

As soon as she got close to the kitchen, though, her musing stopped as she was hit with the smell of seared beef, and her mouth began to water. She hadn't realized the full extent of her hunger until that moment. In the kitchen, Corrick stood at one of the stovetops, which Leena had just noticed had a griddle in the middle of the burners. The griddle had several patties of ground beef the size of saucers on it, and a large stack of buns, just round enough to fit those patties, waiting on the counter next to him. This kid sure knew the way to a woman's heart.

After an attempt to help, and being shooed from the kitchen, Leena sat down at the peninsula, waiting for the burgers to be finished.

"So, Corrick, how old are you?" she asked, hoping to break the silence.

"Sixteen," he answered.

"It must have been nice growing up with a brother so much older than you." She made a point not to put emphasis on, "so much older." Then, after realizing that she was bringing the conversation to Reed, she silently wondered how the brooding man had gotten to her so efficiently. She didn't even realize that from the moment she woke the man had constantly been on her mind until just then.

"If you only knew..." she heard him mumble. "It was nice," he said more audibly, "until recently."

"How so?" she asked, as he scooped the patties onto the buns and carried them over to her. She bit into the first one and couldn't hold back her moan of pleasure. She couldn't even be concerned with being embarrassed by her reverence. It was delicious. Juicy, flavorful, and cooked perfectly.

Corrick gave her a quick smile before answering her question. "Well, you know about our abilities, but do you know what Reed's is?" She nodded, thinking back to her conversation with Reed. "Because of Reed's ability he never really touches anyone, but he has always made an exception for kids. I don't know if it's because their emotions aren't as all-consuming, or if he relishes their pure joy. When I was little, it was like having a second dad, only he was the fun one that never said no." The sad smile that he gave as he thought back to those days just about broke Leena's heart. She wanted to reach over the counter and give him a hug, but instead she put her hand on his and waited for him to continue.

"It all changed when I started my transition this year. I'm only going through stage one, so I developed my ability and I change into my wolf now, along with some regeneration, but I haven't reached full regeneration or my full size yet, that comes with stage two. But ever since the first signs of my transition started Reed has been more distant, which I suspect is because of his ability. My da thinks so too. He says that we have to have faith that Reed will get a better control on his ability and that he'll come around." He shrugged, trying to pretend that it didn't bother him, but the glimmer of tears in his eyes belied his nonchalance. "We'll see."

"Hey," she pulled him closer to her, and set her palm on his cheek. His eyes darted around at first, but after a moment he gave a contented sigh and rested his hand on hers. The poor thing didn't seem to want to show that he craved affection. She would change that. Even if she couldn't get Reed to lighten up while she was here, she would make sure that she gave Corrick the affection that he deserved. "If there was ever a reason for Reed to try to overcome his ability, this has got to be it. I'm certain that he will come around. For you."

He gave a short nod, before changing the subject from him and Reed. "So, do you have any siblings?"

"I do. I have an older sister, and a younger brother." She smiled, thinking back to Scotty at Corrick's age. "He's nothing like you, but I still love him to death. My brother and I actually spent most of our time together growing up. We used to help my dad work on the cars in his shop. He used to tease me mercilessly, though. Girls weren't supposed to do boy things. But then he would tease me even more when I started doing girl things." She still remembered crying to her dad about it, and he always knew what to say to make it better. "One thing that I always knew, though, was that if I ever needed him, Scott would be there for me, just like I'm certain Reed would be there for you if you need him, even with his ability."

"Corrick?"

Leena whipped around in her chair at the sound of Reed's voice. He stood at the other end of the over-sized dining table, his tone was firm but gentle as he spoke. "What are you doing down here? You were supposed to wait upstairs."

Corrick started to answer, but Leena cut him off, hoping that she could keep Reed calm. It was unlikely, but she would rather his anger be directed at her than Corrick anyway. "Well," she started, "I was absolutely famished, so your lovely brother here made me the most delicious burgers ever. I was just begging him to marry me, but alas he refused." She gave a dramatic sigh. "Something about me being older than dirt; but I refuse to let that deter me. He'll come around."

She tried not to think about the fact that Reed actually was ridiculously old, especially when she saw the corner of his mouth lift into the slightest smile. What do you know? He did have sense of humor after all. "If you are quite finished with your delicious burgers and your marriage proposals, I will take you to buy some clothes, and we'll come back tomorrow. My father has set a meeting for tomorrow that I'll need to attend."

"How long will it be before I can go home?" she asked, hoping that she didn't sound too desperate.

"A few days at minimum. A few weeks more likely." Reed answered.

"Can we at least go to my house so that I can get my own clothes?" she asked. "I live not far from here, in Greentree."

"That shouldn't be a problem," he said. "Are you just about ready?"

She looked down at the near-empty plate that she had devoured, and nodded her head. Reed grabbed the last burger from her plate and said, "Let's go then," before taking a bite.

She hopped down from the stool that she was sitting on and turned back to Corrick. "Goodbye, lover. Don't miss me too much while I'm gone," she said in a mock-sultry voice, before giving him a wink and blowing a kiss. Corrick only shook his head and laughed, as he turned to clean the griddle on the stove.

She followed Reed to the front door, and when he opened it to the outside, her jaw dropped. The outside of the house was as gorgeous as the inside. In front of the house was a courtyard of stone, beautiful and decorative. There were a number of cars parked out there, but that didn't detract from the stunning sight. She followed Reed out toward the vehicles, giving her a chance to look back at the house itself. It was made of logs, with log columns the size of hundred-year-old trees. The large window's showing the soft glow of light from the rooms inside, combined with the in-ground lights illuminating the courtyard only added to the beauty. The trees that surrounded the house gave the perfect backdrop to the most perfect home Leena had ever laid eyes on.

She looked back to Reed, prepared to ask him how his father managed to score such a house, when the sight of him took her breath away. He stood in the light of the moon with his face tilted up toward it. He looked serene for the first time. The rays of light caressed every inch of his face, highlighting his flawless features.

At that moment, he turned to her, a heated look in his eyes. He approached her slowly, his gaze never wavering. She suddenly felt like prey being stalked by the big bad wolf. The animal in him was never more apparent than at that moment. Not even when he was walking on four legs.

Reed didn't know what it was about Kalina, but she drove him crazy. Each time he decides to push her away, he feels all the more drawn to her. He had just finished pleading with his father like a child to not make him spend any more time with her, when he followed her scent, only to find her telling Corrick that she was *certain* that Reed would always be there for him when he needed him. After his initial anger that Corrick didn't already know that, he felt grateful that Kalina — Leena, he realized she preferred to be called — would assure Corrick on his behalf. But more than that, he realized that she not only said the words, but she believed them, with conviction. He could feel her confidence in him. It was…refreshing.

How was he supposed to stay away from her and let her find the right mate for herself when his wolf howled for her, and his father insisted on him sticking to her like glue?

It hadn't been but ten minutes, and here he was, standing over her, panting like a wolf catching his mate in heat. Any normal woman should have been frightened by having a six-and-a-half foot tall werewolf towering over her, but the emotions that he felt coming from her were desire, with a small amount of trepidation. Her unease, he could tell, wasn't caused by his nearness, but by her reaction to it. He waited a moment, staring into the depths of her sapphire blue eyes that shone brighter than the surrounding lights, for her to make a move.

His heart skipped a beat when she placed her palm on his chest, but his triumph was quickly doused when she took a step back, using her hand to keep Reed from following. Of course, he could have if he had wanted to, but he would never force her to do anything that she didn't want to do.

"I—" she started, voice trembling. She cleared her throat and tried again. "I need to get home...to my boyfriend."

It was like a punch to the face. A boyfriend... Of course she had a boyfriend. The fact that he expected her to be available just shows how stupid he could be. He cleared his face of all emotion, a talent that he developed over years of feeling an exorbitant amount of emotions while trying to fight and defend his people, and gave a short nod.

"Let's get you to him," he managed to say before he escorted her to his truck. He held the passenger door open while she used the running bar and the handle to hoist herself inside. His body trembled with a combination of pain and anger, his wolf clawing to be freed. "Could you give me a few minutes?" he said to Leena, not waiting for the response before he closed the door, and ran for the trees, pulling his shirt over his head as he went.

The moment he tore off his last garment, he hunched over and allowed his wolf to take over. He barely felt the pain that came with his change through the anger that he felt. Anger that he knew he had no right to feel. Not only had she never given him a reason to believe that she was free to court, but he—as she so graciously pointed out while they were upstairs—had pretty much treated her as if she were a thorn in his paw.

As soon as his change was complete, he shook himself and then tore off through the trees as fast as he could, until the noises of the forest were drowned out by the rushing sound of wind, and the pounding of his paws on the ground. He needed this more than he had known. He needed to shed his human instincts and think like his wolf. At that moment, his wolf was thinking one word. Mate. He didn't understand this overwhelming need to claim her for himself after such a short time, but such things didn't matter to his wolf. His wolf saw a strong, capable woman that would protect their young with her last breath; a woman that offered him peace where no one else could.

Mate.

It sang through his entire body. The most beautiful melody he had ever heard. Where he would have been deterred, his wolf was determined. He had to have her, at all costs. He skidded to a halt, and lifted his muzzle to the sky, singing his declaration to the moon. Even if he had to wait several decades until her mortal boyfriend wasted away, he would pursue her. He had nothing but time.

✥

Leena sat in the pick-up truck, waiting for Reed to return. When he ran off the way he did, she couldn't help but worry. This was the man that wouldn't leave her completely alone in the restroom, and now he was leaving her to run off to the forest by himself. She didn't understand why he had looked so…infuriated. Yes, he had looked about ready to kiss her, but before that he had given her no reason to believe that he even thought of her as anything more than a pain in his ass. Granted, his people skills weren't that great due to his ability, but even he had to see that his behavior wasn't conducive to trying to kiss someone.

And if he had showed interest in her before then, what would she have done? Allowed him to kiss her? Would she have given up her safe relationship with Jason for a shot in the dark with Reed? The sad thing was that she thought she just might have. What does that say for her relationship? Nothing good, she supposed.

In the distance, Leena heard a wolf bay at the moon. The sound was heart-wrenchingly beautiful, and it caused a stirring within her that she had never felt before. It was a vibration that ran through her entire body and made her want to shed her humanity and dart into the woods after that sound. *Mine,* something within her sang.

She shifted in the seat, trying to fight the clawing sensation that started beneath her skin. Everything felt uncomfortable to her. The feel of the clothing she was wearing, the weight of her hair on her head, her own skin felt too tight.

This was it. She was going to change into her wolf, and Reed wasn't even here to help her. She didn't know what she should do. If she stayed in the truck, there was the possibility that she would destroy the interior, not to mention hurt herself. If she got out, there was the chance that she wouldn't know what she was doing, and she could hurt someone else.

Fight it, she urged herself. She squeezed her eyes shut, and dug her nails into the seat, fighting blindly against the wolf inside of her, slowly losing the battle. The door next to her flung open and the hands that grabbed her face felt like branding irons against her skin.

"Leena," Reed said. "What's wrong?"

"What. Do. I. Do?" she gritted out through the pain.

"Leena, listen to me," he said. His voice had taken on a different tone, one of authority that she felt compelled to obey. "I want you to stay human right now, do you understand?"

She nodded her head, squeezing her eyes tighter to concentrate on keeping herself human.

"Leena, look at me," Reed said. She snapped her eyes open to see his emerald green eyes mere centimeters from her own. "I *need* you to stay in your human form. You can do this. Settle yourself and concentrate on the tone of my voice."

Leena did as he instructed, and after a few short moments the pain started to subside. Slowly it faded away, until the only thing that remained was the pounding staccato of her heartbeat.

She concentrated on the eyes still boring into her own, etched with worry as he stroked her cheek. The hands on her face no longer seemed to burn, and her skin lost the feeling of a rubber band being stretched to its limit.

"How did you do that?" she asked breathlessly.

"It's a wolf thing," he answered. "The wolf in you recognizes that I am its alpha, and it obeyed a command. It is compulsory, and has everything to do with the ranking in our pack. We are just lucky that you weren't further along in the change, I wouldn't have been able to stop it." She nodded her understanding, too shaken to speak. "I'm so sorry Leena, I shouldn't have left you. I don't understand, though. What caused your shift?"

She shrugged. "I was just sitting here waiting for you to come back, and then I heard a wolf howl, and I just lost control of my body."

His expression changed from one of concern to one of confusion. She didn't know what he was confused about, but for once she didn't care. She just wanted to get home and crawl into her bed.

Reed must have caught her emotions, because he ran his hands across her cheeks one last time, gave a short nod, and closed her door. Moments later he climbed into the driver's side of the truck, and pulled out onto the driveway. It quickly turned into a narrow gravel path that wound through the trees until they reached the back of a house. The house was a large, colonial home that from the front seemed to be the last house on the very short street. It successfully blocked the view of the access drive to the home that they had just come from, preventing passersby from stumbling upon it. Pretty smart for a group of people looking to hide their nature from the outside world.

"Reed, do all of the werewolves live so secluded?" Leena asked, wondering if it were a requirement for their kind to stay detached from rest of the world.

"No," he answered. "My father's house is the only one that has such measures being taken to keep it hidden."

She sighed, a little relieved, but she couldn't stop herself from asking, "Why?"

He stayed quiet for a moment as he pulled out onto the main road. "Well," he started, "my father is very important."

She quirked an eyebrow, and waited for him to continue. When he glanced over to see her still waiting, he expelled a heavy sigh and continued his explanation. "You'll need to know anyway, but I was trying to ease you in to it. Since you're so persistent...my father is one of the werewolf high alphas. We call them Kings. He is the King of the North American pack. Only werewolves have access to his home, everyone unknown to us requesting an audience with him must be escorted by at least one member of the *Lyca Laochra*, which is a small group of trained warriors whose purpose is to enforce our laws, and protect our kind from both threat and exposure. You will actually meet most of them tomorrow."

She nodded, taking it all in. "And, how did your father become the King?" she asked.

"He was hand-chosen by the oldest of us all, who currently rules over Europe and Asia. He used to be the sole ruler of all werewolves, but in his old age, he decided to choose a few of his most trusted soldiers to take over rule of the other continents. Since he had been a king before he was turned into a werewolf, he kept the title, and bestowed the same on my da. He became the first king because he was the first werewolf ever to exist, and he is the strongest of us all. Most believe that he built an army of werewolves in an attempt to exact his vengeance on the God that made him this way, and that's how there got to be so many of us. My da believes that he started with that goal in mind, but that he began to embrace what was meant to be his eternal punishment, and he forfeited his war against the Gods."

"The first ever?" Leena squeaked. "And he's still alive?" Even after hearing Reed's age, that shocked her. "That would make him..."

"Thousands of years old," Reed finished for her.

Thousands... The thought was unbelievable. How someone could have managed to live so long was beyond Leena.

"Which way?" Reed asked, and it took Leena a moment to remember that she was supposed to be directing him to her house.

When she realized that they were on the parkway headed toward her exit, she directed him through the few turns that it took to get to her home. Declan's house was even closer to the town that she had grown up in than she had realized. It had taken no more than ten minutes to get from his home to her street. "All this time the big, bad wolf was just down the road."

"If you only knew what was the other direction..." Reed mumbled. Leena was just about to ask him what he meant by that, before he cut her off, asking which house was hers. She pointed it out, and Reed pulled into the driveway. She jumped out of the truck, the noises from the traffic on the main road behind her house, and the scents coming from the buildings around her assailing her heightened senses.

She stood facing the home that she had spent most of her life in, a ghost of what it used to be. With her father gone, and her mother moved in with her Nana, the house didn't feel the same. It used to be filled with warmth and laughter, and now the house itself looked saddened and hollow. Leena didn't care for the house anymore. Her brother had been the one that couldn't let it go, but he didn't make enough money at the garage to keep it on his own, so Leena had helped in the only way Scott would accept. She moved back in with him.

Even now, she half expected her father to open the front door to greet her. She'd throw her arms around him, and they would walk back into the house tangled in each other's arms, telling each other how their day was.

When Reed stepped up behind her, he wrapped his arm around her waist, just as she imagined her dad would have done. She allowed herself the brief comfort of his embrace, before she stepped away from him, and approached the front door.

She pulled the hidden key from the notch in the banister and unlocked the front door. As she pushed it open, Reed grabbed her hand, preventing her from opening it any further. "Perhaps we should come back at another time," he said.

Leena stared at him, not quite understanding why he didn't want her to go into her own house, when she heard a pained moan coming from inside the house. Her senses went on full alert, and when she heard it again, she knew who it was.

"Jason..." she let out on a whispered gasp.

Chapter Five

Panic overwhelmed Leena, and she used all of her strength to push past Reed and shove the door open far enough to cross the threshold. Once she stepped inside, she heard the moan again, only this time it was accompanied by a softer, more feminine moan, which caused Leena to stop dead in her tracks. She listened more closely to the noises, honing in on them, and then she realized, the moans were not pained sounds, but sounds of pleasure.

Red clouded her vision as the implication dawned on her. "That son of a bitch!" she snarled. She marched over to the staircase, not needing to bother with turning on any of the lights. Even in the darkness, she could see perfectly. Before she made it halfway up the staircase, Reed jumped over the banister, cutting her off in her pursuit. "Move. Right now," she practically growled in a voice unrecognizable to even herself.

"Leena," he whispered, "you need to calm yourself before you go up there—"

He didn't get the chance to finish what he was saying. One moment he was trying to stop her in her tracks, and the next he went soaring over the banister and landed on the sofa in the living room below. The stunned look on his face mirrored Leena's.

How the hell had that happened? She didn't have long to contemplate it, though, because Reed was already recovering from the shock and he was headed for her again.

She ran the rest of the way up the stairs, noticing that even with her speed her foot falls on the stairs were barely audible.

She stopped in front of her bedroom door, the grunting sounds on the other side now accompanied by the sound of flesh smacking against flesh. Her anger rose to a new level, and without thinking, she raised her left leg and slammed a side kick into the wooden door.

The door stayed mostly solid, falling to the ground in her bedroom. The doorjamb splintered, spraying the inside of the bedroom with chunks of wood. The woman began screaming shrilly, while Jason scrambled off of her, looking wildly about for the culprit. Leena flipped the light switch for their benefit, and the moment Jason's gaze landed on her the color drained from his face.

"Babe, it's not what it looks like," he called out to her.

Leena sneered. "You are really going to try that one?" she asked incredulously. "Exactly how stupid do you think that I am?"

At that moment, the cover fell away from the woman's face, giving Leena a view of her for the first time. "Oh, this is rich..." she spat. The woman was not only familiar to Leena, but she had worked alongside her in Leena's studio for the past several months.

"Babe, please, let me explain," Jason beseeched, stabbing his legs into his pants and walking toward her.

Leena raised her hand to stop him from coming any closer. Her entire body shook with rage, but her hand was steady. As was her voice when she said, "Get dressed, and get the fuck out of my house. I don't ever want to see either of you ever again."

"Babe—"

The sound of his voice was drowned out by the pounding of her heart. Her body shook more forcefully, and her skin started to stretch to the point of pain. A crack resounded through the room, and Leena cried out in pain. She looked around frantically, unsure of what to do. Her gaze landed on Reed who had been waiting out in the hallway, and his eyes widened as realization dawned on him. Another crack and Leena doubled over from the force of the pain.

"Babe, what's wrong?" she heard Jason scream, but she couldn't have answered if she had wanted to.

Before she realized what was happening, the floor was wrenched out from underneath her, and she was clutched to a muscular chest. She recognized the man holding her as Reed from his scent. As he carried her down the hall, she heard Jason screaming after them, asking who the hell Reed was, and what the hell he was doing, as if he had the right. Reed ignored him, and shouldered his way into Scott's room, gently laying her out on the bed, before leaving the room.

Leena screamed out again, as her bones snapped and shifted. Her skin felt as if it were on fire. The pain was worse than she had ever imagined it would be, and the only thing that she could do to combat it was curl into the fetal position and pray that it would end soon. Her cries turned to whimpers as she became accustomed to the pain, until finally it stopped.

The process had taken roughly five minutes, but it had felt like five hours. When she realized her body had stopped shifting, Leena slowly lifted her head, and the first things that she saw were cream and caramel colored paws where her arms should have been. She examined the rest of what should have been her body. Fur: check, haunches: check, tail: check. *Son. Of. A. Bitch!*

At least I'm not a bald wolf, she thought briefly before her vision clouded with red yet again.

❧❦

Well, wasn't that a catastrophe? Reed thought after he managed to throw Jason and his rut-buddy out of Leena's house. He would have never expected what they had just walked in to. In his world, infidelity was practically unheard of. If a werewolf had no desire to be monogamous, they didn't commit. It was as simple as that. Werewolves are far too possessive to even think of sharing what they consider theirs, and a mate is no different. Not to mention the fact that it utterly baffled Reed that anyone could even think to sleep with someone else when he had a woman like Leena. The man was obviously an *eejit*. It had taken all of Reed's self-control not to punch Jason in the face, but that was as much of a courtesy as he could extend to the arrogant arse.

After Reed left the bedroom that he had deposited Leena in, Jason had tried to push past him to get to her, screaming that she would regret her decision to break things off with him, that she would never find someone to put up with her like he had. Reed knew that Leena probably hadn't even heard him past the pain of her first change, but the words enraged him none-the-less. Reed had grabbed the other man by the throat, and lifted him off of the floor, cutting his words short. "Get. Out," was all Reed had needed to say — or rather, growl. The color had drained from Jason's face, and he gathered the rest of his clothes and left without much of a fight after that. The woman needed no more than a look from Reed before she hurriedly ran after him. Reed hovered over them, and stalked them to the front door, the wolf in him disappointed when he let them leave, and just locked the door behind them. There was something more important to take care of than his wolfish desires.

At least one good thing had come out of today.... Reed now knew what kind of power Leena had developed upon becoming a werewolf, and it was one that he had never seen to the extent that she had shown.

Normally when one of the werewolves develops Telekinesis, it is Minor Telekinesis, and they have a hard time actually lifting things. The most they are able to do is skate items across surfaces. On her first display of power, Leena had tossed him across the room. He could only imagine what she would be able to do if given time and a little training.

Reed followed the sounds of wood splintering, and a wolf snarling. The door to the bedroom that he had put Leena in was precariously close to giving way under the weight of her wolf's body as she threw herself against it. He waited for her to do it again, before he shoved the door open, and caught her by the scruff of her neck as she charged it once more. She snapped and snarled as he tackled her to the ground, trying her damnedest to rip into his arms. She actually managed to tear some flesh off before he grasped her muzzle and snapped it shut.

His voice took on the authoritative tone that let their people know that his words brooked no room for disobedience, looked into her deep blue eyes, and said, "Enough."

It took a few moments longer than it should have, but eventually her wolf's body went slack in his arms, compelled to follow out his command. Her wolf was absolutely beautiful, which didn't surprise him, but he had never seen another werewolf with similar coloring. Her snout, underbelly, and insides of her legs were a creamy white, while the rest of her was a golden brown. Her tail and her ears were tipped with black.

She stirred under the weight of his stare, part of her eager to run and rend, while another part of her recognized Reed as an alpha male, and didn't dare contradict him. He let his hold on her slacken, still keeping his eyes on hers, as he guided her through the change back to human.

"Leena, I need you to focus. The wolf is only a part of who you are, I need you to grasp your other half and pull her to the fore. Take control."

Her sides rose and fell slowly as she took deep breaths. It took a few more moments of encouraging words before her body began to tremble and fur was pulled into her skin. Her bones and muscles began shifting next, and that was when Reed released his hold on her completely.

After a few more moments, Leena lay before him, human…and nude. The change had ripped the clothes from her, rendering them useless. She kept herself turned sideways, her arm draped over her breasts and her legs arranged to keep her lower half covered. She would likely lose her modesty after a few changes. Most werewolves did. When you wake up the morning after a full moon, not knowing where you left your clothes, surrounded by several others in the same predicament, you tend to get over your modesty rather quickly. Her hair fell to the floor next to her, giving Reed a view of her back. Unexpectedly, her back and side were covered in tattoos. He could only make out the one on her side, tucked up close to her breast, which looked like some sort of scripture. Interesting.

As she recovered, she dug her fingernails into the carpet, as if she still had claws. Reed had assumed that it was due to the pain, but when he honed in on her with his Empathy the only emotion that he felt was anger. She was furious, at both Jason and herself. He could understand the former, but he couldn't wrap his head around the latter. Why would she be angry with herself?

As if she heard his internal question, she muttered, "So stupid… How could I have been so blind? I should have known."

He placed his hand over hers, which was still hot from the change, and said, "Take it from someone who is practically a walking lie detector, there are people that are so good at deception that even I cannot always tell when they are keeping something secret. Even my Da has been successfully lied to. You can't blame yourself."

She looked at him just then, sapphire blue eyes boring into his own. He could see the emotions in her eyes as well as feel them through his connection. She knew that he was right, but she was still pissed.

She pushed herself up to sit on the floor, keeping her breasts covered with her arm, and took a look around the room to assess the damage. It wasn't too bad. Torn comforter, shredded clothes, splintered door. Worry crossed her face in the next instant, and her search became more frantic. She jumped to her feet, forgetting that she no longer wore panties to cover her, and squealed, "Where is my dog?"

"I'll look for it while you get dressed," Reed told her. She nodded once, and rushed down the hall to her bedroom. Reed swept the house, letting his heightened senses guide him. When he finally heard the whimpering coming from a door leading off of the kitchen, Leena had already joined him, fully dressed in a pair of form-fitting jeans, which showed off her rounded arse and strong thighs, a black tank top, and knee-high black leather boots. The material hugged her curves in all the right places, and the sight of her stole Reed's breath, and he forgot to speak. Even in her casual clothes, she was more stunning than any woman he had ever seen before.

He turned the knob to the door and opened it, without taking his eyes off of her. In turn, he was knocked off balance by a white and copper blur that darted past him and leapt into Leena's embrace. Her face lit up with the brightest smile Reed had ever seen as she allowed herself to be knocked to the ground by the oversized Husky. It burrowed its nose under her shirt and sniffed at her stomach furiously. Reed could understand why. She would smell different to the dog. Her usual scent would still be prominent, but now she would have an underlying musk that came with being a werewolf. The dog nosed at her for quite a while before it decided that it was satisfied and began licking her face.

They stayed that way for several minutes, before Leena set the dog away from her, scratching it one more time behind the ears as she jumped to her feet. Her movements were so lithe and graceful, even for a werewolf, that Reed found himself staring at her, mesmerized. She didn't know it yet, but he would make her his, if it was the last thing that he did.

~⊙⊙~

Leena couldn't help but feel as if she had stepped into some sort of parallel universe. Her world was flipping upside-down, changing irrevocably. She had turned into a wolf—a freaking wolf!—ripped her brother's room apart, and the idiot man that had been so persistent in being a part of her life had betrayed her.

Granted, their relationship hadn't been the best. They were different in so many aspects, some of which Jason had had a hard time with accepting. She was strong and independent, and he had always wanted her to rely on him. The damsel act was one that Leena could never pull off. Her dad had raised her to be tough. He taught her to fight, he taught her how to use a number of weapons, and he taught her how to fix just about anything around the house. The daughter of Jonathan Abrams would never rely on a man for anything.

Still, Leena couldn't fathom why Jason would have stayed with her if he was so unhappy. If he felt that she wasn't good enough, just the way she was, then he should have left. She wouldn't have stopped him. She would have rather been alone than be played for a fool. The thing that made her so angry, wasn't so much his betrayal as the fact that it was done in *her* house, on *her* bed, with *her* employee.

If she would have eventually become saddened at one point by what Jason had done to her, Leena didn't foresee that happening any longer.

There was one thing on this earth that Leena cared about more than anything else, and it was Wraith. Her poor dog had been locked in the basement of his own house for...she didn't even know how long, just so that idiot could sleep with someone else.

She took a few deep breaths to prevent herself from changing again, and introduced Reed to Wraith. Wraith had been wary at first, but it didn't take long for the fluff-ball to warm up to Reed.

When Wraith decided that he was done with his greetings, Leena let him out into the backyard, leaving the door open for him to come back in at his leisure.

"Wraith?" Reed questioned. "It's an interesting name for a dog. How did you come up with it?"

Leena thought back to the day that she found Wraith and her anger for Jason intensified. Her sweet dog had been through so much in his lifetime that she had vowed to keep him safe and pamper him for the rest of his life.

"My father and I were driving home from a trip into the city. He had just sit through a ballet production of Dracula at the Benedum for me, and on our drive home we saw a box on the ramp leading to the bridge. As he passed the box, I looked back in the side mirror and saw a lump of fur. He pulled the car over, stopping traffic in that lane on the bridge, and when we came upon the box we found a litter of Husky pups left out in the cold. They must have been newborns, each one was small enough to fit in the palm of my hand. We never knew if it was the cold or the manner in which they had been dumped, but five of the six pups had been dead before we got to them. Wraith was at the bottom of the pile, kept warm by the bodies of his dead brothers and sisters. He was close to death himself, but we were able to get him to the vet in time to save him. That's how he got his name. My dad and I pulled him back from the brink of death. He's my little wraith."

Leena had always known that there were horrible people in the world, but she had never been able to comprehend why someone would have disposed of a litter of newborn pups in such a manner. Never mind the fact that people would have paid a small fortune to own those pups, if the owners hadn't wanted to raise them they could have given them to a shelter. Their death was more than unnecessary, it was cruel.

Reed reached out a hand to her and she took it for a moment, knowing that he felt her emotions and meant to give her comfort. While Leena wanted nothing more than to go to him and bury her face in his shoulder, she was stopped when she remembered Reed's aversion to physical contact, and in particular his distaste for their situation.

Instead, Leena gave his hand a light squeeze and brushed past him to return to her bedroom. She needed to pack a bag to take to Reed's, and she also needed to take her mind off of the situation by cleaning the splinters of wood.

Even knowing that Reed wasn't thrilled with their situation, Leena could see now after her episode with Jason just how much she needed to be around Reed. Her shift had come unexpectedly, and once she had changed, she had lost herself to the desires of her wolf. The wolf had wanted to hunt. To rip its fangs into flesh.

Leena had no idea that when she shifted she would be fighting for control of herself, that she would have to fight the nature of the wolf. She was under the assumption that she was still herself, just in wolf form. What a wake-up call this had been.

What was worse was what she had done to Reed. Even as he tried to hide his arm from her, she smelled the blood, and caught the glimpse of red where she had torn into him. If that had been anyone but Reed, she likely would have torn them to shreds, just like the wolf in South Carolina had done to her.

At least Jason's indiscretion had given her a viable excuse to use for not living in her own house for the next few weeks. She had wondered what she would say to Scott about staying somewhere else, and this gave her the perfect justification. She still didn't know how she would gloss over the fact that she would be staying with a man that she had just met, but she at least had a reason not to stay here.

She also hadn't known how she was going to explain Scott's room to him, but when she called him, the lie flowed from her lips more easily than she cared to admit. Jason had locked Wraith in Scott's room, and Wraith had become distraught and lost himself. Truth be told, Wraith would never have destroyed anything, but Scott seemed so upset by what Jason had done, that logic was beyond him.

All packed up, in true female form—with more clothes than she would likely need, of all different fashions—Leena looked around her room for anything else that she may need. Her gaze landed on the bed, and she tried to ignore the scents that floated up to her nostrils. With another wave of fury, Leena dropped her bags to the floor, marched back to her dresser, and ripped one of the drawers from its track. After dumping its contents onto the bed, she repeated the process with three other drawers, until all of Jason's clothes lay on her bed. She pulled the corners of the sheets up from her bed, tied them together, and then chucked the bundle into her bathroom.

When she turned back to her bedroom Wraith sat in doorway watching her, with Reed standing right behind him. They both had their heads cocked to the side as they watched her move about the room. She had known when they had arrived, presumably so that Reed could make sure that she didn't go wolfy on him again, but she hadn't cared. If Reed had a problem, he could kiss her ass. But, rather than the derision that she expected to see on his face, he looked somber, as if he felt sorry for her and understood why she was so angry.

It wasn't that the idiot had shoved his cock into someone else; it was that he had made a mockery of her. She remembered back to earlier that night when Reed had loomed over her with a heated look in his eyes. She had pushed him away claiming that she had a boyfriend. What. An. Idiot. She should have kissed the sexy werewolf when she had the chance, and vowed then and there that if she ever got the opportunity again, she wouldn't hesitate.

As Leena contemplated how she would move forward from here, footsteps sounded on the walkway outside. After her initial shock that she could hear them so clearly Leena slipped past Reed and rushed to the door, Reed and Wraith right on her heels. The door flung open to reveal her baby brother in all of his protective anger. She could have kissed him, but instead she jumped into his arms and squeezed him in the tightest embrace that she could without breaking something.

Even covered in grease and dirt, her little brother was more handsome than ever. With his brown hair cropped close to his scalp, and his easy grin, he looked like a spitting image of their dad. The thought squeezed at Leena's heart, but she didn't let it show.

Quickly her brother's expression turned serious, and he clasped his hands on either side of her face and put his forehead against hers, looking into her eyes. "Don't you ever scare me like that again," he demanded. "I can't lose you."

With one last fierce hug, she pulled away from her brother, a man well beyond his twenty-three years of age, and turned to introduce him to Reed.

"Scotty, I'd like you to meet Reed. He is the one that saved me."

Scott outstretched his hand to Reed. "Thank you so much, man. I owe you."

"Don't mention it," Reed said coolly, grasping Scott's hand tightly. He stared at him intently, assessing him. Scott made no objections, and showed no signs of pain, but Leena could tell that Reed's grip was debilitating. She didn't understand the power play, but then again, she never did understand why men did the things that they did. And they had the nerve to call women complicated.

She lightly placed her hand on Reed's shoulder, and he released Scott's hand. She made sure he felt her irritation before she said, "Scott is my brother."

If he felt contrite, he showed no sign of it, but he did lighten his tone when he proclaimed, "Nice to meet you."

Scott nodded. "You also." He turned back to his sister and asked, "Lee, you want to help me with the new hardware while I get the doors?"

She moved to follow him out the door, but Reed stepped in front of her and said, "I'll do it." Whatever. If he wanted to do it, she wasn't going to gripe about it. Instead, she went into the garage to get the power drill and a few screwdrivers so that they could replace the bedroom doors, and change the locks to the house. She found the drill easily enough, but the screw drivers were missing from their usual spot. As she sifted through Scott's toolbox, she heard footsteps approach the garage door and stop.

"That's a beautiful car," Reed said.

She looked up to see him admiring her dad's old Mustang Fastback. The one that her and Scott had helped him rebuild from the ground up. It was her grandfather's before he passed, and when her dad had inherited it, it had become a family project to get it back to its former glory. Leena had done the body work, Scott, had done the mechanics, and Dad had redone the interior. Reed was right, she was beautiful, but her beauty hadn't been shared with anyone other than her brother and sister since her dad had died a few years back. Not even Jason had been allowed to get inside that car.

"May I?" Reed asked, reaching his hand toward the handle. He could have had his father's ability to read minds with his timing.

Leena just stared at him for a few moments as he waited with his hand outstretched, not touching her most precious possession until she gave her consent. With a short nod from her, Reed opened the door, and instead of getting in as she had expected, he knelt beside the car, running his fingers lightly over the supple leather. She returned to digging through the toolbox, entrusting the large, Irish werewolf with her father's car.

By the time she found the screwdrivers, Reed had moved on from the Mustang to her own Jeep Wrangler. Next to the sleek classic, her Jeep was nothing special, save for the modifications that she had made to it. The front bumper, the useless plastic that it was, was now encased with a sturdy, black metal brush guard that attached to the frame, and she had bent to resemble black flames licking the grill of the Jeep. Along the top were automated, swivel spotlights, attached to the black metal roll cage that framed the top of the vehicle. Leena knew that most people assumed that her Jeep was owned by a male when they saw it, but she had never cared. Ever since she was young she had been obsessed with making things out of metal. Put something in front of her that can have metal tacked to it, and she would go crazy. The result: her badass, one of a kind, off-road vehicle.

This time, without looking to her for permission, Reed stroked his hand along the folded steel bars, tracing the curves and points of the metal. "I've never seen one of its like. Where did you get this?"

"I made it," she said simply, waiting for his disbelief.

He surprised her again by saying, "I would love to have you make one for my truck one day."

Gobsmacked…that's what she was. Here was a man that knew nothing about her, and he not only appreciated the work that she could do, but he didn't even judge her for it. Most people couldn't understand what a nice, pretty girl like her was doing working with fire and metal day in and day out, and they couldn't understand that she found the act comforting. That seeing something as tough as metal bend and form to her will gave her satisfaction. She could learn to get used to Reed…so long as he wasn't stomping around and brooding.

"Consider it done," she said before returning to the main house, tools in hand.

It didn't take long for Scott and Reed to get to work, leaving Leena and Wraith to stand around uselessly. That was never really Leena's forte, so instead, she slipped out the back door as quietly as possible—which she learned was pretty stealthy, if she said so herself—with Wraith in tow, and she walked across the yard and through the thin stretch of trees. Her usual path to her studio.

Chapter Six

After his initial encounter with Leena's brother, Scott, Reed actually found that he rather liked the young man. He was hardworking, strong, and he loved Leena with all of his heart. Not only as a brother, but as a friend. He had discovered that the two of them still went on the annual camping trips that they used to take with their father. Just the two of them, some firewood, and a case of beer. That explained the roll cage and spotlights on Leena's Jeep. Scott had confessed to him that he always thought that Jason was envious of how close he and Leena were, but Reed couldn't understand why.

She no longer had her father, so Scott had become the man in her life. Nothing to be jealous of there. In fact, the only thing that Reed was jealous of was that the two of them were able to do those types of things together. He wondered if Corrick would die of shock if Reed would ask him to go camping with him for a weekend. Most likely. He didn't even know how he had let their relationship get to the point where it was, but after overhearing the conversation between Corrick and Leena, Reed had every intention of salvaging his relationship with his baby brother. The time for letting his ability overwhelm him was over. Leena had been right. If there was ever a time to try to overcome it, now was it. He couldn't lose his brother.

As soon as the new bedroom doors were hung and the locks were changed on the outer doors, Reed looked around for Leena. He hadn't heard from her or her dog, Wraith, in a while. He knew that she wasn't upstairs, because he would have heard her, or sensed her. The rooms on the first floor showed no signs of her either. Reed discreetly sniffed the air, trying to catch the freshest trail, but it was no use, she had moved around far too much.

"Where is she?" he practically snarled to Scott, as he rechecked every room. Just in case. She should have known not to go anywhere, especially after her change earlier. That should have been enough to show her that she needed to stay close to Reed. Headstrong female...

"She probably went to her studio," Scott said. "She's been through such an emotional roller coaster that she's going to need to release it all. She does that through dance."

"Where is it?"

"It's just located out on the main road, but if you walk it's even easier to get to. The trees that line the back of the property separate the houses from the businesses on the other side. Her studio is the one at the corner. I can take you there, if you want."

"That's okay, I'll find my way. Thanks."

With a shake of Scott's hand, Reed left the house and started walking across the lawn, picking up Leena's trail the moment he passed their pool. He followed it through the trees at a diagonal, noting the wear in the path that was obviously taken daily before he was deposited onto a parking lot. He followed her trail to the side of the building where there was a door that accessed the back of the building. Reed could tell that she used this door often, but she hadn't used it today. Still, he looked through the glass of the door, noting the machinery and a wall that housed shelves of varying types of metal.

Reed backed away from that door to follow her fresh trail, which led him to the front of the same building. The entire front was made of glass, including the door, giving Reed a full view of her dance studio. The right wall was lined with mirrors from floor to ceiling, the left wall had ballet barres bolted to the walls. The back of the studio had a wall that had mirrors on the left half, but not on the right. It also had two doors. The door next to the mirrors also seemed to be made of a mirrored glass, while the door on the right was solid. In front of the solid wall was a table holding a large stereo system with an iPod docked in the middle of it. Under the table Wraith lay on a large dog bed, watching Leena as she danced. From the stereo, a song that Reed had heard a few times before blared loudly enough that the lyrics could be heard clearly from outside, even if he hadn't had supernatural hearing.

> *...This is my fight song*
> *Take back my life song*
> *Prove I'm alright song*
> *My power's turned on*
> *Starting right now I'll be strong*
> *I'll play my fight song*
> *And I don't really care if nobody else believes*
> *'Cause I've still got a lot of fight left in me*

Leena floated across the floor, her feet moving so fast that Reed could barely keep track of them. Punctuating the emotion in the song, she jumped around the room, often popping up onto her toes. She even managed a series of flips and leaps that defied gravity. Her long hair whipped at her face, and sweat dripped from her skin, but she didn't seem to notice or care. Through the glass, Reed could feel the emotions leaking out of her. The fainter emotions were anger and hatred, but the one that seemed to consume her was freedom. Being on that floor, allowing her body to move however the beat of the song carried it brought her a kind of joy and release that most people wouldn't understand. Hell, Reed wouldn't have understood it if he hadn't seen it. Felt it. Her eyes were closed, her movements lithe. Each movement looked both practiced and effortless, and she molded them together as if it were a routine that she had been learning since she was a child, but he somehow knew that she was making it up as she went. The sight of her was absolutely mesmerizing.

Reed had been prepared to come here and ream her a new arsehole for leaving the house, but just watching her move across the floor calmed even his emotions.

When the track ended, Reed entered the studio. He expected her to be startled, whipping her head in his direction, but she made no jerky movement at all, just walked to the stereo to turn it off.

"I knew that you were there," she said, answering his unasked question.

"How?"

"I could feel you watching me," was all she said, and Reed decided not to press her on the matter.

"You shouldn't have left the house. I can't protect you if I don't know where you are."

She glared at him then, frustration rolling through her. "Spare me. You've made it quite clear that you don't care to be my babysitter. Besides, it's not like I went somewhere with a lot of people, or somewhere that I may run into someone that could spark a change. I walked through trees and came to my own establishment, which is currently closed to the public. I would have been more of a danger at the house."

Reed opened his mouth to snap something back at her, but quickly clamped his mouth shut. Her emotions were still raw, and she was lashing out because of it. He could feel it. He certainly wasn't used to having people talk to him the way that she did, and while he didn't find it quite as refreshing as his da had, he couldn't fault her for it either. Everything she said was true. He had griped about being her "babysitter" and had given her no reason to believe that he had her interests in mind.

Right now, she needed his understanding and compassion. He took a deep breath, trying to calm himself before speaking. He was spared from having to decide what to say to her when she expelled a deep breath and said, "I'm sorry. I shouldn't have said that. And you're right, I shouldn't have left without informing you."

He nodded, accepting her apology. He hadn't expected her to get control over her emotions so quickly, and even less had he expected to hear her apologize to him. She certainly wasn't like anyone he had ever met before, and he marveled at how easily she was able to release her hold on her anger. He admired that about her.

He let out a sigh. "It is getting late. When you're ready we'll get your things and head back to my place."

Well, there was something he had never said to a woman before…

Leena raised her eyebrow at him, catching the double entendre of his words. Instead of remarking on it, she simply said, "I'll get a shower and we can leave."

She turned on her heel and stopped, turning back to him. She looked as if she wanted to say something, but didn't know how to phrase it. Finally she took a deep breath and just spit it out. "Would you mind if I brought my dog?" she asked quickly. "You don't have to say yes," she continued, "Scott would be more than willing to watch him, but—"

Reed stopped her from rambling on any further. "You can bring him."

Her face lit up in a bright smile and she thanked him more than once.

He nodded, and watched as she went through the solid door at the back wall, Wraith right on her heels. Before the door snapped shut, he caught a glimpse of lockers and stalls. A changing room, equipped with showers.

Out of curiosity, he opened the mirrored door at the other end of the wall. An office. From inside the office, Reed realized that the mirrors were actually one-way glass. He could see every inch of the studio from here, and on the other side of the room, one-way glass showed him another vantage point of the workshop that he had seen from the side door. From this view, Reed could see that she had two clamps in the floor hold up a nearly-complete motorcycle frame. A woman who danced like an angel and yet pounded metal into subservience...such a contradiction of soft and hard, and yet, it fit Leena. She was beauty and grace, and at the same time she was fierce and strong. She would be the perfect fit for their alpha female.

✥✥✥

Once her hair was dried, Leena hung up the blow dryer, got dressed and met Reed out in the studio. The walk back to her house was uneventful, aside from a civilized conversation with Reed about her and Scott's relationship. She was learning that Reed was actually trying not to be an A-hole, and she couldn't help but be grateful. While she had fun poking the bear—or wolf as it were—she liked this side of Reed far more. He was relaxed and chivalrous, holding his hand out for her to step over a tree root. She took it, just to keep him reposeful. She could have sworn that she even saw him smile at one point, and if she were being honest, even his half-smile was enough to have any woman stop and stare at him, if there were any women out at this time of night.

With her luggage on the back seat of Reed's truck, and Wraith in the bed, they made the drive back toward his home. It had seemed as if they were going back to Declan's at first, but rather than taking the access road, Reed stopped at the colonial home that appeared the be the last house on the street. The house was so modest that Leena was shocked that it belonged to Reed. The Prince of Werewolves lived in a house that you would expect to see a tire swing in the front yard and apple pies baking in the kitchen. It was beautiful.

Reed parked the truck in front of the detached garage, next to a first-generation Hummer Alpha in pristine condition. He looked surprised to see the vehicle there, so Leena assumed that it wasn't his. He leaned over to her in the truck and whispered, "Listen, before we go inside, I am sorry in advanced," and then he slipped out of the truck, not giving her time to respond.

Well, that was cryptic. She couldn't help but wonder what would possibly make Reed apologize to her. Whatever it was it wouldn't be good, of that she was certain.

She and Wraith followed Reed toward the front porch. She made a grab for at least one of the bags that bogged him down more than once, but he moved them out of her reach and glared at her. She raised her hands in defeat and opened the front door for him instead.

Once inside, Reed deposited her bags at the bottom of the stairwell in front of them and continued into the living room off to the left. The furniture was white leather, oversized, and comfortable looking, and in one of the chairs sat a man that was beyond sexy, and his expression told her that he knew it. With his wavy blond hair brushing his collar bone, his perfectly groomed beard, and his silver eyes, he was the type of man that probably had women throwing themselves at him when he went out in public. His lean, muscular frame and wicked grin only added to his sex appeal, but there was something about him that screamed to Leena that he was a heartbreaker. Perhaps it was the way he carried himself as he stood and gave her a slow, lingering perusal. Yeah, yeah. Get your fill, pretty boy.

The man only took his eyes off of Leena when Reed growled low in his throat and said, "Shaun, what're you doing here?"

"Your aul man said you'd be coming back here soon, so I thought I'd come and check on the lovely new she-wolf," Shaun answered. He also had an Irish accent, but it sounded slightly different from Reed's and Declan's. Thicker. "She is quite the lash, isn't she? Please tell me you've rattled her," he said to Reed.

She turned to see Reed's face go expressionless. She raised her eyebrow at him questioningly, but he didn't enlighten her as to what Shaun had meant. "Fecking gobshite," he muttered, and punched Shaun in the arm none-too-gently. If the punch had hurt, Shaun showed no signs of it, just grinned like a fool.

"Come off it," he said. "She doesn't even know what I've said. At least tell me you've dropped the hand a bit. Given the Aussie kiss? Had her shift your flute?"

With each new phrase, Reed's fists balled tighter and tighter. Leena could tell that he was trying to decide if it would give him satisfaction to punch Shaun in the face this time, but he must have decided against it.

She placed her hand gently on Reed's arm and asked, "Which room am I staying in?" He seemed to be relieved that she asked, and told her which direction to go once she reached the top of the stairs. Wraith followed closely behind her as she went up the stairs and to the right. The first door she came to was the bedroom that she would be staying in. The décor was very simple. A queen-sized bed, two dressers, and a television. It was perfect.

❧❦

The moment that Leena was out of earshot, Reed punched Shaun as hard as he dared without trying to break anything. The *eejit* just stood there, laughing. "You're a fecking tool."

Shaun shrugged nonchalantly, and returned to the chair that he had been sitting in. Reed grabbed two beers from his refrigerator, handed one to his best friend — although, after today he may have to reconsider their friendship — and joined him on the adjacent sofa.

"You like her, I can tell," Shaun accused. Reed didn't bother denying it, just drank from his bottle. "It's about bloody time."

"You didn't come here just to bust my balls, and you would have seen Leena tomorrow night. Why did you really come?"

"Perceptive bastard." Shaun took another swig from his bottle before answering. "I went out with Lucan tonight after chasing down a rogue in the city, and he was telling me that your da was raving about this new she-wolf. Of course, raving by your da's standards are pretty much just saying that the girl is tough as nails, but it was more than that. Lucan says that your da thinks that she'll be the females' new alpha bitch. That she exhibits all the signs of a true dominant; protective, strong, and resilient. Of course, he's telling me all of this, and I look up, and a few tables over are Jasmine and Annabelle, and they've heard every word of what Lucan has said. She slammed some cash down on the table and stormed out of there. I just wanted to give you a heads-up. She'll be at the meeting tomorrow night, and she'll likely try something. You know how she is."

Reed nodded. Unfortunately, if Annabelle had heard that conversation, it was more than likely that she would test Leena somehow. The woman had always played games, and the only reason she had remained the alpha bitch this long is because she had never been challenged. She won't take an overthrow lightly, but if she were a true dominant, she would do what was best for the pack, even if that meant stepping down in her role. That would be a cold day in hell.

Knowing Annabelle, she would challenge Leena in a way that meant he or his da could not interfere. The only thing that he would be able to do to help her is try to prep her before the meeting. They would have to go to his da's house early to get started. He had to try to fit years' worth of training into a few hours' time. She would probably hate him afterward, but if it helped her hold her own against Annabelle, he would do it.

He and Shaun talked a bit longer, telling each other what they've done the past few days, and then he left. Not long after, Leena reemerged, redressed in loose cotton pants and a tank top that hugged her frame, her hair tied back in a long, thick plait. On her heels was her furry sidekick. Reed wondered if the dog would ever leave her side if he didn't have to. Probably not; and he couldn't blame the pup either.

"He was an...interesting character," Leena said. Reed couldn't help but smile. Shaun definitely took some getting used to, but when he was at your back in a fight, you knew that you were protected. He may blow through women swift as the wind, but he was loyal to the death when it came to his friends.

"Don't pay him any mind. He's actually not too bad once you get past the philandering."

She grimaced. "So he's always like that?"

Reed took a minute to think about it. Shaun didn't often talk to women quite in that way. He was normally flirty and sly. He usually only spoke like that in front of the people that he wasn't trying to impress, most often the other men. He also spoke like that to the women of the pack that he didn't particularly have an interest in, most often Annabelle. It was hard to tell why he spoke to Leena that way, but considering that he was able to guess that Reed was attracted to her, he probably wanted her to see the real him.

"He's not always, but certainly more often than not. I'm not going to try to make excuses for him, but he is the way that he is for a reason." He took a swig of his beer as Leena tucked her feet up under her and settled into the oversized chair that Shaun had vacated. "He lost his entire family at such a young age that he doesn't let himself become attached to mortal women. There aren't any women in the pack that he can see himself settling down with long-term, so he takes the playboy route. I believe he put on that display for you to show you a courtesy, in his own right. That's his way of showing you his worst side, hoping that you can see past it, and at the same time, letting you know that he doesn't plan to try to bed you."

She raised her eyebrow at him. "You got all of that from him asking if I 'shifted a flute?' What does that even mean, anyway?"

"You really don't want to know," he said, not really knowing how to explain it to her without an image of her on her knees in front of him invading his mind. She shrugged her shoulder as if she didn't much care what it meant, and shifted her gaze. She looked around her, for what, Reed didn't know. "Can I help you find something?" he asked her.

She looked almost embarrassed, but she said, "I'm really hungry."

Of course she was. She had gone through a change and a lot of physical exertion since she last ate, burning off all of the burgers that she had eaten. He led her to the kitchen, where he began making her some steak and filling her in on the meeting tomorrow, leaving off the part about Annabelle likely challenging her.

"So you're going to discuss what to do about the werewolf that attacked me, and assign someone to go down and take care of it?" she asked around a bite of meat.

He nodded, "Pretty much."

"I want to go," she said, not so much asking him for permission as telling him that she intended to go.

"No."

"It wasn't a request," she snapped.

"The answer is still no," he said. "You're too new, and no matter which of my men goes, they'll worry more about keeping you safe than doing what needs to be done with this rogue. You're not going."

"Did it ever occur to you that I can take care of myself?"

"No. Not up against a werewolf that has let his wolf instincts overrule his humanity. He would tear you to shreds."

She growled low in her throat, a sound that would never come from a human, but he knew that he made the noise himself when he was frustrated. In the next instant she pulled the paring knife from his butcher block, held the blade with her left hand, and tossed it at the corkboard on the other side of the kitchen. The blade stuck with a loud thud, and when Reed looked, he saw the hilt protruding out of the gag photo that Shaun had tacked to the board. It was of Reed, sitting at a bar with a woman grinding in his lap. Every time he ripped the photo down, a new one was put up in its place, so Reed had eventually given in and left it. He expected to see the blade sticking into his face, but when he looked closer, he saw that it was stuck in the woman's neck. For some reason, that made him smile, which only infuriated Leena more.

"Impressive," he said to her. "But you're still not going."

"We'll see about that," she mumbled, swiping the rest of her steak off of the plate and carrying it up the stairs as if it were a sandwich.

Of all of the people for him to be drawn to, it had to be this headstrong woman. The gods must truly hate him.

Chapter Seven

The next morning, Reed woke Leena up at a most ungodly hour. She figured that it was punishment for stabbing his bimbo in the throat the night before. If he harbored any ill will toward her, he hadn't shown it, other than pounding on her door loud enough to wake the freaking dead.

She was so close to ripping his jugular from his throat with her bare hands, when a plate of heaven saved his life. He was standing on the other side of the door with a plate full of omelets, stopping her dead in her tracks. The smell of bacon, ham, and cheese wafted up to her nostrils, causing her mouth to water.

She thought of those omelets now to stop herself from ripping his pretty face off. They had been at his father's house for hours already. The first few hours Reed had her sniffing absolutely everything, committing it to memory. She sniffed the wood of the house, the leather furniture, and the contents of the refrigerator. Hell, he even had her sniff his father. While the King smelled like a wonderful mix of tangerine, and what she later discovered was a hint of teakwood, it was probably one of the more awkward things that she had ever done.

The sniff tests had continued for a while, apparently they had a whole room devoted to it. She now knew the scents of herbs that she had never even heard of before today. Somewhere in that time he fed her again, and now, she lay on a black dojo mat, sweating profusely, having had her ass sufficiently kicked. He was trying to kill her, she determined. She could see it in his smug look.

She had been fairly confident in her fighting abilities, before today. Reed put her to utter shame. He knew each moved she was going to make before she made it, and he head her off. When she made a false step, he struck out at her, when he caught her punch, he'd strike her again, when her kick didn't withdraw fast enough, he flipped her onto her ass. Her body was so sore, that she doubted that there would be any flesh left on her that wasn't bruised.

She pushed herself to her feet, and approached Reed again, going back for more. That was one thing that she could say for herself; she was too foolish to give up. She looked to his left and made a move to lift her right foot to kick him there, changing it at the last moment to kick her left foot dead center in his chest. Her blow landed, but she was surprised that she didn't shatter the bones in her foot. It was like kicking a brick wall. She went for him again, glancing down to his feet, but jumping up instead. She wrapped her legs around his chest and dove for the mat behind him, pulling him down to the floor with her. Before they hit the mat, Leena twisted her body to land on top of his chest, digging her knees into his biceps. Finally.

Her triumph didn't last long. Being so high on his chest left his legs free, which he used to kick up and wrap around her torso. He pulled her onto her back, flipping on top of her, pinning her knees to her chest. The weight of him pressed her into the mat, and she couldn't move. Crap.

"If you wanted to be on top, all you had to do was ask," she said.

The corner of his mouth twitched, but he didn't let the smile break. "This is serious. You are the new wolf, you haven't proven yourself yet, and you'll likely be challenged by the other females. You need to learn to fight, and win."

"I doubt the other females are built like brick shithouses like you. I should be able to throw their weight, or land a devastating kick."

He did grin then, but it was more feral than sexy. "Even if you can beat the females, how do you plan to bring down the werewolf near Charleston? He was most definitely male, I could smell it."

Damn... He had her there.

"With this," he said, pulling something out from behind him. A dagger. She took it from him by the blade, and the metal burned her hand. It started as a slight discomfort, but built to a burning inferno until she had to release the blade. "Silver," he said. "Silver will cut through a werewolf like butter. Bury it into the heart, or cut off the head and there is no regeneration, just dead. The head can be cut off with any blade, really, but to cleave through it, you would have to have a great deal of strength behind your swing. You probably wouldn't manage it without silver."

He let her up, and when she got to her feet, she tested the knife. Slightly back heavy, but not drastically so, dual edged, and extremely sharp. She grabbed it at the point and whipped it in the direction of the sparring dummy across the room. The blade buried into the dummy's throat, causing it to sway back and forth.

"Where did you learn to do that?" Reed asked, and she could hear the awe in his voice.

"My father was a military man, and a weapons master. He was a perfect marksman with just about everything, but the one that I liked was the throwing knife. Guns are loud, and can misfire, but if a knife misses, it's due to a lack of skill on the part of the thrower. I spent a great deal of time perfecting it with my father's help. He was the only person who ever understood my need to learn so much, because I got it from him. I may not be good at this werewolf thing yet, but I will be before long, you just watch."

Just then he smiled in that way that had Leena's stomach doing somersaults. "I'm looking forward to it. For now, though, I'll settle for watching you change into your wolf at will. You changed at your house because the wolf is protective, and it is drawn out by strong emotions. She will do anything to protect you. What you have to learn to do is to call on her, but stay in control. She gets her chance to run wild and free at the time of the full moon, but any other time, you are in charge."

"You talk as if she isn't a part of me," Leena said.

"She is a part of you, but she is everything that humans learn to repress throughout their lives. She is impulsive, feral, and dangerous. She could rip the throat out of your neighbor and feel no remorse. Wolves do not show remorse and she is all wolf. Now, call her to the fore."

Leena closed her eyes and tried to envision her wolf. She didn't exactly know how she was supposed to pull the wolf out, but she was willing to try just about anything. Shouldn't she be able to just say, "Go, go wolf form," and spark the change? "Wonder-wolf powers, activate!"

Come on. She squeezed her eyes tighter and concentrated. She pictured the trees around Declan's home, imagined herself running through them as fast as four legs could carry her. If she turned around, she would see a black wolf practically nipping at her heels, but she knew that he wouldn't catch her unless she let him.

She felt it then. Her skin began to crawl, burning as if someone had run a blowtorch over her skin. After a few moments, fur began to shoot from her pores. Her muscles and bones began to snap and tear, shifting around. She bit down on her lip to keep herself from screaming out in pain, the metallic taste of blood settling in her mouth.

Her T-shirt stretched across her back before bursting at the seams and falling from her. After a few more moments, she stepped her back paws out of the material that used to be her pants, but now lay in a heap of torn fabric. Once the change was complete, Leena stretched out her back, planting her hind legs into the mat, and using her front paws to pull the muscles taught and release them slowly. Her legs trembled with need. A need to run.

She danced in place, eager to let her new legs carry her away from this room that she had been trapped in for hours, but she knew that she had to stay put. With a great deal of effort, she plopped her haunches down on the mat, and looked up at Reed, her tail swishing back and forth across the mat in excitement. Reed knelt in front of her, studying her for a while, before he pulled back and punched her in her flank. Red covered Leena's vision, but when the wolf in her wanted to launch herself onto Reed and tear him to shreds, Leena held her back, using up a great deal of effort. She knew that it was meant to be a test of her control on her wolf, but she didn't understand why he had to punch her already abused body as a means of a test. Leena snarled at him, letting him know that she didn't appreciate being punched, but she did manage to quench the need to tear him apart limb by limb—although the wolf wasn't the only one that wanted to bite his favorite appendage off for that punch.

Leena focused on pulling her human body forward. This part she had already done consciously, and she managed to duplicate it after just a few moments effort. She waited for the pain to subside and as soon as it did, she pulled her own fist back and punched Reed as hard as she could in the shoulder. "I just wanted to make sure that you knew that was from me and not my wolf," she said, satisfied to see that Reed actually had to rub his shoulder after that hit. Served him right.

"Do it again," he growled in response. And she did. She changed her form over and over again, until her legs were about as stable as two rubber bands. With each attempt, the change came quicker than the last until she barely had to think about it.

With each shift, her body became weakened, and each time she looked to Reed to see a look of satisfaction on his face. Was this meant to be another test? If so, she was determined not to let him see her weaknesses. It wasn't until she switched back to her human form for the eighth time that she tried to push herself up from the mat, and her arms gave out.

Reed moved to help her up, but she shrugged him off. "I'm fine, my arm just wasn't back in place yet," she lied. She knew damn well that Reed would know that she was lying, but she didn't care. She was not going to give the bastard what he wanted. She would keep going until she passed out if she had to. Stupid? Yes. Stubborn? You bet. Did she care? Not a lick.

Instead of trying to get to her feet and risk falling on her face, Leena managed to push herself into a sitting position, pulling her hair forward to drape over her breasts. Just then she was thankful that she never talked herself into cutting off her long hair, it had its uses after all.

"Here," Reed said, throwing her a white, fluffy towel. "We're done for the day. Dry off, get dressed, and we'll go downstairs and wait for the others to show up."

Thank Heaven for small mercies. Keeping her butt on the floor, she turned away from Reed to dry the sweat from her skin.

"Dragons," he mumbled.

"Excuse me?" Leena said, unsure that she had heard him correctly.

"Your tattoo, it is of two dragons."

She grinned. "Is that what they are? I didn't know."

Without commenting on her sarcasm, Reed knelt behind her, "May I?" he said. Well, since he was being polite… She clutched the towel to her chest, leaned forward, and swept what was left of her hair out of the way so that he could see her tattoos. The dragon lovers dominated her back, entwined in each other, with their outstretched wings spanning her shoulder blades. His finger brushed her skin, tracing each one. From there, he moved to the one on the lower left of her back. A pair of throwing knives crossed over each other in an X, over a target. To its right, Reed ran his finger along her most feminine tattoo; two fairies dancing the tango, the woman's leg draped over the man's lunging thigh. "What do these say?" he asked, brushing her sides.

"They are spells written in Iroquoian. They're ineffective without the proper herbs and ingredients and without being verbalized, but they are supposed to be protective incantations. My Nana taught them to me, but even when I cast them properly, they don't work for me. Not much does." Leena didn't really know why she got them tattooed on her body, other than the fact that they were something that she shared with her Nana.

"They're lovely," he said, rising to his feet. "And the one on your chest…Wings?"

She nodded and resumed drying her skin, running the towel across the tattoo in question. It was positioned just above her left breast, over her heart. "Angel wings, for my father."

Leena didn't understand why he was being so nice to her all of a sudden. He had just put her through the wringer, grinning each time he slammed her onto her back. His hot and cold mood swings were so confusing to her. She almost preferred it if he would just be a jerk to her all the time.

Sensing her confusion, Reed said, "You did really well today. Most new werewolves wouldn't have made it past the second or third shift." He handed her the second set of clothes that she brought so that she could get dressed. "I know it seems like I pushed you unnecessarily hard, but there truly was a reason for it. You'll see it in time."

❧❧

Reed hoped that Leena would eventually see that he pushed her so hard to keep her alive. Looking at her now, though, he couldn't help but wonder if he may have pushed her too far. In a few short hours the meeting would start, and Leena couldn't even push herself to her feet. He had kept himself linked with her the whole time, trying to judge when she had had enough, but with each shift she had become more and more determined. It wasn't until he saw the tremble in her limbs that he realized that he had let things go too far. She wouldn't even stand to shimmy into her jeans. When he offered her a hand, she just glared up at him from the floor and rocked her hips side to side to coax the fabric up around her arse.

Once she was fully dressed, she tried again to push herself to her feet. She actually managed to stand, but the moment she took a step her leg refused to support her weight and she toppled forward. Reed lunged to catch her before she took a dive into the mat. She muttered a "thank you" and tried to push him away, but he didn't move. There were over thirty stairs between her and the first floor, and he wouldn't watch her fall down any of them.

He wrapped each of his hands around her thighs and lifted her off of the floor, twining her legs around his waist. She tried to push at him again, shouting indignantly that she didn't need his help, but he just ignored her. By the time he made it to the flight of stairs leading from the third floor to the second, she had given up on pushing off of him and rested her head on his shoulder. *Jaysus*, she felt wonderful. He was ultra-aware of every inch of her body, from the press of her breasts against his chest, to the feel of her strong thighs on his palms. Her emotions had calmed significantly as well. Instead of the determination and anger that she had felt before, she had grown weary and contented. It was as if she had gone from a feisty tigress to a purring kitten. Of course, he would never tell her that. He liked his bollocks right where they were, thank you very much.

She turned toward him and buried her face into his neck, burrowing her fingers into his hair for something to hold on to. That act set him over the edge. A trail of heat shot down to his sack giving him an instant hard-on. Feck. He hoisted her up higher on his waist to keep her ignorant to his predicament, and continued down the second flight of stairs. *Almost there,* he told himself.

"You can put me down if I'm getting too heavy," she mumbled.

Again he ignored her. He couldn't even think to form cohesive words let alone allow them to spew from his mouth right now.

Each of his senses were honed in on her, overwhelming everything else. Everywhere her body touched his felt as if flames were licking at his skin. The slight staccato of her heart beat pounded in his ears, the feel of her breath on his neck feathered lightly across his skin, cooling the heat that her closeness caused. Even his empathy was honed in on her. He could tell that there were other people in the house, but he couldn't feel them. It was as if she was the only person that his ability cared to read at that moment.

When he finally made it to the kitchen, he deposited her on the stool that she had occupied the night before, sidestepping to the other side of the peninsula to shield himself from her view. "Do you like lamb?" he asked her, as he tried to will the blood from his groin back to his brain.

She nodded, and he quickly turned from her to the refrigerator. One thing that he knew, if he couldn't get this damn thing to go down before the meeting, he would never hear the end of it…ever.

❧❧

Leena couldn't quite understand Reed. For someone who dealt with emotions on a day-to-day basis, he didn't really have a good handle on his own. Just in the last few hours alone he had been frustrated with her, somber, tender, sweet, hot—and boy, had he been hot—and now he seemed distant and couldn't put enough space between them. He barely spoke, grunting a few monosyllabic words that were meant to be sentences. What had happened? She hadn't even said much, so she couldn't possibly have upset him, could she? It was possible—if anyone could pull that off, it would be her—but it was highly unlikely, she thought.

She watched as he focused on searing the lamb chops. He didn't say a word, and he refused to look in her direction. Even when she asked him where he learned to cook, he mumbled something that sounded like the word, "practice," and went about his business. Alrighty then.

Not wanting to be a pain, Leena stayed quiet as Reed finished cooking. She thumbed the knife that he had given her, when a thought came to her. She hid her hand under the counter of the peninsula as she concentrated on her fingertips. She had gained a fair amount of control over calling on her wolf, but she was still shocked when, after only a few attempts, she actually managed to push a set of ebony claws from her fingertips. The pain was immense, akin to growing razor blades, and they receded rather quickly.

It was then that Reed set a plate of lamb chops in front of her, her stomach growling loudly as if she hadn't eaten in weeks, and her mouth began to salivate. How. Freaking. Embarrassing.

She dug in, savoring each bite. "This is delicious," she said around a mouthful of meat, and meaning it wholeheartedly. Never had she tasted anything so wonderful. She groaned in delight, and actually managed to crack a smile out of Reed.

"Thank you," he said, scooping another heaping serving onto her plate before getting a plate of his own. "Are you nervous about meeting the others?" he asked out of the blue.

Leena scrunched her eyebrows in confusion, but rolled with the conversation. Reed was just now getting back to an enjoyable mood, and she wanted to keep him that way for as long as possible. "Not really," she admitted. "Should I be worried?" He shrugged. "Do you have any advice on how to keep my head through tonight?"

He thought about it for a moment, and then deadpan, he said, "Don't insult my da." As if she had intended to. "Even in jest. Each one of my men is honor-bound to serve my da, and they take it very seriously."

"Your men?"

"Yes. We have one woman, but she won't be here tonight. She and her brother are investigating a mauling in California. The rest of the warriors—or *Lyca Laochra* as we're known by—will be here. My da may be the ruler of our kind, but I am the leader of this chapter. It was created to help take some of the weight off of my da's shoulders."

"So, if you're the leader, wouldn't it be unwise for me to insult *you*?" she asked.

"You would think," he replied with a tilt of his mouth, "but no. These men are the closest friends that I have, and more than anything they enjoy fecking with me. If you were to say or do something at my expense, they would probably laugh their cacks off."

He said it as if they annoyed him to no end with this, but when she looked in his eyes she saw the spark of amusement. Reed loved those men, she could tell just by watching him as he spoke about them.

She finished the rest of her lamb, and slowly slid herself to the ground. Her legs trembled slightly, but held. That was a good sign. She managed to walk all the way to the dishwasher and back without falling on her face, although the trip felt more like she had run several blocks and back. At least she was regaining her strength.

Reed led her to the sitting area around the fireplace, allowing her to make the trek all on her own, where they waited for the rest of the men to arrive. He sat next to her on one of the sofas, and he managed to stay complacent through an entire conversation that they had while they waited.

The first person to show up, Leena recognized, and she couldn't have been more surprised to know that he was one of the warriors of an entire pack of people that could probably fight better than any military man. Although Shaun had muscles to the nth degree, Leena pegged him as more of a lover than a fighter.

Shaun greeted Reed with a grin and a punch to the arm, before he sized her up and gave a nod of approval, as if she wore her outfit just for him. She bared her teeth at him, which only caused him to throw his head back and laugh. She wondered if Reed would let her shove her new pretty knife into the idiot's eye. A look to him, and a shake of his head, confirmed that he wouldn't allow it. Damn.

The next man to walk through the front door and into the sitting area definitely looked like a warrior to Leena. Perhaps not as muscled as Shaun or Reed, the newcomer was built more for speed and agility than brute strength, but he moved with the grace of a panther ready to strike at the slightest provocation. His long dark hair fell loosely around a face that screamed "killer" when you looked at him. Leena knew with one look that she never wanted to get on this man's bad side. He looked as if he would kill his own mother of she displeased him.

The man approached the sofa where she and Reed sat, clasping Reed's hand when he got close enough. He didn't touch Reed for long, withdrawing his hand quickly, and Leena remembered what Declan had said about Reed's aversion to being touched. Oddly enough, she realized that this was the first time that she saw him act on that declaration. He had seemed to have no problem touching her, which she made a note to ask him about at a later time.

"Lucan," Reed said, "This is Kalina, but she prefers to be called Leena. Leena this is Lucan." She didn't know how

Reed knew that she preferred her nickname to her given name, but she didn't feel that now was the time to ask. She extended her hand, and Lucan took it in his own. He bowed gracefully over it before laying a soft kiss on her knuckles.

"A pleasure," Lucan said. Leena didn't expect for him to be so formal, or so polite. She would have been less surprised if he had given her a good punch to the throat. She also hadn't expected his voice to be a deep, soothing timbre, with a hint of an accent that Leena couldn't place.

"Thank you," she said, not really knowing how else to respond. With a slight nod of his head, Lucan moved to the armchair closest to the hearth.

The next two men entered together, and Leena couldn't decide which she should focus on more. The man on the left had tanned skin, a shade or two darker than her own. His features were sharp, highlighted by the medium brown hair brushing his shoulders, and the light stubble on his face. When he glanced her way, she saw that his eyes were a striking amber color. He was light on his feet, and even with her enhanced hearing, she noticed that he barely made a sound as he entered the room.

The man to the right—Leena gasped. When he turned to face her, Leena noticed a long angry scar that ran from his forehead, across his eye, to his chin. On closer inspection, Leena realized that the scar was actually a tattoo and that his face wasn't the only place he bore the tattoos. They ran all along every bit of exposed skin. She wondered why on earth he would purposely tattoo his body to look desecrated, noting that he was actually quite attractive behind the tattoos, but she knew that it wasn't her place to ask.

Reed introduced her to the two before they took their places on one of the other sofas. The first man, Leo, had possessed an odd scent that Leena couldn't place. The second man, Milo, had grinned at her, and the effect was absolutely breathtaking, even with his "scars."

The final member that they were waiting on walked through the front door, and Leena's jaw dropped to the floor in a most unbecoming way. She couldn't help it. In a room full of sexy men, her eyes were drawn to this man. He was extremely tall, approaching seven feet; his broad chest was so muscular that the t-shirt that he wore threatened to tear at the seams. His black, tightly curled hair was cropped close to his head, and he had a neatly trimmed chin-strap beard. His skin was the color of coffee with a splash of cream, showcasing his dual heritage. The feature that caught Leena's attention most, though, was the color of his eyes. The ice blue stood out against his mocha skin even from a distance.

With a huge, bright smile on his face, he marched up to Reed, pulled him up from the sofa into a bear hug, and clapped him on the back twice before releasing him.

"Reed," the man said by way of greeting.

Reed smiled back at the man that dwarfed even him, and said, "Tresize, how was your trip home?"

"Long, but I'm glad to be back. This must be the newbie that you and Corrick found. Shaun told me quite a bit about her, but he failed to mention how lovely she was." He held his hand out to Leena, and she took it. "Spencer Tresize. It's a pleasure to meet you."

"Kalina Abrams," she replied, "but please, call me Leena."

He nodded once, "A beautiful name. It suits you well."

She opened her mouth to say that a name like Tree-Size fit him as well, but she clamped it shut, determined not to insult him. "Thank you," she said instead. He still held her hand in his massive one, his gaze boring into hers. She felt as if he were looking into her soul, getting a read on her from a level that couldn't be falsified. She could feel it as he recognized some of her worst habits and faults, as well as her more admirable traits. A grin spread across his lips, the type of grin that said that he discovered some sort of secret just from looking into her eyes.

"Spencer," a familiar voice said, "Please release Kalina. She has been through quite enough already."

Declan.

He strode into the sitting room, followed closely by Corrick, who had also acquired a new shadow. Wraith. She didn't know how Wraith got here, because she and Reed had left him at his house when they left. Corrick must have been the one to rescue him, because he now stuck to the kid like white on rice.

Tresize released her hand the moment Declan approached them, bowing his head slightly before taking a seat. Corrick sat on the sofa next to her, sandwiching her between the McAndrews boys. When she raised her eyebrow at Corrick questioningly, he simply winked. Wraith sat on the floor between Leena and Corrick nudging the boy's hand until he pet him. Interesting. He had never taken a liking to someone so quickly before.

"Alright," Declan said, "I'm sure you all know already that we have a new addition. Kalina is here with us now due to a rogue in the Charleston area—" Declan stopped mid-sentence. Leena looked around and saw every head turn toward the front door. She heard it then, a click-clack of heels on wood.

The knob turned, and the door was thrust open. A beautiful blond woman entered, dressed to impress in a pair of white slacks that hugged her hips and thighs and a brown blouse. Leena looked down at her own ensemble and felt like a bum in comparison. Truth be told, she would never be able to pull off an outfit like this woman's. When she wasn't sweating, dancing around a studio, she was working with metals that gave off a black deposit as soon as you heated them. Her wardrobe, even her nice clothes, was primarily made up of dark colors. You would never find her in white pants, that was for sure.

The woman sauntered toward them, obviously putting on a show but Leena couldn't decide whose benefit it was for.

She stopped in front of Reed, running her fingers along his face in a caress. Reed stiffened, likely getting hit with the emotions that the woman was projecting.

"Baby, you brought home a stray for me to play with. How thoughtful." From Leena's other side, Wraith growled low in his throat, as if he realized that the woman was insulting Leena. Or it could have just been because he realized that he didn't like her, either way was fine by Leena. She pet him on the head, scratching him behind the ear to reward his efforts. The woman turned on Leena just then, "Little pup, you're going to have to move, you're sitting in my spot."

"There wasn't a 'reserved' sign on it."

"It is Pack dynamic. I am the alpha female, the third in command here. Therefore, I sit next to the second, Reed. You, little stray, can sit on the floor with your mutt."

What the hell was this bitch's problem? Leena straightened in her seat before replying, "Well, when the second in command asks me to move, I'll consider it." She looked to Reed, who looked to his father. Declan was obviously trying not to smile, but Leena had a hard time seeing the humor in the situation.

"Annabelle," Declan interjected, "just take a seat somewhere, there are plenty." Annabelle shot Declan a glare, but didn't dare say a word back to him. She may be the third in command, but when the first tells you to sit your ass down, you listen. Leena had only been a werewolf for two days and she knew that rule. Declan spoke in a soft, polite manner, making you feel praised and welcome, but he had an air about him that told Leena that he earned his spot as the king of North America for a reason, and that she never wanted to see that reason in action.

"As I was saying," he continued as Annabelle sat next to Tresize, glaring daggers at Leena as she went. "There is a rogue near Charleston. He is responsible for turning Kalina against her will. After a recount of the events, it was apparent that rogue was actually going for her sister, but Kalina interfered to save her sister's life. We need to stop this rogue as soon as possible. Another woman's body was found this morning. The police don't know what to make of the girl's body, so I should be able to convince them to accept our help in this. They aren't releasing any information to the public at this time."

"What does Steven have to say about this?" Leo asked.

"He claims to know nothing of the attacks. He has, however, agreed to meet with whichever one of you goes down. Access to his territory would be paramount to finding this Rogue, so I need you to try to play nice with him."

The men all around Leena nodded. She took this moment to seize an opportunity. Here went nothing... "Excuse me, Declan? Your Majesty? My Lord?"

Declan smiled at her. "'Declan' is fine. Yes, Kalina?"

"I would like to go to Charleston to hunt the rogue," she said quickly.

Next to her, Reed stiffened, waiting for his father's answer. Leena knew that it was practically a slap in the face to go above him, but this was something that she needed to do.

"Kalina, I understand your desire to go, but I think it would be safest for you here. Besides, I need to send a member of the *Lyca Laochra*; that is the way we've always done things. I cannot have untrained werewolves hunting down rogues. It would be a suicide mission."

Reed relaxed slightly, but Leena was too determined to put this to rest that easily.

"Then how does one become a member of the *Lyca Laochra*? Are there certain requirements?"

"You would become a member by petitioning Reed. He would watch you fight and make a decision based on what he saw. If he thinks your skills are of use to his warriors, then he may recruit you."

Well... there went that idea.

She turned on the sofa to look at Reed and whispered to him. She knew that everyone else in the room could hear her clearly, but somehow whispering made what she was about to do sound less pathetic. "Please, Reed." She put her hand on his so that he could feel her desperation. "I need to do this. Not for myself, but for my family. That asshole went after my sister, and I need to see with my own eyes that he is no longer a threat to her. I need to protect her, in the same way that you are trying to protect me by keeping me here. The only difference is that you know that I am capable of defending myself." He stared at her for a moment, and it almost looked as if he were contemplating saying yes. The fact that he was at least considering it was enough to make her grovel if she had to. "Please," she said again, squeezing his hand. "I'll do anything."

She waited for him to make a decision, aware that everyone else was watching the two of them. He seemed to think it over for a long time before he turned to his father and said, "I have already seen her fight, and while her skills are adequate, I do not believe that she is ready to take on a rogue by herself." Leena's heart plummeted into her stomach, she didn't know why she expected him to say yes, but she had hoped that she could appeal to the side of him that would do anything to protect those he loved.

She withdrew her hand from his and turned back toward Declan, feeling utterly defeated. "However," Reed said, and she snapped her head back in his direction, "I do believe that she can be trained quickly, and that the skills that she does possess can help us in many ways. I accept her request, on the condition that I accompany her to South Carolina."

Leena hadn't expected that. Just yesterday he was all too ready to get rid of her, and now he wanted to take her to hunt the werewolf that had endangered her family? If it was his condition, though, she would agree to it, even if she didn't understand it.

"I agree," she said.

"It's settled then," Declan said, "Reed and Kalina will go to Charleston—"

"I object," Annabelle said, launching herself off of the sofa onto her feet. Oh, this Leena had to hear. All eyes turned to Annabelle, waiting for her to explain her objections. "I don't believe the pup is capable. In fact, I am challenging her for her position."

Leena turned to Reed. "What does that mean?"

"It means, little pet," Annabelle answered, "that you and I shall fight, and if I win, you are not only no longer a candidate for the *Lyca Laochra*, but it will secure your status in this pack as my little bitch."

Next to her, Reed sighed. He knew. He had known that this would happen today, and that's why he had pushed her so hard all day long. She could have kissed him right then. The whole time she thought that he was just angry with her and that's why he was pushing her, but he had done it to help her. She squeezed his hand one last time, hoping that he could feel how grateful she was, and she pushed herself to her feet. Thankfully her legs held her up. No longer weak and shaking, but not quite a hundred percent either. It would have to do.

"You're on," she said. "And when I wipe the floor with you, you can tell the rest of your little bitch-clique that I'll be more than willing to serve them their asses on a plate as well, the moment I get back."

The men all stood and pushed the sofas and chairs out of the way to give Leena and Annabelle some room. They formed a circle around the two women, all too ready to watch this girl-fight that wouldn't be all slaps and hair pulling. Although, there probably would be some clawing.

Leena waited for Annabelle to make the first move, watching her as Reed had done to Leena earlier that day. Women were thinkers. They thought about moves before they made them. Annabelle would do the same. Leena would just have to try to be more spontaneous in her movements so that she didn't telegraph her next move.

Annabelle looked to Leena's right, assuming that Leena was right-handed, before she threw a punch. Leena blocked the blow, and landed one of her own, right in Annabelle's gut. They pushed off from each other and without waiting to think, Annabelle side-kicked Leena in the chest.

Leena felt her sternum snap, causing her breathing to become more labored, but she refused to let the pain show. Annabelle lashed out again, this time using her fingernails to cut the side of Leena's neck. So close to the carotid. She was trying to kill her.

Enough of this shit. Leena bent forward and plowed into Annabelle in a football tackle, absorbing the blows to her exposed back and shoulders. She flipped Annabelle onto her back, using her weight to pin her down, and grabbed her by the throat. Without much effort, which Leena chalked up to her wolf's need to protect them from danger, her fingertips once again sprouted wickedly curved ebony claws. Before they had a chance to recede again, Leena pressed the tips into the flesh of Annabelle's neck.

"Admit defeat, and I won't rip your fucking throat out," Leena growled.

Annabelle glared back at her for a long moment, even daring to try to move until Leena dug her claws in a little further, piercing the skin. Blood beaded underneath her claws, and that was enough for Annabelle to realize that she would not survive this fight if she didn't tap out. "You win," she gritted out.

Leena withdrew her claws, and got to her feet. Just as quickly as they came, her claws receded, replaced once again by her human fingernails. *That* was pretty freaking awesome.

"Well that settles several things," Declan said, causing everyone to turn their attention to him. "Kalina has not only secured her spot in the *Lyca Laochra*, but as the pack's alpha bitch."

Wait. What?

Chapter Eight

Reed watched as Leena's face scrunched in confusion. She had no idea what she had just done. By defeating Annabelle, she had just secured her position as the alpha bitch, third in command of the entire pack, and the females' go-to person for all issues and disputes. Reed and his da knew that she was bound to take the position eventually — she was far more dominant than Annabelle — but they had planned to give her time to acclimate to the pack dynamics, and to train her. With Annabelle's challenge of Leena's position, she had put her own on the line, and lost it.

He pulled Leena to the side to explain all of this to her. With each word that he spoke, her eyes rounded in a mixture of confusion and shock. "I don't understand why she would do that." Leena said, completely awestruck. "I was a nobody. Why would she put her position on the line just to prevent me from helping to hunt down the guy that attacked me?"

"That's the thing. You weren't just a nobody. You were already in line to take her position from her, and she caught wind of that. This was her attempt to prevent it while she thought that she could take you down."

"What if I don't want to accept the position? I'm certainly not qualified enough. I don't even know anything about the pack dynamics, how am I supposed to help other people figure them out?"

"The only way to not accept this position is to not accept your place in our pack. That may sound harsh, but this position isn't like a job. It's not like your acceptance into the *Lyca Laochra,* where you can opt out of it. This is your rank amongst our people because you are the most suited for it." He could sense her fear at his words, and while he didn't want to scare her, he needed her to see that this was for the best, for all involved. "If you did decide to relinquish your position in the pack, you could probably go to the Shifters. They have a small number of us within their ranks, mainly due to marriage. If you are actually considering that, please think of this first: you would be leaving every female in our pack under the leadership of Annabelle. Annabelle has never truly cared for those women; the only thing that she cares about is having people that have to obey her. They are subjects to her, not people who need her help and protection."

"If that's the case, then why haven't you overthrown her already?"

Reed shrugged, "She is the strongest, and most capable. One of the other women would have needed to challenge her for position, and win, and those types of challenges normally end in death. Not many of the women were willing to risk it, and the ones that were weren't successful. The only other thing that my da and I could have done is to take a mate, but not only is that an *eternal* bond with someone, but we also haven't found anyone that we think would help the women enough to consider taking someone that we don't love as a mate."

Leena nodded, and he could feel her understanding start to overshadow her anxiety. She didn't much like the idea of being thrown into the position of alpha female, but Reed could tell that she was resigned to it. She would do it for all of their women. They were people that she hadn't even met yet, and she was already putting their well-being above her own. A true dominant.

"Fine," she mumbled, as she turned away from him and approached his da, who wore the largest smile that Reed had seen on the man's face since before his mum's death over a hundred years ago.

As Da debriefed them on approaching Steven, Reed noticed that Annabelle had disappeared. It was probably for the best. Just as Leena's broken sternum was healing, Annabelle's neck wounds would also heal, but her pride may never. A "pup" had handed her arse to her in a matter of minutes, pulling off a partial shift that the majority of their people couldn't have managed. A large portion of their women will find pleasure in that knowledge, and give her hell for it after what she has put them through over the years. Of course, there would be a few women—Annabelle's inner circle—that will likely push Leena to her limits, just out of loyalty to Annabelle.

After his da finished, all of his men gathered around to congratulate Leena. The moment she opened her mouth to speak, she unknowingly grabbed each one of them by the bollocks. Reed had thought that they would bust his balls for how enthralled by her he had become, but they had fallen just as easily under her spell.

As she told them about herself, from the death of her da, to her studio that doubled as a workshop, to the close bond that she shared with the rest of her family, each and every male hung on her every word, including Reed.

When she laughed, seven male voices boomed with laughter right along with her. When she frowned, each man turned deadly, ready to destroy whatever would cause her the slightest pain. Not one of these men had ever taken to another person so quickly. Reed didn't know what it was about her, but he was glad that she was going to play such a large role in their lives from this point on. Each of these men had had a hard go at life, and it was nice to see them enjoying even a small bit of it.

Tresize seemed to be the most taken by her. Reed found himself thanking the heavens that Leena wouldn't be near the big man for the next few days, before he caught himself and shame washed over him. Tresize was like a brother to him, and he deserved to be happy, but Reed feared that if Leena started to fall for the oversized teddy bear that his only chance at happiness would slip through his fingers. She was it for him, and he knew it. He would never find another woman to spark desire in him the way that she had.

If he were a good friend, he would back off and let Tresize move in on her. She would probably be happier with him anyhow. He watched as Leena laughed, and playfully swatted at Tresize's arm. The two had an easy, lighthearted rapport that Reed could never hope to accomplish. Just when he decided to forgo his attempts to win her heart, she turned to meet his gaze and rewarded him with a coy smile that caused his chest to tighten. He was already lost to her.

It was a few hours before Reed realized how late it was. He hated pulling Leena away from the others, but the two of them needed to leave if they were going to fly out in the morning. His da was already making the arrangements to have the pack's plane ready for them in the morning, and coordinating a landing with the Mt. Pleasant Regional Airport.

Leena grinned as the others voiced their reluctance to let her leave, before giving each of them a kiss on the cheek — even Shaun, who Reed knew she was slightly repulsed by. She also pet and cooed to Wraith, who would be staying behind with Corrick.

The little sneak had known all along that Reed would cave and allow Leena to accompany him, and that was why he went to fetch the dog from Reed's house.

On their walk back to Reed's house, he could feel Leena's happiness as if it were a warm embrace. He found it amazing that she was able to be so happy so soon after her experience with Jason, but he was glad for it. He didn't know if it was due to being able to avenge herself and her sister, or if it was due to having six grown men and a teenaged boy that could kill someone in less than two seconds turn to putty in her hands. Perhaps it was a combination of the two.

"Thank you," she said softly. "I know that you were pushing me so hard earlier because you knew that Annabelle was going to make a move for me. Thank you. You probably saved my life."

"You're welcome," Reed replied. "And thank you, for taking this position that you are by no means ready for. You have no idea yet, but you took an enormous weight off of my da's shoulders. A lot of the women had started bypassing Annabelle and going directly to him with their issues, and he would try to solve them, on top of everything else that he has to do."

"You're welcome," she said. "Although, I'm still a little confused on how your dad couldn't have just done away with her position, especially if he was doing it all himself anyway."

"It's not as easy as it sounds like it should be. There has to be a woman in charge. There has to be both a male and female alpha. It creates a balance that is needed in our world. It would be more effective if the female and male were mated, but this was the best that we could come up with. The most dominant female will take the role until my father or I decide to mate."

She smiled, "So I may not be in this role forever?"

He grinned. He knew it looked somewhat maniacal, but she had no idea that he had the mind to pretty much seal her fate in that role.

"I wouldn't count on that too much if I were you," he said to her. "Only a mate of my da's would be the undisputed alpha female, and he hasn't had any relationship with a woman in one hundred and eighty years."

Her mouth hung open, and he could feel her surprise. "But, what about Corrick?" she asked.

Reed knew what she meant by the question, and he shook his head. "Corrick's mother was just a one-night-stand that ended in a pregnancy. My da rarely feels the need to go out looking for women, but he still does it now and then. Probably every ten years or so. He pretty much scoffs at the use of protection, seeing as his body would heal any disease that he may get, and since our kind welcomes babes. He monitors the women that he sleeps with, and watches for any signs of pregnancy. Corrick's mother had been on her way to a clinic when my da caught wind of what she was doing. He got to her just in time, and offered her an obscene amount of money to sign over her rights to the babe to him instead, and she accepted."

Reed hadn't meant for the conversation to take such a turn. He had merely meant to thank her for taking on such a huge responsibility. He just hadn't wanted her to expect to have someone come along anytime soon to take the role from her. It would pretty much be a cold day in hell for it to happen.

"Wow…" she breathed out slowly. "Poor Corrick."

Indeed, poor Corrick. He never seemed like it bothered him that he didn't have a mother, but Reed could tell that when he saw any of his friends with their mothers, that it saddened him. Of course his da had told Corrick the truth about what happened with his mother, and he had no desire to meet the woman that didn't want him, but he longed for a female figure in his life.

Silence hung between Reed and Leena for a few moments. He could tell that she was thinking about something that didn't quite make sense to her, so he waited patiently for her to ask him about it. Sure enough, she said, "That was your mom all those years ago, right?" He nodded, and she continued. "If your dad was so in love with her, why aren't they together now? Was she a human?"

He stopped walking for a moment and turned to look at her. "She was not human, she was a werewolf. They are no longer together because she is dead."

Leena gasped. "I'm so sorry," she said with the utmost sincerity. "Do you mind if I ask how?"

Reed barely ever told anyone about his mother. No one had ever really asked him other than Tresize and Corrick. He certainly never expected to be telling a virtual stranger, but he couldn't seem to refuse her, especially when she stared at him with such sympathy in her dark blue eyes. "She was killed, when I was still a boy. We were still living in Ireland at the time, and Lucan had just come in for a visit—he and Da have been friends since well before I was born. They were taking Shaun and me out to teach us to fight."

Reed remembered that day as if it were just last week. *His mum, Nia, sat at the table chopping vegetables for their dinner for that night. Helping her was Lucan's mate Gwenna, several months pregnant and ready to deliver at any moment. That was the reason for their visit. Mum would be delivering Gwenna's babe when the time came.*

Shaun, a scrawny little boy of nine, was following Reed's da around their house begging him to teach him to fight on a daily basis. Each time Declan had said no.

Shaun's own da had been a human, and before his mother ever even knew that she was pregnant with Shaun, the man had been killed by raiders. Lycaon had moved the pregnant she-wolf to a village where one of his best soldiers resided, knowing that Declan would watch over her and her babe.

For Shaun, the village had become his own personal hell, rather than the salvation that it was intended to be. Short, underweight, and a bit timid, Shaun was the target for every other boy around their age. Declan didn't approve of solving the boy's problems with fighting, but when Shaun came home to his mother with a bloodied nose and a gash across his cheek, Reed's da had seen no other alternatives. So he asked her if he could teach the boy to defend himself, and with a grateful sigh, she had agreed.

Of course, he couldn't teach Shaun without Reed. The two boys had grown to be inseparable over the years. With Lucan and his mate in town, Declan had decided that it was the perfect time to teach the boys how to defend themselves. Declan had been sure to drill that into the two boys, that these teachings were to be used for defense only, and that if either boy used what they were taught to start a fight, they would be punished the same as any full-grown werewolf would for defiance.

It had been Lucan's idea to take the boys into the woods, away from the over-protective, ever-watchful eyes of their mothers. Shaun had been buzzing with excitement to the very end. Bruised and bloody, the lad had a grin spread from ear to ear.

When they returned to the village, Declan watched as the boy trudged toward his home, across the farm from their own, before opening the wooden gate to his property. Immediately, he stopped dead in his tracks. Reed had walked into his da, unaware that something was wrong. An emotion crossed over Declan's face that Reed had never seen the man show before...fear.

With no more than a look to each other, Declan and Lucan took off at a run that Reed had no chance of keeping up with. The two moved as swift as the wind, barely making a sound. Reed pushed himself to run as fast as he could after them, not caring for a moment that he sounded like an elephant thundering through the weeds.

As Reed approached the stone cottage, twin howls of agony rang out into the night. He stumbled over the threshold to find his da clutching his mum to his chest, shaking with a barely controlled rage. The front of her dress was covered in blood that had spread from the identical puncture marks at her neck, and the knife protruding from her chest. She had managed to kill a few of her attackers before they got to her, and they lay on the floor between Reed and the only woman he and his da had ever loved. In the room beyond, Lucan howled. The overtly wolfish sound was so odd coming from the mouth of a man that at first Reed didn't notice that he was covered in blood.

He knelt by the prone body of what used to be his beautiful Gwenna, butchered. Her large stomach had been sliced to ribbons, and a dagger had been thrust into her heart. Presumably silver. In Lucan's hands, the head of a babe rested carefully, the body unattached.

The stench of blood and death permeated throughout their home, causing Reed's stomach to churn. He made a dash for the door to the outside, tripping over a vampire head as he went. The moment *he stumbled outside, the contents of his stomach emptied into the flowers that his mum had tended.*

Tears streaked down his face, and no matter how many times he swiped at them, they kept coming. Movement out of the corner of his eye drew his attention. Shaun had just jumped their fence, running toward Reed as quickly as he'd ever seen the boy run. The image of him flickered between blurry and clear as Reed tried to focus on him through the tears that refused to stop. It wasn't until his best friend was standing right in front of him that he noticed the blood.

"Reed," he shouted, his voice catching on a lump in his throat, "my mum is dead!"

❧❦

Leena walked quietly next to Reed, listening intently to every word of his story, tears flowing freely from her own eyes as he spoke. She reached out and took his hand in hers. "That must have been hard on you to lose your mom that way," she said, her voice cracking. He nodded, not daring to look her way.

She glanced down at their clasped hands, wondering when he would pull away from her. Instead, he surprised her by squeezing her fingers tighter, and her heart swelled even more.

"To be honest," Reed said, "I didn't get much of a chance to grieve. My da and Lucan were the only guardians that Shaun and I had left, and after that, they spent the next few months exacting revenge on the coven that killed my mum and Lucan's pregnant mate. Shaun and I had to grow up quickly, and learn to take care of ourselves. Even after every last vampire involved was slain, my father went into a dark depression that I wondered if he would ever recover from. It was as if he was a walking shell, no emotions, he barely spoke, and we had to force him to eat. If it hadn't been for the livestock that we kept, we wouldn't have survived.

"Slowly, he started coming back to us, but it wasn't until a few years later, when Shaun got extremely sick, that he snapped out of it. We didn't know what to do, and I came so close to losing him, the friend that had become a brother, that my da rallied and found a way to save his life. He resumed his duties as the second-in-command of the European pack, and it wasn't until the famine came to Ireland that Da decided to leave and come to America. Shaun still hadn't come into his regeneration, and Da wanted to keep him safe. Lycaon put my da in charge of the small group of werewolves that decided to emigrate, naming him King."

Leena didn't much care for Shaun, but just then her heart went out to him. He had been through so much. They both had. She wondered if his easy smile came from seeing so much death, and still being alive, and if his lack of inhibition was because he knew that death could take him at any moment, so he better live his life to the fullest. Leena couldn't blame him for that. She didn't have to like it, but she wouldn't judge him for it.

As they reached Reed's front porch, he stilled her before going inside. "I'm sorry to lay all of this on you. Giving you my sob story was never my intention. Let's go get some sleep."

She nodded, but before he opened the door, she stopped him by tugging on the hand that she still held and she said, "Please don't be sorry. I'm glad that you felt comfortable enough to tell me about your mom, and your suffering. It makes me feel like I know more about the real you, and not just the tough guy that you portray to the new werewolves that insult your dad."

His smile actually touched his eyes then, and he pushed the door open to allow her to precede him, placing his hand at the small of her back as they entered. She was surprised to see how much he was allowing himself to touch her since they left his father's house. It was as if he was trying to prove that he could withstand their contact, and the fact that he seemed to want to touch her caused a swarm of butterflies in the pit of her stomach. She had never felt so much like a teenager — even when she had been one — than in that moment, tucking her hair behind her ear nervously, trying to ignore the way that he made her feel.

They stayed that way until they reached the landing at the top of the stairs inside. Before making her way down the hall to the bedroom that she had been occupying, Leena pulled Reed down to her for a hug, brushing her lips across his cheek. She could feel Reed's gaze on her back as she turned away from him, not daring to look back at him. If she did, she knew that she wouldn't be letting him sleep that night. Something had changed between them. Previously, when he hadn't been glaring at her, or brooding, she had been attracted to him, and now that she was seeing a whole new side to him, she feared that she might actually fall for the large werewolf.

Leena was starting to understand why Reed had such a hard time dealing with his own emotions, let alone absorbing everyone else's. He had gone through a lot in his childhood, but he never had a chance to deal with his emotions because he had to take care of himself and his friend. She wondered how Reed hadn't been driven crazy by the emotions from everyone around him. Although, she realized, perhaps he was a little crazy, in his own way. She had watched him change over the course of a few days between a man of indifference, a man ready to rip her face off, a man with an easy smile, and a man that looked at her as if little stood between him tearing her clothes from her body. Oddly enough, it was the last one that had scared her the most.

᠗᠗

Reed waited until he heard the sheets rustling from Leena's bedroom before he went back down the stairs, and out the back door. He ran for the trees, shedding his clothing as he went, grateful that his closest neighbor was several hundred feet away, and not likely to see him unless they decided to go for a stroll onto Reed's property.

He shouldn't have needed to run again so soon, but the emotions were consuming him; and this time, they just so happened to be all his own. Throughout his lifetime, he had learned to use the wolf to escape the onslaught of emotions. The wolf didn't feel the same emotions that humans did, and when Reed was in his wolf form, he could ignore those emotions until he got a grip on himself. Normally, he only needed to use this means of escape once a week, at most, never twice in as many days.

The moment he shifted into his wolf, Reed let go of everything and simply ran. He didn't let himself think of his mum, lying in a pool of blood, or the crazed look that his da had worn on his face for the ensuing years. Instead he focused on the feel of the dirt slipping between the pads of his paws, the rush of the wind against his face, the scents and sounds of the woods around him.

He could feel the muscles in his shoulders slowly begin to loosen, and as soon as he felt relaxed enough, he did allow himself think of Leena. He looked forward to a time that he could share this experience with her. She would adapt so quickly as she had with everything else, of that he was certain.

The images sprang to him now as he ran. Her light brown wolf, darting through the trees ahead of him, her jasmine and citrus scent carrying to him as he chased her through the brush. They would hunt, and play until their wolf bodies collapsed in the dirt and curled up for the night, waking with each other's scents absorbed into their skin, so that every other werewolf would know that she was his.

His tongue lolled out of his mouth as he loped back around to the house.

By the time he collapsed onto his bed, all thoughts of his past were gone; replaced by ones that he was determined to make his future.

Chapter Nine

The sun was shining brightly in South Carolina when the pack's private plane touched down on the air strip. Leena could feel the heat rush in the moment the hatch was opened to the outside. Why anyone would want to live in a place that got so hot in late September was beyond her. She hoped that there would be enough time for her to jump into the hotel's pool in between everything they had planned for the day, but it didn't seem likely. They were already arriving a little later than Reed had intended, and they had a lot to cram in to the afternoon.

On the plane ride, she and Reed had ironed out a game plan. After checking-in to the hotel that Shaun had booked for them, they would go for the meeting that Reed had scheduled with this Steven character.

Leena had learned that Steven was one of the leaders of the race of shape shifters. Reed had mentioned the Shifters to her briefly the night before, but the fact that there were other races of people that could shift into animals, and enough of them that they had a council of rulers, had shocked her. What Reed told her next had flummoxed her even further.

Of the entire race of shape shifters, from weasels to bears, the races combined were matched in number by the werewolves. The shifters and werewolves had come to some sort of understanding a long time ago, to stay out of each other's way. That was why they had to meet with Steven. As a courtesy, since Charleston was where he kept territory, Reed had to ask for Steven's permission to hunt the rogue werewolf inside the shifter territory in the event that their hunt carried them in that direction. Political bullshit, Reed had called it, and Leena couldn't have agreed more.

After their meeting with Steven, they would try to pick up a trail from the location that the wolf had attacked Leena and Amy, and fled from when Reed had shown up. Leena would have Reed on a leash in his wolf form, so that no one would notice the enormous black wolf wandering around aimlessly. Yeah. Right. Even with a leash strapped to him, Leena knew that Reed would attract a lot of attention due to his size. The most the leash would do was prevent people from running from him screaming, and even that wasn't a guarantee.

In the meantime, Declan was in contact with the local police force, trying to swing details on the death of the girl, and photos of the crime scene. Leena had no idea how he was managing that, and she didn't much care to ask. She just hoped that he was able to move quickly.

She wondered more than once why this rogue seemed to be targeting women. Was it because he viewed them as easier prey? Was he so unsure of himself, that he didn't think he could take down a human man? Or was it for sexual reasons that he targeted women? He had seemed to make his mind up about going for Amy rather than Leena that night, and from what she had been through in her own changes, she knew that this werewolf hadn't simply lost control. He was too calculated.

Leena thought this through for the entire drive to the hotel, no closer to figuring out this guy's motives by the time they rode the elevator to their floor. Reed slid the key card into the slot on their door, and pushed the door open. The room was beautiful, as far as hotels went. There was a full sitting room and kitchenette, and through the open door at the back, Leena could see the massive king-sized bed.

"Fecking Shaun," Reed muttered, and Leena looked up to see that he was also looking at the single bed. "Right dirty bastard." He shifted uncomfortably, which made Leena smile. He was a man that ran toward danger, fighting supernatural beings on a regular basis, but this made him uncomfortable. It was actually pretty comical.

"Don't worry about it," she told him. "We'll figure something out." She deposited her suitcase in the bedroom, opening it to grab a cute blouse that hugged her chest, cinching under her breasts, before flaring out to hang loosely around her stomach and waist. She took it to the bathroom to replace her t-shirt with it, leaving her jeans on. She swapped out her tennis shoes for her knee-high heeled boots. The heels wouldn't hinder her, since she was used to soaring across a dance floor in them all the time. Hell, one of her training exercises had been running in heels, so she had no worries about her mobility in the boots.

The reason for the boots had absolutely nothing to do with aesthetics. She had no intention of carrying a purse, and the boots would conceal the sheath with her silver dagger that she strapped to her calf. When the boots were zipped, she checked her reflection in the mirror, and was pleased to see that the ruffles in the leather hid the bulge of the knife perfectly.

She emerged from the room to find Reed sitting on the sofa in a white button-down shirt, opened at the collar, and black slacks. The sight of him stopped her dead in her tracks. He was absolutely gorgeous. The sleeves to his shirt were rolled up to his elbows, showing off his muscular forearms. The thin material was taught against his massive chest and shoulders, highlighting his superior strength.

Heat rushed through her body, and her mouth went dry. She couldn't think of the last time any man had caused such a reaction in her, but she had a feeling it was somewhere around...never. The funny thing was that Leena could tell by the way that he carried himself that Reed never really considered himself to be someone that women would fawn over. His ripped muscles were merely a tool that he used for fighting. That endeared him to her even more, making him even sexier.

His eyebrows rose into his hairline at the sight of Leena, and she smiled. Perhaps he had been expecting her to come out dressed in a t-shirt and some work boots, calling that "formal wear", but that was never the case with Leena. Even when she was under the hood of a car, Leena took some pride in her appearance. It must have been an effect of the dancing.

She knew that without dance, she probably would dress more of a tom-boy, instead of the walking contradiction that she had become — a harmonized balance of hard and soft.

Reed cleared his throat and stood from the sofa, offering Leena his arm in a flourish that dated him. She took it with her right arm, sliding the extra key card into her back pocket with her left as Reed led her to the door.

❧❧

Reed hated the political bullshit of the supernatural world. A rogue was out there killing women, and here he was dressing up in slacks and a dress-shirt, getting ready to pretend that a worthless arsehole like Steven had to give him permission to hunt this tool. He understood that having the shape shifters as allies was preferable to having them as enemies, but this was the twenty-first century and he grew weary of the games of the past.

His irritation didn't even stem from the fact that Reed hated Steven. Well, not entirely anyway. The man thought of himself as the ruler of all of the shape shifters, but in actuality was one of seven council members. If you asked Reed, he didn't even deserve that role. If Steven had been a werewolf, he would have been punished severely for the things that he had done over his lifetime. As it was, he was seemingly rewarded for the way he treated those that he was entrusted to protect. That fact grated on Reed's nerves more than anything else.

If Reed had thought that he would have gotten away with it, he would have killed Steven a long time ago, sparing his da and the entire race of Shifters a load of grief. The only problem with that plan was that Reed's da would have been left with no choice but to punish Reed to the full extent of their laws. That would mean death for Reed, and as much as he may not have minded that fate before, he knew that his da would have been the one to have to deliver the death blow, and he also knew that going through that would have killed the man.

Reed was not just a son to him, which already meant a great deal to their kind, but he was also the only thing that his da had left of his precious Nia. If he had to kill Reed, it would be as if he were killing the woman that he had loved all over again, and this time by his own hand. It would destroy the last hold on humanity that his da had, and he would either seek death himself, or he would be consumed by his wolf, likely killing his closest friends in a wild rage.

That had been what had kept Steven alive these past years, and what Reed reminded himself of now, as he maneuvered his truck through the streets of Charleston toward Steven's home.

Something lightly touched his arm, and he looked down to see a small hand. He followed the length of the arm to its owner, struck dumb once more by the sight of her. He had thought that she was beautiful in the men's t-shirt and sweat pants that they had given her to wear; gorgeous in her own t-shirt and jeans; and now she was breathtaking. She had left her long hair down, even though he knew it must have made her feel the heat of the south all the more to have it so. Her jeans were so tight that they left little to the imagination of what you might find beneath them, and he wouldn't even go into what that top did for her already magnificent breasts.

He had to make the conscience effort not to stare at them on several occasions.

Now she looked at him with concern on her face, and the emotion flowed through him at the touch of her skin on his. "Are you alright?" she asked.

"Yes, I'm fine. What makes you ask?" he replied.

She shrugged. "You had that hard expression on your face that you affect when you don't want anyone to know that something is bothering you. You seem to do it when you're picking up on too many emotions."

He stopped at the red light ahead, and turned to stare at her. He could still feel her concern for him, but now it mingled with unease at the weight of his gaze. He had been around people for almost two hundred years that hadn't picked up on his tell, and she had him pegged in just a few days. Reed didn't know if he should be concerned that he had been so transparent, or flattered that she paid such close attention. He decided to go for the latter.

Looking back to the road, he let his expression soften. "I am fine. I'm just trying to decide how to approach Steven today. The main purpose for us getting Steven's permission to enter his territory is so that he doesn't view it as a slight from my da if we end up hunting within his borders. If he does, he could start a war with our kind, and it wouldn't bode well for either species."

"Wow. That's a lot of pressure to be under," she breathed out, and Reed nodded.

"It would have been easier on our kind if we had stayed in our own parts of the world and not tried to integrate with other species. That, however, is my own opinion. My da sees it differently. Since he is King, I can do nothing but follow his orders."

This time Leena nodded in understanding.

They drove through a guard station and followed the winding driveway through a wooded area. When the house came into view, Leena snorted. "Dracula called, he wants his digs back," she muttered, and Reed smiled, the stress that he was feeling forgotten with one sardonic comment.

The gothic stone house looked at odds against the afternoon sun. The gargoyles and the wrought iron fencing were almost comical. Leena was right about one thing; the place had the type of flair for the dramatics that vampires were more accustomed to than shape shifters.

He parked his truck and turned to Leena before getting out. The serious look on his face wiped the grin from hers. He lowered his voice to make sure that the men just inside the house couldn't hear them. "Leena, you have to let me do the talking in here. If Steven talks to you directly, be courteous, but keep things short. He is old enough that he most likely will not regard you at all unless he finds you intriguing, which I am hoping that he will not."

❧❧

The ominous tone in Reed's voice sobered Leena. She didn't think that Reed was afraid of Steven, but he was afraid of what might happen if Steven took notice of Leena.

"Why? What do you think would happen?" she asked.

Reed shrugged as if it was no big deal, but the look in his eyes belied the movement. "The wolf in me would probably try to kill him," he said bluntly.

Leena stuttered for a bit, unsure of how to reply to a comment like that. She thought that maybe he had been joking, but the deadpan look on his face let her know that he wasn't. Would he really try to kill someone just for showing an interest in her? She couldn't say, but for some reason the thought of it caused a delicious tremor to course through her body.

Before she could question him further, Reed opened his door and stepped out of the truck, into the South Carolina heat. Leena followed suit, meeting him at the front door of the gothic monstrosity. Reed lifted his fist to knock, but before he fist fell, the double doors drew open slowly, revealing four of the largest men Leena had ever seen, aside from Tresize. At six and a half feet tall, Reed had to look up to meet the gaze of the man closest to him.

"We are here to meet with Steven," he said. Without a word, the men stepped aside to let Leena and Reed enter. The moment they were fully inside the house, the men surrounded her and Reed. Leena hadn't been intimidated before, but being flanked by men with biceps thicker than her waist, and guns strapped to their hips, was enough to put a spark of fear in her.

One of the men stood in front of her, looming over her. She squared her shoulders back, affecting a stance of bravado that she didn't truly feel. The act was intended to show the man that he wouldn't intimidate her, but when he looked down to overtly stare at her breasts, her fear flew out the window, replaced by ire. The man licked his lips suggestively, lifting his gaze for a moment to gage Leena's reaction before returning to his ogling, daring to take a step closer to her. Now she was getting pissed. Of its own accord, her hand flew out toward the boulder of a man, but it never made contact with his face. Reed caught her hand in his, threading his fingers through hers to prevent her from doing anything stupid.

When she turned toward Reed to glare at him, the look on his face told Leena that he hadn't only grabbed her hand to stop her from slapping the man, but also to prevent himself from punching the bastard in the throat. His usual impassive expression around others had been replaced by a heated look of ferocity. His jaw clenched, and his grip tightened to a painful degree on Leena's hand, but he didn't say a word.

The man grinned at her before turning his back on her and leading the way down the torch-lit hallway. She and Reed followed, taking in their surroundings — what she could see of them around the barrel-chested guards, anyway. Even though it was the middle of the day, the interior was dark and dreary.

The rug was a deep crimson, and the few decorations on the walls were intricate ironwork sculptures. They were absolutely beautiful, but in the setting they only accentuated the look of the Middle Ages that Steven must have been going for. Leena wondered if the place had indoor plumbing, or if that would have ruined the vibe that they were going for.

At the end of the hallway, the guards stopped at a set of double-doors. Leena's nose told her that there were at least a dozen more men inside, and at least two women. The first thought that came to Leena after she realized that she had been able to differentiate between the men and women was one of awe. Reed hadn't even tested her on that, but she knew without a doubt that she was right. Her next thought was that these Shifters were really going all out for this visit. She wondered if this was meant to intimidate Reed, or to put on a show for him. Perhaps it was a combination of the two.

The guard in front of her pushed the doors open, and that was when Leena realized that her numbers were slightly off. The room was the size of a small amphitheater, emptied of furniture, aside from the fainting couch in the middle of the floor. All along the walls, men stood at attention. As if it were a uniform, they each stood bare-chested, wearing nothing but black slacks…oh, and the arsenal of guns and knives at their hips. There had to be at least thirty men.

Lounging on the fainting couch was a man so average looking that Leena had a hard time believing that this could possibly be Steven. His height couldn't be more than six feet, his hair, a mousy brown, and his frame was so unassuming that Leena was certain that even her sister Amy could take him down in a fight. At his feet, two women knelt in garbs that could only be called togas, as they fed him from a plate of berries.

Leena couldn't help it, she snorted at the sight. She was quieted by a squeeze of her hand, and that was when she noticed that Reed still had a hold of it. With a look to him, she realized that he was using the contact with her skin to ground himself to her, focusing on her emotions to ward out the emotions of the men around them. Now she wondered if that wasn't Steven's plan in the first place; to overwhelm Reed with the emotions of all of these people. If so, she hated the man already.

As they approached the fainting couch, Steven turned toward them, a feigned look of delight on his face. "Ah, Reed MacAindris; the wolf-prince himself. To what do I owe the pleasure of your visit?"

Even his voice was average, Leena thought. Even though he tried to affect a gentlemanly demeanor, he didn't pull it off. He didn't give off the same vibe that she got from Declan. The one that made you want his approval, and also made you all too aware that he wasn't someone that she ever wanted to piss off. When you were in a room with Declan, you knew that he was in command. In this room, Leena was worried more by the men with weapons than the man in front of them.

That thought was cut off the moment his words registered in her brain. Had he just called Reed *MacAindris?* Reed and Declan had introduced themselves as McAndrews.

"Steven," Reed said, by way of greeting. "We are here because there is a rogue wolf running around the Charleston area. He is attacking people on the outskirts of Charleston, but in case he enters your territory, we are requesting your permission to continue to hunt him."

Reed said all of this with cool and collected composure, but Leena could tell that having to ask this man for permission grated on him. She didn't know how she was so sure of it, but it was almost as if he were projecting it through the link of emotions that Reed had created between the two of them.

Steven stood from the fainting couch and approached them. He stopped just in front of Reed grinning maliciously. "It kills you to have to ask this of me, doesn't it?"

Reed squared his shoulders, looking down on the man in front of them. "My king has requested that I ask your permission to hunt in your territory. Whether or not I like to do so is irrelevant."

"So, you're a submissive little pup, then?" Steven said derisively.

Leena was so close to punching him in the face, but since Reed had her left hand — the one that would do the most damage — tightly gripped in his, she somehow managed to refrain.

"I choose to be subordinate to one man, and one man only," was Reed's reply. "Do not confuse such for submission. With or without my father, I have the power to drop you and your men on your arses, make no mistake."

Steven stiffened as if Reed had slapped him across the face. At the same moment, Leena heard weapons being unsheathed, and guns being cocked. The air around them turned absolutely deadly in a split second. That probably wasn't the smartest thing that Reed could have said, but she couldn't be sorry that he had.

"I'd love to see you try," Steven spat, dropping all pretenses of this being a friendly visit.

"One day, Steven. One day."

Furious whispers sounded all around them. The one word that Leena could make out above all others was the word "threat." They thought that Reed was threatening Steven. If there were any guns left uncocked, that was no longer the case. The room echoed with the ominous clicks of slides being drawn, and she looked around to find each of those guns directed at Reed's head. Even if the bullets in those guns weren't silver, which she suspected they were, thirty shots to the head was more than enough to incapacitate Reed for good.

The thought of Reed being hurt caused an emptiness in Leena's heart that she didn't even want to begin to contemplate. As the wolf in her howled for blood, a snarl sounded from low in her throat. A light tremor ran through her body, one that caused her to sway from loss of strength, and before she knew it, the clicking sounds of bullets being released from their chambers was followed by the scraping of metal against marble, along with gasps of disbelief.

She looked down at her feet to see the arsenal of guns and knives scattered about her. The clips were separated from their guns, the bullets popped from the chambers lying harmlessly on the floor next to them. *Oh shit,* she thought.

For the first time since they entered the room, Steven looked to her. It was obvious that he had known what Reed's ability was, and it damn-well wasn't telekinesis, so that left one person. Leena.

Steven evaluated her for a moment, noting her hand clasped in Reed's, before smiling mischievously. "Reed, I tell you what," he said slyly as he perused her, "you leave your little pet here with me, and you will not only have my permission to hunt this rogue if he comes into my territory, but I will provide you with as many of my men as you like to assist you."

Leena gaped at him, uncertain that she had heard him correctly. Was he honestly bartering for a living person? How sick was this guy? Leena looked to Reed and was shocked to see that he appeared to be contemplating the deal. Asshole. Even if she had only imagined that there was a spark between them, she couldn't believe that he would be willing to trade for her as easily as boys trading snacks in a lunchroom.

She made the attempt to wrench her hand from his, but he held it tightly, stroking the palm of her hand with his thumb. He glanced at her for a moment, his eyes beseeching her to trust him before he allowed his expression to go blank again.

"I don't think that I can do that, Steven," Reed said, as if he regretted it. "You see, my father rather likes her. In fact, he likes her enough to have named her Alpha Bitch. If I go back without her, he will have my hide."

Steven switched tactics, speaking to her directly for the first time. "Darling," he said silkily, but to Leena his voice was as slimy as a snake, and she wondered if maybe that was what he shifted into. "You don't want to live with these wolves, do you? I can tell that you're new, that you haven't seen your first Pack meeting with them yet. The games that they play, as well as the actions of their women, will appall you. They will not easily accept you. You are but a pup to them. They will not take to you. Stay here, with me, and I will see to it that your every desire is fulfilled." The last was said with a sultry wink, as if Leena were too stupid to catch his meaning on her own. He stepped forward, brushing her hair back from her shoulder and then he ran his hand down her arm.

Reed's grip on her hand tightened to a painful degree. She gave him a reassuring squeeze back, before addressing Steven. "My every desire?" she said, lowering her voice to a seductive level. "You can start...by never touching me again," She gritted out the last bit, pushing his hand away from her. "First, you treat me as if I'm a piece of property to be bartered with, and then, while I'm standing next to the most drop-dead gorgeous man in existence, you try to appeal to me sexually? Nice try, but I think not."

Next to her, Reed let out a snicker. Steven glared back at her. In a final, desperate attempt, Steven said, "You think that this damaged piece of shit could please you? He'll be the biggest disappointment you've ever had, and you'll come crawling back to me, begging me to satisfy you where he couldn't."

"I doubt I would remember your name, much less request your services, after he fucks me senseless. Come on, Reed. We don't need him. We'll keep the rogue out of his territory, and if he enters it, we'll wait him out. Let's go."

She turned on her heels and stormed toward the doors, Reed following close behind her. Before they reached the double doors, Steven called after them. "Reed, do give my regards to my son."

Leena didn't know what that was all about, but she had no desire to stick around to find out. As one of the guards stepped in front of her to block her path to the door, he was shoved out of her way by an invisible force. She could get used to this ability.

Chapter Ten

Reed had been overcome with a myriad of emotions, and surprisingly they were all his own. First he was struck with a jealous rage when Steven had dared to touch Leena. That was quickly replaced by satisfaction when she had called him the most gorgeous man in existence, which gave way to amusement when she insulted Steven. Now he was in awe, and completely turned on by her. The moment that she had mentioned being fucked senseless by him…that was all Reed could think about as he followed her across the room and down the hall; openly staring as her arse swayed temptingly in her tight jeans. Her irritation and her display of power as she plowed through guards without so much as touching them only added to his arousal.

Only one thing was able to douse his attraction for her, and that was Steven's assessment of what would come of their relationship. Not that he was certain that there would ever be a relationship, but he did hope for it.

What Steven had said was so paralleled to Reed's own fears that he couldn't help but wonder if it *was* possible for him to satisfy her. He hadn't been able to fully enjoy the act of sex, ever. He could never lose his control, and he could never endure the bombardment of uninhibited emotions. He was always on guard, always trying to shield himself, however unsuccessfully.

Over the past few decades, Reed had pretty much given up all hope of having relationships with women. Of finding the one woman that he wouldn't mind getting to know on every level, and letting her emotions flow into him freely.

When the pent up frustration became too much to handle, he used them, just as they used him, but he never let go of the tight leash that he kept on his control.

Reed stopped and stared at Leena as she stood under the rays of the setting sun. He could sense her apprehension, but as he noticed before, it was nowhere near as strong as anyone else's emotions. At this distance, he really had to focus on her just to get a reading on her. The fact that he often found himself delving into her emotions to get a read on her spoke volumes. She had to be it for him; that one person.

Already he felt more for her than any other woman he had ever met. What was there not to be attracted to? She was strong and fierce, loyal, beautiful. She laughed easily, living every moment to the fullest. She was intelligent, and thoughtful, often catching herself doing something that Reed may not be comfortable with, and adjusting. What she didn't know was that he wasn't uncomfortable with anything that she did. Maybe, just maybe, it could work out with her.

With a renewed smile on his face, he went to the truck and opened the door for her. Her somberness intensified as he drew closer to her, but he didn't press her on the cause of it right away. As they drove down the driveway and out onto the main road in silence, Reed could feel her struggling to find the words that she wanted to say to him.

Finally, she said, "I'm sorry about what I did back there. You told me to let you do all of the talking, and I should have listened. I blew it."

He reached across the bench and took her hand in his, noting again how soft it was despite what she did for a living. "You didn't blow it. As you said, we can hunt outside of Charleston. Besides, if the rogue enters Charleston, and we can't draw him out, my da can petition the rest of the shifter council members for the right to hunt him in Charleston."

Leena relaxed a little, but that didn't stop her from feeling contrite. "What do you think he'll do in response to the way I spurned him?" she asked.

Reed thought on it a moment and he really couldn't decide on what he thought Steven would do. The man was usually calculating and intelligent, but with the way he was humiliated, there is a chance that he would throw caution to the wind at a chance for revenge. Still, he would be an utter fool to try something once they got back to Pittsburgh, and Steven was anything but foolish.

"If he knows what's best for him and his people, he won't retaliate. My da wouldn't stand for an attack on his alpha bitch," Reed answered honestly. If there was one thing that his people revered, it was their women. Women carried the next generations of werewolves. If their numbers dwindled, they would need the women to replenish the pack.

While human women could carry werewolf babes, not many human women could endure such a pregnancy. Not to mention, there was only a fifty percent chance that the babe would even be a werewolf. With the women of the pack, they were stronger and more capable of carrying the babes to term. And with a werewolf male to impregnate them, the child would most definitely be a werewolf.

As the king, it would look poorly on Reed's da if he let anything happen to the alpha of all of their women. If she were harmed, they would have to respond tenfold. The remaining council members wouldn't allow Steven to start a war that they didn't stand a chance of winning. And he wouldn't risk his leadership, and quite possibly his life, just because his sexual proposition was turned down.

"Also," Leena said, her face still etched with confusion. "What was he talking about when he asked you to give his regards to his son?"

Reed had almost forgotten about Steven's parting dig. He had to have known that there was no way that Reed would carry out his request, but what Reed hadn't understood was why Steven would even bring up his affiliation with Leo in front of so many people. The man had spurned Leo from the moment that he was born, even going as far as trying to have him killed while he was still in the womb.

"Leo is his biological son," Reed answered, hoping that Leena would leave it at that. He should have known better by now.

"I don't understand, is Steven a werewolf?"

"No, Steven shifts into a snow leopard, as does Leo. His mother, however, is a werewolf. Steven had hated Iris from the moment that she told him that she had grown pregnant from a one-night-stand, and he hated her even more when he found out that she had planned to keep the babe. She never asked him for anything, though, and the day that Leo was born and we found out that he carried the scent of a snow leopard and not a wolf, my da made sure that she knew that Leo was, and always would be, a part of our pack for as long as he wished it. That was roughly one hundred years ago, and he's been with us ever since."

"Poor Leo," she whispered, before turning to look out the window, the sadness in her eyes punctuated by the connection that he kept with their linked hands.

Reed had used the words "one-night-stand" loosely in his explanation to Leena. He didn't want to lie to her, but letting her know that Iris had actually been raped by Steven that night was not his place. Iris had left the pack when she thought that she had fallen in love with a bear-shifter and moved to Charleston with him. A few weeks later she showed up on Declan's doorstep, telling him of how the man that she hoped to mate with had presented her to Steven for him to use to his pleasure. She begged for Declan to take her back, and he had without hesitation, threatening to report Steven to the rest of the council. Iris had asked him not to, and reluctantly he had agreed. She had only ever told Reed and his da what had happened to her, and then later on, Leo.

Bringing him back to the moment, Leena cleared her throat and asked, "Is it going to be a problem to visit the marsh in the dark?" She pointed out the window, indicating the waning sunlight.

He smiled, surprised that she hadn't noticed yet; but then again, there had been lamps illuminating his da's house and the street when they were out before. "The dark has little effect on us. And when I'm in my wolf form, I'll see just as well as if it were daytime. This will actually be more beneficial, because there won't be as many people out."

She nodded and turned to look back out the window, not realizing that he still held her hand. Oddly enough, he felt comfort touching her. Her emotions were so mild compared to everyone else's. Even linking to her, her emotions were like a hum compared to the roar of a person standing several feet away. Not to mention the fact that he liked knowing how she was feeling. Her emotions were always so pure, even her frustration and rage. She telegraphed her feelings in a way that hid nothing, so that when Reed absorbed her emotions, there were no surprises. He liked that about her.

Reed parked his truck several blocks away from the marsh that he first found Leena in. He didn't realize until now how lucky he was that his brother was able to see the street names on a sign that Leena had run passed in his vision of her. There would have been no way for him to figure out which marsh she was going to be in without that intersection. Then and there, Reed vowed to start showing his appreciation for his brother and his ability. Without him, Reed would have never found the beautiful woman next to him that promised to make the rest of his unnaturally long life worth living.

That thought shocked Reed. He had known that he was falling for Leena, but to consider her being in his life forever? Even as he thought that it was way too soon to think that way, a part of him was already resigned to the fact that he did anticipate spending the rest of his life with her. Even if he couldn't convince her to be with him romantically, he already couldn't imagine going back to the way that things were before she came into their lives.

❧❧

Leena slid out of the truck and followed Reed as he carried a drawstring backpack underneath the cover of two trees. With the sun completely set, his silhouette could barely be seen even with Leena's heightened vision. Before she had only had a hint of what her eyes could adjust to when they had gone to her house two nights ago, but now, as she looked around at the houses without the harsh light of streetlamps in this area, everything was so clear to her. She could even make out the couple a few houses down making out in their darkened bedroom. She averted her eyes, stepping under the shadow of the trees that Reed had disappeared under.

He handed her the drawstring bag. "The collar and leash are in there," he informed her, as he began unbuttoning his shirt.

Leena glanced around nervously. "What are you doing?"

"I don't want to tear my good clothes. Would you mind carrying them in the backpack while I'm in my wolf form?"

Leena shook her head, unable to speak as Reed slowly exposed his broad chest and tightly chiseled abdomen. Her mouth dried as the fabric slid off of his shoulders and down his thickly corded arms. He handed the shirt to her and reached for the fly of his pants. Her fingers fumbled with the buttons of the shirt as she refastened them and folded it. She kept her gaze on the shirt and backpack, not letting herself focus on the whir of a zipper and the brush of fabric against skin.

Reed cleared his throat, and Leena held her hand out in his direction. She heard him snicker just before he stepped into her line of vision, laying his pants over her outstretched palm.

Oh. My. God. She may have forgotten to breathe for a few moments. He had only given her a glimpse of his fully nude body, but that was all that she needed. Her heart pounded against her rib cage as a flush covered her entire body.

Trying to ignore the way her body shook, she folded his slacks and stuffed them into the backpack with his shirt, donning it after she withdrew the leash and collar. Had he done that on purpose? He had to know that the fleeting look of his body was enough to keep her distracted for the rest of the evening. The image of it was burned into her retinas, causing a huge grin to spread across her face and a delicious heat to course through her body. She hadn't been lying to Steven earlier...Reed truly was the most gorgeous man she had ever seen in her life.

Leena barely registered the sounds of bone crunching and skin tearing as she daydreamed. It wasn't until the enormous black wolf that was Reed nudged Leena's hip with his muzzle that she was broken from her reverie. She should have been embarrassed, but she couldn't bring herself to muster the emotion. If she died tonight, she would die with a smile on her face, and the most magnificent image etched into her brain.

As she strapped the collar around Reed's neck, she ran her fingers through his soft fur once, out of habit. She straightened, and waited for him to lead the way, since her surroundings didn't seem familiar to her yet.

They only passed a few people on their way to the marsh, earning glances from each of them. People don't often see a woman in a blouse and heels walking a wolf-like dog whose back reached her hip. Then again, in a world where Lady Gaga and Nicki Minaj are idolized, who's to say that walking a huge dog in boots and jeans in ninety degree weather is unordinary?

When they reached the fenced-in portion of the marsh, Leena looked around for any prying eyes before kneeling in front of Reed and unhooking the leash from the collar. She watched as he easily leapt the fence in a single bound, using his nose to guide him through the slush.

Leena looked around again, making sure that no one saw her release Reed. From this point on, if anyone saw her wandering around with a leash, or happened to see Reed on the loose, she had the excuse of looking for her dog that had escaped her.

She jogged down the road to the bridge that she knew led to the other side of the marsh, gaining one wary glance from a runner in shorts and a tank top as she passed. On the other side, she would meet back up with Reed after he locked on to the rogue's scent.

She arrived shortly before the black wolf dropped down onto the pavement next to her. She strapped the leash back onto his collar, almost disappointed that she hadn't needed to use her fantastic(ly horrible) acting skills. She followed behind him as he tracked the scent of the other wolf.

After a few minutes, their surroundings started becoming familiar to Leena. At first she couldn't figure out why, but when it dawned on her it was as if her heart had turned into lead. They crossed over another short bridge, drawing closer to the one place that Leena was hoping they wouldn't go. *Please don't turn right,* she begged silently; hoping beyond hope that it was just a coincidence.

Despite her plea, Reed turned right into the housing plan, causing her heart rate to accelerate. After turning left and then taking another right, Leena's heart dropped to the pit of her stomach. He stopped in the middle of a cul-de-sac, under the grouping of trees and flowers in the middle of the road, staring right at Amy's house.

◈◈◈

Reed could hear Leena's heart pounding in her chest as the rogue's trail grew stronger. At first he thought it was anticipation, but then he felt her dread flow from her. When the trail ended, Reed had stopped, and he barely heard the pained moan that escaped her. "Amy," she breathed out, and Reed finally understood. He trotted off between two houses, his leash slipping easily from Leena's trembling fingers.

Thankfully his human neck wasn't as thick as his wolf's, so he was able to shift to his natural form without strangling himself. He looked around before emerging from the cover of the houses, stepping up behind Leena, resting his hands on her shoulders. She shuddered, and he knew that it had nothing to do with his touch, but the fear that still rolled through her.

He slid the cords of the backpack from her shoulders and down her arms without her so much as moving. She was in a daze, staring at the house across from them. The light was on inside, which was a good sign, but Leena didn't seem to register it.

Quickly, he slipped into his slacks and button-down and then stepped in front of her, grabbing her arms to get her attention. "Leena, listen to me. His scent does not cross the street, so he hasn't yet approached your sister. She is still in there. It does, however, get very strong at the end of the street, all the way to this spot, as if he has visited it numerous times."

Her face hardened as soon as his words registered. "That son-of-a-bitch is stalking my sister."

It wasn't a question, but Reed nodded anyway. She had believed his words when he said that the rogue hadn't crossed to her sister's house, but he could feel that she still needed to see her sister with her own two eyes. Without a word, she strode across the street, and rapped on the door.

After a few short moments the door flung open, revealing a stunning woman that looked similar enough to Leena that he knew that this was Amy. There were major differences between the two, such as Amy's darker skin and hair, and Leena's thicker muscles, but the biggest one to Reed was their emotional signature.

Amy gave off a confidence, the kind that he felt in Shaun, whereas Leena gave off a relaxed vibe, the kind that said that she didn't prefer the spotlight, but she had no problem commanding it when it became necessary. Leena was a balanced contradiction of soft and hard, especially when meeting new people, but Amy gave off a free spirited and trusting vibe. The one thing they had in common? The fierce loyalty and protectiveness of those closest to them.

Amy was projecting that now, as she glared at Reed, even as she squealed her sister's name, and threw her arms around her in a tight embrace. "What are you doing down here?" she asked Leena. "I thought you were back up in Pittsburgh."

Leena hesitated for a moment, clearly uncomfortable with keeping things from her sister. In that moment, he knew with certainty that Leena had never lied to her sister, and the fact that she had to bend the truth with her now sat ill with her. "I flew back down this afternoon," she answered truthfully.

"Well, come in!" Amy said, ushering them into the house. "Who is your friend?"

Leena hesitated again, trying to decide how much to tell her sister, before Reed absolved her of the responsibility. "My name is Reed McAndrews. My brother and I scared off the dog that attacked your sister. I have been by her side the entire time, making sure that she pulled through."

At that, Amy's demeanor toward him softened exponentially. She no longer cared that she didn't know him, he had saved one of the most important people in her life, and that was worthy of her acceptance. "Nice to meet you, Reed," she said, holding out her hand for him to shake. He accepted it, returning the nicety, and Amy continued. "Thank you for saving my sister. You have no idea what you have done for my family."

He gave a wry smile before answering, "I have an idea."

"Amy," Leena interjected, "we have to talk to you. Why don't we take this into the kitchen?"

Amy nodded and led the way. Leena hung back several steps, whispering to Reed so that her sister wouldn't hear her. "How much am I allowed to tell her?" she asked.

He thought on it a moment. According to their laws, humans were to be kept in the dark on their existence, but exceptions were made. Family was one of the exceptions, as long as the person took responsibility for the actions that family member took against the pack. "As much as you think she can handle," Reed responded.

She gave a short nod and entered the kitchen. When she sat on a bar stool at the island, Reed sat next to her. Amy handed Leena a small handbag and a mobile phone before she took the seat opposite her sister.

"I've kept it charged, but it is on silent now. Jason called the day we were attacked, and I told him what happened. He didn't call again until two nights ago. It was late, so I didn't answer, but I answered yesterday morning and he started screaming at me. He asked me where the fuck you were, and told me that you'd regret leaving him, and where the hell do you get off having Scott *schedule* an appointment for him to come and get his things. I hung up on him, and when he kept calling back, I turned the ringer off." She grinned then. "Did you really break up with that tool finally?"

Reed decided in that moment that he liked Amy just fine. He tried to suppress his own grin, grateful that Leena didn't have the ability to feel his emotions.

"I did," Leena responded. "He decided to mourn my possible demise by fucking Sandra...in my bed."

"What a douche-bag," Amy spat vehemently. "I knew that there was something not quite right about that asshole."

Leena heaved a sigh. "Go ahead, give it to me...'I told you so.' I deserve it. You had been right all along."

"Would I do that to you?" Amy said looking aghast.

Amy and Leena both smiled after that. "Yes," they said in unison, breaking into a fit of laughter afterward.

Reed loved seeing Leena this way. The comfortable banter that she had with her sister—despite their differences in personality—left him both amused and slightly envious. He didn't expect that he and Corrick would ever sit around discussing relationships, but it would be nice to be able to have a lighthearted conversation with the kid, without worrying about how someone could use his brother to hurt him.

After a few more friendly quips at each other, Leena's face turned grave. "Amy, there's a reason that we've come here tonight. You may not believe any of this, but I need for you to keep an open mind."

Amy opened her mouth to respond, but with a look at her sister, she closed it again, and settled for a nod. Leena heaved a deep breath, and let the words tumble from her mouth. She told her sister everything, from the rogue wolf attacking them, to the showdown with Annabelle earning her the title of alpha bitch. She went on and on, until she finished with, "and he has been revisiting you here the past few days, watching you."

At first Amy looked disbelieving, but before she spat out denials she stopped to think things over. Reed could feel her internal debate. What Leena had told her couldn't possibly be real, but then again, her sister had never lied to her before in her life. She knew that Leena wouldn't make something like this up to yank her chain, but she just couldn't fathom it.

To help Leena get her point across, Reed pushed himself to his feet, and stripped out of his clothes for the second time that night. Amy watched him, transfixed, as he stood naked in her kitchen. Leena had turned to watch him also, and when he caught her gaping at him, he gave her a wink. Her blush amused him, but he didn't comment on it. Instead, he knelt on the tile, and called his wolf to him.

As his bones snapped, and his skin shifted, he heard Amy's shocked gasp, and Leena's reassurances. When he stood fully changed, there was an extended silence before Amy let out an, "Oh. My. God."

Chapter Eleven

Leena was grateful that Reed had decided to help her show Amy what they were. If she had been forced to shift for Amy, it wouldn't have been pretty. Not that Reed's change was pretty, in fact, it looked rather gruesome, but his wolf came to him so much faster than Leena's did. That, and Amy would have been more horrified to see her baby sister breaking apart and reforming than this man who was a stranger to her.

She had been holding her breath during Reed's shift, and for the extended silence afterward. When Amy finally spoke, Leena had let the breath rush out of her in relief. She looked to her sister, whose eyes were wide, and mouth agape.

Amy stuttered over what to say, before the words finally came to her.

"Leena, I know that Nana has done some pretty outrageous things, but this one takes the goddamn cake.... A man just turned into a wolf in my kitchen!"

Amy paced back and forth in the kitchen, glancing down at Reed every few seconds, and muttering the words "oh my God" over and over. She swiped a hand down her face, and fixed her gaze on the giant wolf sitting patiently on the tile floor, shaking her head slowly.

"Amy, look at me," Leena said, and Amy pried her eyes away from the wolf to look at her sister. "There are more important things to worry about right now. The reason that we're here is that a man is stalking you. Have you left the house at all the past few days? Seen what you thought was a dog watching the house?"

She shook her head and continued pacing. "No, I haven't gone anywhere. I'm still on vacation from work, and I've spent most of my time waiting by the phone. Matt has been taking care of everything lately; I've just been looking after Aiden." She said the last part with a mixture of relief and regret. Amy was always self-sufficient, so to rely on Matt was something new for her. He probably enjoyed being able to do something for her for once, but she would see it as taking advantage of him.

"When are you set to go back to work?"

"On Monday."

It was Friday. That gave them two full days to track down the rogue and dispatch him. "What are the chances that you could take a few more days off, if it was necessary?"

"If I tell them that my sister was hospitalized, I could swing a few more."

Leena nodded and turned back to the wolf that sat on the floor watching their exchange. "We should probably get going," she said to him. It was getting pretty late, and she still wanted to check in with Declan to see if he had been able to get the photos of the woman's murder. Leena wanted to set up a game plan for trying to catch this bastard as soon as possible.

Reed dipped his muzzle in a nod, and she watched as he burrowed his snout underneath his button-down and tossed his head back, launching the shirt onto his back. She tried to hold back a snicker as she watched him repeat the action with his slacks, and trot off into the hallway to change back into his human form.

The moment he was out of earshot for a normal person, Amy whispered, "Please tell me that you are rebounding with that sexy piece of meat. He is yum-my!"

Leena laughed. She probably should have mentioned the enhanced senses to her sister, but she hadn't seen the need to at the time. "He can still hear you, Amy," she whispered back to her sister.

"I don't care," Amy responded.

Leena should have seen that one coming. Her sister would have said something like that in front of Reed on normal circumstances. She probably only waited for him to leave the room for Leena's benefit, knowing that her baby sister would have blushed from head to toe. "Dish," Amy said more forcefully.

Leena thought for a moment about the feelings that she had been developing for Reed over the past few days. Yes, the man was sexy enough to tempt a nun, but when she actually allowed herself to think about it, she had to admit that it was more than that. Shaun was drop-dead sexy as well, but he hadn't nearly stirred the emotions in her that Reed had. Even when Reed had been infuriating, she knew that he got that way in an effort to protect his people, including her. He was a warrior that was tasked with protecting every North American werewolf, but he knew when to let that go and be sweet and attentive instead of fierce and deadly. He was everything that she had ever imagined a man should be, and she definitely wouldn't call him a rebound.

She knew that her sister was asking her if she had had sex with Reed yet, but the phrasing of her question had left Leena curious about her and Reed's situation.

It had only been two nights since she found Jason in bed with Sandra, but somehow it felt like weeks had passed. When she thought about it now, there was no sting from his betrayal. She barely even felt anger towards him anymore, she just felt indifference. Would it be considered rebounding if she never felt as if she had lost anything? In truth, she felt liberated from him. He had walked into her as she was leaving her studio one day, seeing her in her dance garb, and assuming that she was delicate and feminine. When he found out that she was hard and tough, he had slowly tried to change her. Reed, on the other hand, had been trying to help her hone her skills, making her even tougher. If she punched a man out for grabbing at her, Reed would probably praise her rather than scold her.

Her sister waited patiently for her answer, and she could hear Reed go still in the next room, undoubtedly waiting to hear what she had to say. *No pressure, guys...*

"Well, even if I do end up pursuing a relationship with *anyone* right now—sexual, or otherwise—I wouldn't call it a rebound. I'm not only *over* Jason, but I realize now that there was never really anything there. If I'm being honest, I believe that I only even let him move in because no one else seemed interested, and the illusion of companionship was better than spending every day alone. I was a coward. Me...do you believe it? The Abrams girl that would jump into a fight to defend someone that she didn't even know, with boys twice her size, was too cowardly to be alone."

Amy settled her hand over Leena's until she looked up to meet her sister's eyes. "Hey, everyone is afraid of something. That doesn't make you a coward, it makes you human." She paused, thought about her wording, and then rephrased it. "Or rather, a person." After a moment, she put her finger under Leena's chin, forcing her to look into her eyes. "Just do me a favor," she said, waiting for Leena's nod before continuing. "Don't let your fear of being a coward again stop you from pursuing relationships—sexual or otherwise."

Leena snorted at Amy's use of her own words.

"Besides, Lee," she went on, ignoring Leena's snort. "The boys were always interested, you were just too introverted to notice. You think that those friends of yours saw you as nothing but one of the guys, but I saw the way that they looked at you, and I see the way that *he* looks at you now." She pointed her thumb in the direction of the hall to indicate Reed. "The difference between them and Jason is that Jason wasn't afraid to be persistent. Even when you said no, he didn't give up pursuing you."

Leena had no idea what she meant. Not about Jason, that bit was true, but about Reed. Amy had only seen Reed as a man for no more than fifteen or twenty minutes. Not to mention, Leena had been talking the entire time, so of course he would be looking at her. She opened her mouth to say as much, when she was cut short by Reed clearing his throat. She had almost forgotten that he could hear everything that they had been saying.

"Are you ready to go, Leena?" He asked, his face devoid of all emotion.

She nodded, not trusting herself to use words just then. She stood from the stool, and walked around the island to hug her sister. "Please remember what I told you, and don't leave the house."

Amy squeezed her back, saying, "You remember what I said also."

"I will."

❧❦❧

Reed waited while Leena ran up the stairs to grab the suitcase that she had left when she was attacked by the rogue. When she met him outside, a heavy silence hung between them that Reed didn't know how to break. He could feel the disbelief still rolling through her at her sister's proclamation. He tried to give her the time to sort through her thoughts, but when she settled on a resolve, Reed knew that it wasn't her resigning to the fact that men felt her desirable. He didn't know what had happened to her that made her think that she had nothing to offer men, but he was determined to have her see herself the way that he saw her.

"You know, your sister is right," he said, as they turned off of her sister's street and headed back toward his truck. She shot her head up then, looking at him questioningly. "You are extremely beautiful, and I'm certain that a fair share of men find you desirable."

She shrugged. "I know that guys think that I'm pretty, but the minute they find out that I'm not the girly-girl that dancing portrays me to be, they're put off. I'm the girl that hammers out metal and throws knives, the girl who has been known to jump into fights instead of squeal and call out for a rescuer. Men want feminine, and that's just not all me. It's a part of me, but the side of me that isn't dainty overshadows it."

Reed let out a derisive snort. "Only the weak men want a dainty woman. They don't want a woman who is stronger than them, because it makes them look like less of a man. You need a real man."

"Like you," she scoffed.

"Yes," he said flatly.

She looked at him as if he had grown an extra head. She still didn't believe that he could be interested in her, even though he knew that she could sense his attraction to her. He sighed inwardly and said, "Becoming a werewolf will help you to see how much men will desire your strength. We are a race of brutes who revere fighting. Look at Annabelle, for example. She is beautiful, but she is tough as nails. Her fighting skills are what the men of our pack find attractive in her. It's her personality that no one likes."

Leena let out a bark of laughter as Reed had intended, and the sound was like music to his ears. He just couldn't believe that she had no idea how she affected him, and not just because she was beautiful.

"May I ask you something?" Reed said, and when she nodded he continued. "Why did you tell Amy everything about what happened to you but not Scott? You seem to be so much closer to Scott."

She tilted her head to the side in a wolf-like manner before answering. "I am closer to Scott, but he would be so much harder to convince than Amy. If you hadn't changed into your wolf in front of Amy, I could have still convinced her that I was telling the truth. Scott hates the idea of magic.

Even after seeing the things that my grandmother could do, he would convince himself that it was coincidence, or that there was a trick to it that he was missing. Not to mention, that I was pretty livid by the time Scott came home, and I had no desire to try to convince him that I wasn't crazy on top of it."

"Understandable," was all Reed said.

After a few more moments of silence, Reed felt amusement roll through Leena again, just before she said, "So… you think that Annabelle has a terrible personality?"

He grinned. "The worst," he admitted. "When she's not busy being vain, she splits her time between trying to weasel her way into a permanent position as Alpha Bitch, and fighting with absolutely everyone. She reacts as if everything is a personal attack against her. A few years ago, she tried to get Tresize into bed with her, and when he turned her down, she forced one of the other females to put a dozen Brazilian Wandering Spiders into his Range Rover. The first bite would have killed a normal human, but thankfully, Tresize managed to heal a few days after Shaun found him."

She gaped at him. "Isn't that…"

"The most poisonous spider in the world? Yes."

"Jesus…" she breathed out. "The woman is crazy. I can't imagine what she'll have in store for me when we get back."

"If she harms you, I'll end her," Reed said matter-of-factly.

Leena smiled. Not quite the reaction he had expected. Most women would either demurely accept his offer of protection, or rail at the fact that he assumed they needed it. She did neither.

"I appreciate the offer, but I think that I can handle her."

If anyone could it was the scrappy woman next to him.

Finally Reed's truck came in to view, and he could feel the fatigue coming from Leena. They hadn't eaten much since they got off of the plane, and they had expended a lot of energy. He wouldn't be surprised if she fell asleep the moment she laid her head down on her pillow. One thing that he knew about women, thanks to his da, was that their guard was down when they were this tired. They were more likely to say what they were thinking, or feeling, without their usual inhibitory inclination.

He had to make a decision now. If he chose to pursue this thing between them he had to act, and if he acted now, he would have to commit. It was now or never. Was he ready to try one last time to get close to someone?

He looked down at the amazing woman next to him, and grinned mischievously. "So, your sister thinks that I'm *yummy*?" he said.

"Hmm? Oh, that." A lovely shade of pink tinted her cheeks. "Just ignore her."

"Do you?" He asked her.

"Do I what? Ignore her?"

"Do you find me to be *yummy*?"

❧❧

Leena had started to lose track of their surroundings a few blocks after they left her sister's house. It had been such a long day, and she was ready to fall into bed. She had barely registered what Reed had said to her when she caught his amused tone. She could have punched Amy if it wouldn't have taken too much energy to stomp back over there and lift her fist to launch the blow. Next time.

She didn't actually think that Reed would drop it when she told him to ignore Amy, but she hadn't expected his question either. The word "yummy" should have sounded so ridiculous coming from such a large, overtly masculine man, but it hadn't. The purr of his voice as it rolled over the word sent shockwaves of heat coursing through her body. Yummy didn't even come close to describing Reed. He was a delectable feast laid before a starving woman, and just then she longed to take a bite.

"You have to know that you're attractive," she said, not quite answering his question but not quite denying the truth. He had to feel the desire now coursing through her with his ability.

She stopped at the passenger door to his truck, waiting for him to unlock it. He stepped in close to her, bracing his hands against the truck on either side of her, blocking her in. Her heart rate sped up, and awareness shot through her, chasing away the fatigue.

"I know that some women believe so," he said. His voice was low, and his accent thickened. "I want to know what *you* think."

His face was so close to hers that she could feel his breath on her lips. Centimeters. She would only have to move a few centimeters for his lips to touch hers. Oh what the hell?

"I meant what I said to Steven. You're the sexiest man that I have ever seen."

The moment she got the last word out, his lips crushed hers. She let out a gasp, and he took full advantage of her opened mouth. His tongue slipped between her lips, and as it stroked hers her brain fled and her body took over. She snaked her arms up around his neck and pulled him in closer, deepening the kiss. *Oh. My. God.* He was just as delicious as she imagined he would be, and he kissed like a man who had decades of training. Fitting, she supposed.

Reed moved his hands from the truck to her ass, lifting her off of the ground. She wrapped her legs around his waist and he pinning her to the truck with his long, hard body. The truck rocked on its axis from the fervor of his movements. She broke off the kiss long enough to laugh, only to be cut off by Reed devouring her mouth once again.

She didn't know how long they stayed that way. It could have been minutes, it could have been hours. The only thing that Leena knew was that she could stay that way forever. It was unlike any kiss she had ever experienced. It was as if they had formed a soul-deep connection. One that she never wanted to sever.

One of his hands moved from her ass to her waist, burrowing underneath her shirt. His skin on hers was as hot as a branding iron.

A high-pitched wail pierced the silence. Leena broke apart from Reed, and looked around to see if anyone was out on the street with them, but she saw nothing. It was then that she realized that the noise came from Reed's pocket. His cell phone.

With a growl that was more wolf than man, Reed ignored the incessant ringing to reclaim her mouth. The phone went quite for just a moment, before it resumed its ringing. It was as if it were louder and more persistent this time around. With a look of regret, Reed broke away from her and let her slide down his body until her feet reconnected with the ground. He reached into his pocket, and without looking at the screen, slid his finger across it to answer the call.

"What?" he barked into the receiver.

"Reed," Leena heard Declan say on the other end. "Another woman has been found dead."

Chapter Twelve

Reed listened as his da gave him the details of the girl that had been murdered, most likely by their rogue wolf. The moment that his da had said that another woman had been killed, Leena had gone stone white, clutching the front of his shirt like a lifeline. It wasn't until his da gave them the location of the woman's death that Leena had relaxed her grip and expelled the breath that she had been holding.

While his da gave him the name of the detective that was expecting them as well as their cover story, Leena typed the address into his truck's GPS.

The town was just north of them. A ten minute drive. He had offered to take Leena back to the hotel so that she could sleep, but she gave him a look that told him that if he offered again she'd shove her blade into his chest.

Over and over again, he wanted to say something to her about their kiss, but each time he shut his mouth the moment it opened. Now wasn't the time, but he wanted her to know that he had enjoyed every second of that kiss. He hoped that it was something that they could duplicate—preferably every day for the rest of his life. That kiss had been unlike anything he had ever experienced. He could sense her desire, but he could differentiate hers from his own. It was muted, allowing him to savor other things, such as the taste of her lips, and the feel of her body against his.

"I remember this road," Leena said, interrupting Reed's thoughts. "Amy and I drove this way to get to the night club that just opened. This area didn't used to have any, and now a few have popped up in the past three years. Amy made me go to each of them under the assumption that because I like to dance, then I would like to gyrate on total strangers."

Her revulsion at the thought was the only thing that kept him from snarling at the idea of anyone else being able to feel her body the way that he had, and from launching himself across the seat to mark her neck with his bite. His wolf instincts were far too close to the surface. If he was going to think levelly, then he needed to get a grip on himself. He didn't know if he could do that with her so close to him.

"Do you think that this girl was at one of these night clubs?" he asked her, proud with himself for not growling as he did so.

"It's possible," she answered with a shrug.

Up ahead, Reed saw the flashing blue and red of several police vehicles. He pulled his truck as close as possible to the scene, and killed the engine. To reach the scene, he and Leena had to push through a large crowd of people. Curiosity, sympathy, amazement, sorrow, and grief flooded his emotions. He absorbed them, trying to keep them separate from his own, and trying not to let the effect they had on him show.

Reading him like a book, Leena slipped her hand into his. The second her skin came into contact with his, all of the other emotions were cut off. It was as if she had slammed a two-foot thick steel door in the faces of a screaming crowd— silence. The only emotion she gave off was concern, and it was so diluted that he had to concentrate just to feel it.

He couldn't figure out what it was about her, but touching her, skin to skin, had the same effect as being in the same building, but not the same room, as anyone else. If he believed in fate, he would say that perhaps it was because she was meant for him. That she was his gift for having to go through so much grief over the past one hundred and eighty years. Since he didn't believe, he would just continue to marvel at it, and revel in the feel of it.

They reached the police tape, and when Reed lifted it for Leena to step under, they were stopped by a large police officer. Well, large compared to Leena. He towered over her, glaring down at her. The body mass that Reed carried in muscle, the officer made up for in fat. With one beefy hand, he grabbed Leena by her bicep and shoved her back toward the tape. She was strong enough that she could have resisted, but she didn't.

"You can't be here," he snapped at her, not bothering to look at Reed.

Before she had a chance to open her mouth, Reed had a hold of the officer's wrist, squeezing until his grip on Leena went slack. "Don't ever touch her again," he said, pronouncing each word slowly. Just a bit tighter and all it would take was a flick of his own wrist to break the officer's. The officer knew it too. He glared back at Reed with a look that dared him to try it, while his outrage flowed into him. Reed could barely differentiate it from his own fury.

"We're here to meet with Detective Bradley," Leena rushed out, resting her free hand over the one Reed still grasped the officer's wrist with. "Darling, let go," she told him before addressing the officer again. "You'll have to excuse my husband, sir. He's on the force back home, and if there's anything he has a hard time dealing with it is mistreatment of women and children."

At her first words, Reed had released the officer. When she had called him her husband, all of the anger had fled from him. It was as if she was using her words to stroke the beast in him; lulling his wolf into a state of calm. In front of this crowd, she had declared herself his, and that was enough to sate his need to dismember the next person to touch her.

He knew damn well that her words were just an alteration of his da's cover for them, but that did not matter to his wolf. To his wolf, she had just accepted that she was his mate. It didn't matter that he hadn't officially staked his claim on her yet, or that she thought that him being her husband would have been the only logical reason for him to have reacted so forcefully to her being touched, it only mattered that she had called him her own.

The wolf in him seemed to purr — PURR! As if he were an oversized cat and she had just found that sweet spot to pet.

The officer sized up the two of them, his gaze lingering on their clasped hands, before pointing to a detective several feet away. Leena nodded to the officer and thanked him.

Reed squared his shoulders and moved his hand from hers to the small of her back. Her low-slung jeans helped him to keep his skin in direct contact with hers, and it didn't hurt that his hand was close enough to her arse to have the image of her pressed against his truck and squirming against his body resurface. "Come, *mo ghrá*," he said, leading her toward the detective, a renewed smile spreading across his face.

This man looked more like an officer of the law than the man that had grabbed Leena by leaps and bounds. His dark skin was pulled tightly over ropes of muscle, mostly hidden by his dress shirt. His stern features and knowing gaze dared you to try to pull something over on him and try to get away with it. Reed watched him as they approached, and he noticed how easily the man moved around the scene. He knew every inch of his surroundings, and caught every detail of the scene. If Reed's nose hadn't told him differently, he would swear that Detective Bradley was a werewolf.

The detective's gaze raked over Reed as he approached, and then he did the same to Leena. In his perusal, he studied her hands and legs, noting the way she moved gracefully and silently in her heels and the barely perceptible calluses on her hands. Despite her soft, sweet face, he saw her for what she was, swift and deadly.

Reed extended his hand to Detective Bradley. "Detective. My name is Reed, and this is my wife, Kalina. You spoke to my superior earlier."

He grasped Reed's hand and nodded. "Yes, Mr. McAndrews said that you were working on a case similar to ours. This is our second girl in this area that has been killed, and we have nothing. Any help that you can give would be appreciated."

"Do you have the file on the first woman?" Reed asked, and Detective Bradley passed him a manila folder. Reed opened it, quickly glancing through the photos before passing the folder to Leena and returning his hand to her back.

When she opened the folder a soft gasp escaped through her lips followed by a wave of sadness.

≪�⌒≫

Leena had braced herself for pools of blood, torn flesh and unrecognizable features. Instead, she was met with a photo of a beautiful young woman staring up at the camera, her lifeless eyes frozen in terror. The only marks that marred her skin were twin holes just above her left clavicle.

When she flipped to the next photo, she found that similar holes marked her back, stopping just short of piercing her scapula. From the looks of it, Leena would guess that the wolf had bitten the girl at the junction of her neck and shoulder.

The next photo was a close-up of the back of the girl's head. Her skull was misshapen, and dried blood matted her hair around raw flesh. It looked as if her head had been smashed by something big and heavy. Leena couldn't believe that the rogue would bash her over the head with something just to shift to his wolf and bite her neck. Perhaps he knocked her to the ground, causing her to hit her head off of the pavement.

"Where was this girl found?" Leena asked Detective Bradley.

"Just a few blocks from here," he answered, pointing in the direction that Reed and Leena had approached the crime scene from.

She nodded and closed the folder, holding it close to her stomach so that it couldn't be snatched from her hands.

"Can we see the new victim?"

He led them over to the mouth of an alleyway, handing Reed a card as they walked. "The girl's name is Megan. We found her license and credit cards in one of her pockets along with some cash."

Reed passed the license to Leena and she tried to ignore the tightening in her chest as she looked at the ID. According to the birth date, Megan was only twenty-two years old. A few years younger than Leena was.

Leena shook slightly as they drew closer to the girl, the scent of blood assailing her sinuses. This was the first dead body that she would ever see up close, if you didn't count her father at his funeral. She tried to force herself to look at the woman objectively, but it wasn't working. All Leena could think about was how Megan would never get the chance to live out her life, and a part of Leena wondered if it was her fault.

A spotlight from a police vehicle was pointed at a spot a just a few feet into the alley. The officers standing around the body dispersed as Detective Bradley drew near, giving Leena a view of the dead girl. Megan looked closer to what Leena had expected than the woman in the photographs had. Her blouse had been ripped in several places, her arms torn and bloody. There were marks at her neck also, but along with the larger holes that mirrored the first woman's, there were smaller holes in between each set. He had bitten down harder on Megan than he had on the first woman.

When Leena looked at Megan's face, she saw her own features instead of the girl's for a brief moment. This is what would have happened to her if Reed hadn't saved her life. She glanced over at him, the man that had given her her life back, and projected her gratitude to him. She knew that he would understand.

Through the flush of fever on Megan's skin, Leena could tell that she was tan; at least a shade or two darker than she was. Her eyes had been closed, but her sweet face was contorted with pain. The werewolf virus had started to course through her system, but instead of saving her, it had killed her.

Leena cleared her throat, trying not to let her emotions show. She pulled her newly recovered cell phone from her pocket and held it up, "Do you mind if I snap a few pictures?" she asked.

Detective Bradley waved her on, and crouched next to the girl's body. "The state of the women is so different from one another that we wouldn't have assumed that they were related if it weren't for the puncture marks at their necks and their proximity. These holes—" he indicated the two larger ones, "—are the same distance apart, and almost the same size in diameter as the marks on the first victim. They look like they could be from an animal, but we don't have any animals indigenous to the area that could make these marks. Your superior says that you specialize in animal attacks, what do you think?"

Reed and Leena shared a look. "We were thinking along the same lines, but there are a few things that don't add up." Reed responded, skirting the truth. "The markings look canid, but we haven't been able to determine species. From the looks of it, I'd say your first woman was incapacitated by the blow to her head, causing her to not put up much of a fight. It looks as though the animal jumped her, latched on to her neck, and knocked her to the ground. Your second woman must have struggled to try to get away."

As Reed spoke, Leena could see the images of it playing across her mind. Her blouse being torn by the claws seeking purchase on the hard ground; his teeth sinking into her forearms and tearing her flesh as he tried to get to her neck;

finally managing to lock onto her as her body weakened from the venom and blood loss.

What Leena didn't understand was the significance of the bite on the neck. She would have to ask Reed if he knew why the rogue kept going for the neck when they were away from Detective Bradley.

"These marks on her arms," Leena said, pointing to Megan's forearms, "are deeper down by her elbows and get shallower toward her wrists. I'd say that she was gripping the animal by the neck or chest, holding it away from her, while it dug its teeth into her arms and sliced upward."

"That would have to be an enormous head to reach down that far on her arm," Detective Bradley said.

Reed nodded. "Indeed. That's why we've had a hard time determining species."

Leena touched the girl gently on her head, vowing to catch the son-of-a-bitch that did this to her, before rising to her feet. Reed and the detective followed suit. Leena had been determined to capture this rogue when he had attacked her and her sister. Now, looking at the innocent girl at her feet, she would see to it that this rogue died a most painful death.

She swayed on her feet, somehow managing to stay upright. She had to get out of there soon. It was a little after two o'clock in the morning, and that, mixed with the fact that she had barely eaten anything since they stepped off of the plane, had her legs shaking. Her body was ready to collapse. The burst of adrenaline that she had received when she heard about the attack had worn off.

Sensing her fatigue, Reed held his hand out to Detective Bradley, letting him know that they appreciated his help, and that if they found out what animal they were dealing with, they would let him know.

As they walked away from the scene, Reed tucked Leena into his side, wrapping his arm around her waist. To onlookers, they would simply look like lovers embracing, but Leena knew that he did it to help keep her on her feet. The fact that he didn't sweep her up off of her feet and carry her to the truck meant a lot to her. The last thing that she wanted was to appear weak. Not that she hadn't enjoyed it when he carried her through his father's house, but that was after having her ass handed to her several times, and a few taxing shifts. Not to mention that no one had seen her weakness at Declan's house. Reed had made sure of that.

"Our rogue killed her, for sure. I could smell him on her," Reed said, the moment they cleared the crowd.

Leena nodded, she had figured as much, but it was good to have the confirmation. "It definitely looks like both women were coming from one of the night clubs," she whispered back to him. He raised his eyebrow at her, so she elaborated. "You can tell from the clothes and make-up. The first woman was wearing a tiny black dress and silver heels, and Megan was wearing a shimmery blouse with black shorts and strappy sandals. Their make-up was heavy enough to be seen in dim lighting."

"It's a good place to start," Reed said.

"I can play the bait while you scope the places out," she offered, not entirely fond of the idea of dressing up to be groped and fondled, but if it helped find this rogue, she would do it. If she wasn't mistaken, Reed looked about as thrilled with the idea as she was.

"He could recognize you," Reed said. "If not by sight, then by smell."

"I have an idea for both of those problems," she responded, the solution coming to her quickly. "I'll just have to go shopping tomorrow to get a few supplies. I can temporarily alter my physical appearance, and mask my scent."

He opened the truck door and waited as she hoisted herself inside. He still didn't look happy about it, but after a few moments he nodded. "Just don't use perfume. It is off-putting to our kind."

That was something that she had discovered on her own. Walking through the crowd of people to get to the scene had been like walking through a Macy's and having each sales representative spray a bottle of perfume in her face. She had noticed that the scents hadn't even smelled the slightest bit pleasant, like they must have to the wearers. Only the sharpness of mixed chemicals was perceptible. No, she had a much better idea.

❧❧

The drive back to the hotel was practically unbearable. Reed knew that Leena was tired, but not hearing her voice or the ringing of her laughter as she swayed in and out of consciousness was akin to giving a child a toy, letting him play with it for a bit, and then snatching it from his hands. He could feel the sting of loss, and more than once he contemplated asking her questions just to make her answer, but he had stopped himself. It had been a long day, and she needed her rest. Even he was starting to feel heavy with fatigue.

A few times, when Reed thought that Leena was asleep, he would steal a glance in her direction, only to find her head braced on the window, but her eyes wide open. Finally, as he pulled into a parking space in front of the hotel, he said something to her about it.

"I thought that you would have fallen asleep. I can feel how exhausted you are."

She shrugged and said, "I don't fall asleep in vehicles."

"Ever?"

"Never," she said. "I don't like the idea of not knowing what's going on around me while I'm trapped in a big metal box that someone else is in control of. Even if I wanted to fall asleep, I couldn't."

She and his da had that much in common. His da was actually worse. He would not even get into a vehicle unless he was in the driver's seat. He had to be in control, which Reed had never understood, because even if they did get into a car crash, his da would not die from it. Any injury would heal after a few hours, or days depending on severity.

Leena opened the door and slid out of the truck. As tired as she was, she still landed quietly and gracefully on the pavement. She held the folder from Detective Bradley close to her abdomen, and let the little purse that her sister had given her dangle from her fingers as she wheeled her suitcase to the doors of the hotel.

Reed got out of the truck, and followed her through the automated glass doors. When they were encased in the elevator, Leena perked up as a thought came to her.

"Do you know why the rogue is biting the girls on the neck?" she asked.

He had noticed that also, and it was something that worried him. "When wolves mate they mark each other on the neck. It is usually done on the full moon, and the magic of the mating ritual makes the scar permanent. That's what I don't understand about what he's doing. The full moon isn't for another week, so the bite on the neck is insignificant."

The door slid open, depositing them on their floor. As soon as the light on the card slot on their door turned green, Leena pushed the door open and marched straight into the bedroom. Reed thought that she would plop down on the bed and be out for the rest of the night, but she surprised him by grabbing a few garments from her bag and going into the bathroom.

While she muddled about in the bathroom, Reed changed into a pair of sleep pants, and then searched the room for extra bedding. He found some in an armoire and used them to create a pallet for himself on the floor next to the bed. He eyed it dejectedly wondering if it might be more comfortable if he slept as a wolf, when the bathroom door opened. Leena emerged dressed in a black tank top that hugged her body and a pair of tiny black shorts. He had half a mind to track down the person that designed those shorts and thank them. They hugged the curve of her arse, cutting off just below the junction with her tan, smooth thighs.

He shifted as his pants became a tad tighter, but she hadn't noticed. She was staring at the makeshift bed on the floor, her contrition flowing through him. He didn't understand what she felt guilty for. It wasn't her fault that Shaun had set them up in a room with a single bed.

"Please take the bed," she said. "I'll sleep on the floor."

He just glared at her. There were no words. He knew that he could be an asshole sometimes, but if she honestly thought that he would sleep in a big comfortable bed while a woman slept on the floor, then she didn't read him as well as he thought she did.

She shifted uncomfortably under his gaze. "You're paying for this room; you should sleep in the bed." When he continued to glare at her, she said, "At least share it with me, it's more than big enough."

Share the bed with her? He may be chivalrous, but he wasn't an idiot. Besides, it would be as if he was doing her a favor if he slept in the bed with her. She would likely have a hard time falling asleep by worrying about him being on the floor. He couldn't allow that. He would be doing her a disservice if he didn't accept her offer.

"Fine," he answered, trying to sound defeated rather than eager.

"Thank you," she breathed out. She burrowed under the blanket, facing the edge of the bed and leaving enough room for three of Reed behind her. He grinned as he turned off the light and then crawled into the bed. He waited for her breathing to slow to a steady rhythm before he slid closer to her, tracing his finger over the wings of her dragons before drifting off to sleep.

Chapter Thirteen

Leena woke to the sound of light snoring behind her. It took her a few minutes to comprehend where she was, who she was with, and why there was a muscular arm draped over her waist. Normally being touched while she slept would have roused her, but she had remained dead to the world as Reed had molded his body to hers and held her.

Even more shocking to her was that he was touching her when no one else was around. He didn't need to anchor himself to her emotions, but he was subjecting himself to them anyway. She wondered what her emotions did to him while he slept. Did they affect his dreams? Did he even register them?

Slowly she extricated herself from his arms, tucking her pillow in her place. He looked so peaceful without his inscrutable mask, and it made him even more handsome, if that were at all possible. Her chest ached as she stared down at him. She never would have expected to feel such a strong attraction to someone at all, let alone so soon after meeting them, but here she was, staring down at a man that had awakened things in her that no one else ever had. Even if he didn't have a face that could have been carved by angels, she feared that she would still be falling for him.

When she first met him, she didn't think that she was ever going to like him. He had grated on her nerves. He was miserable and touchy, and she could barely stand to talk to him. It was as if someone had flipped a switch in him. Now he was sweet and protective. He had trained her to defend herself against Annabelle, he had accepted her into his group of warriors without knowing anything about her, just to make her happy, and he had been kind and friendly to the two people that meant more to her than anything else in the world. He touched her often to prove to either her or himself that he could. When it was just the two of them he let his guard down, smiling and laughing and telling her about the saddest parts of his life.

In less than a week she felt closer to him than she ever had with Jason, or anyone else for that matter. And that kiss.... She had tried all night not to think of that kiss. The blood and gore had only deterred her a little, but even that hadn't managed to douse the heat that Reed had sparked in her. Never had she had a kiss that was so passionate. Even now, just the thought of that kiss caused a shiver to course through her. She hadn't thought that he had it in him. He had told her that he didn't have physical relationships with women thanks to his ability, so in the brief moments that she had wanted to throw herself at him, she thought it over and stopped herself for his benefit. Now that she knew that he craved her touch as much as she had come to crave his, there was nothing that would stop her from throwing him down and having her way with him.

For now, though, she decided to let him sleep. She pulled her phone from the charger on the nightstand, surprised to find the blue light flashing, letting her know that she had messages. She had cleared all of the missed calls from Jason the night before, when Amy gave it back to her. These were all new. Three calls, five text messages, and one voicemail.

The text messages and voicemail were pretty much the same in content. Jason was drunk, and he went from grief-stricken and apologetic to an asshole in seconds. First telling her that he was sorry and he needed her, then blaming her for his needs not being met, causing him to sleep with someone else, and then informing her that there had been multiple women over an extended period of time. Her guess was that on a last-ditch effort he was trying to hurt her. Whatever. She was over it. If she never saw Jason Wright again in her life, that was fine by her.

His messages had served one purpose, though. They reminded her to talk to her assistant Chloe. At least it was unlikely for Jason to have slept with her considering that it was illegal...she was only fourteen. Chloe had been working for Leena for the past five years in return for dance lessons. Chloe had grown up in foster care since before she could remember. She had lucked out with a wonderful foster mother whose only fault was that she took on more kids than she could comfortably afford.

For weeks Chloe would come and stand at the window of the studio, watching Leena teach her beginner's classes. Some days, she would stay there for hours, just watching, until one day Leena pulled her chair from the office and waved the little girl in to sit. She had been hesitant at first, but she came into the studio and sat down, watching with such longing.

After Leena's class ended, she approached Chloe, asking her if she would like to sign up for classes. She had dropped her gaze and shook her head no, telling Leena that she hadn't the money to pay for classes. When Leena told the girl not to worry about the money, she shook her head even more vehemently. She would not accept a hand out, but she was willing to work for it. Leena agreed, on the condition that Chloe's foster mother approved of it. She had met with Mrs. Jameson later that evening, and Chloe started working at the studio the next day.

Leena had grown to love that little girl as if she were her own sister, and tried to do as much for her and her foster mother as the two would allow. She invited the family to barbeques, cooking far more food than could ever be consumed and sending home the leftovers; she commissioned Mrs. Jameson to help her make costumes for her dance students, and for herself; and she had bought Chloe a cell phone so that Leena could call her whenever she needed her, and so that Chloe could get in touch with Mrs. Jameson when Leena had her running errands.

She put that cell phone to use now. After checking the clock, and seeing that school would be in session, Leena sent her a text message instead of calling. She told her that she was okay, that she would be stuck in South Carolina for a few extra days, and asked her if she could call and reschedule Leena's classes when she got out of school. Leena also let her know that if either Sandra or Jason showed up at the studio, that she should call Scott right away.

As Leena set up her laptop on the desk in the main room and pulled the file out on the first murdered girl, she got a reply message from Chloe.

Aye, aye, Captain!

Leena's mouth split into a grin before she returned her attention to the case file, flipping through the details while the photos that she took the night before uploaded to her computer. When she dug deeper into the report, she discovered that the first woman's name was Heather. She was twenty-nine years old when she died. Her hair was blond, while Megan's had been brown. Her skin was pale, and her eyes were blue, while Megan's license had reported brown eyes. The only similarity that the two girls seemed to have was their location the night that they were killed.

Leena lost track of time as she worked at her computer, until a rustling noise drew her attention to the door to the bedroom. Reed was standing there, watching her, his short black hair mussed from sleep. His arms were crossed over his bared chest as he leaned against the doorjamb. The hungry look in his eyes mirrored her own, and it had nothing to do with the lack of food in her stomach. She had had a taste of him the night before, and now she longed to have the rest of him.

He moved from the doorway, and came to stand behind her, bending down to read the screen of her computer where she had listed the differences in the girls, and her plans for changing her own scent and appearance for her attempt to play bait.

"These are actually really good ideas," he said, his voice deep and rumbly.

She was relieved that he thought so. She didn't intend to make too many changes to her physical appearance, figuring that the slightest differences would work in hiding her identity from the rogue.

"I have already looked into the places that I can find everything that I need, I just need to go and get them," she said, noticing that her own voice had gone a little husky from his nearness.

"I will take you wherever you need to go, as soon as we go for a run."

Leena turned to look at him then. A run? Why on Earth did he want to go for a run?

Sensing her confusion, Reed said, "Before we landed, I researched places to run nearby, and there is a forested area near the Regional Airport. I wanted to take you and teach you how to track and hunt as a wolf."

Deep inside her something stirred. It was as if his words had awoken a part of her. Suddenly her skin felt tight and itchy, and she wanted nothing more than to leave her human form behind and run as a wolf.

She nodded, too afraid to let herself speak. Fighting the urge to shift into a wolf at that moment, she stood from the desk and went to the bedroom to change out of her sleep clothes.

∽⭗⭗

Reed had been able to feel Leena's wolf perk up at the thought of a run, but she had done an excellent job of tamping her down. During the entire drive, her body shook with little tremors of anticipation, but still she held her human form. She was exerting such tremendous control over her wolf for a newly turned pup, that Reed was stunned. He and his da had known that she would be powerful, but this was far beyond what they had expected from her.

He pulled his truck off of the road, and into the trees to keep it from being spotted, before leading Leena deeper into the wooded area. He could feel the buzz of excitement flowing from her as they trekked through the trees. When he decided that they had gone far enough, Leena wasted no time. She stripped out of her shorts, t-shirt, and under-things, stuffing them into her tennis shoes, before she hunched over and called her wolf to her.

Reed followed suit, completing his transformation seconds after hers. She was getting better at her transformation as well.

Before he had a chance to shake off the last tingling sensation, Leena nipped him in the leg and darted off through the trees. He laughed, the sound coming out as more of a wheeze in his wolf form, and then gave chase.

He never really played like this with anyone else, but it was something that he had anticipated doing with Leena from the beginning. With the guys, he rough-housed—throwing them around, fighting, and pinning—but they never chased. It was something that was done between mates and couples that were courting each other, never between friends. He had never even done it with Annabelle in the brief stint that they had. It hadn't felt right to him.

Dipping his head, he took off after Leena, letting his nose guide him to her. She had run in zigzags, trying to throw him off, but it didn't take long for him to find her. She was running at an easy pace, letting him catch up to her. Her ear twitched as he drew near, and she didn't look back to see how close he had come, she just took off like a rocket.

Her wolf was smaller than his, and she used that to her advantage. She dove under low branches, and through gaps of brush that were too small for him to fit through unscathed. If he didn't know any better he'd say that she had been a werewolf for decades. It was if she was born for this, it came to her so effortlessly. Her foot falls were nearly silent as she ghosted over the terrain, dodging trees and other obstacles that Mother Nature threw her way.

Up ahead, Reed spotted a boulder protruding from the ground that could be used in his favor. Leena darted to the right of the boulder, but Reed leaped on top of it, pushing off of the rock to get airborne. When he landed back on the ground, he was right on Leena's haunches. He dove under her legs, causing her to lose her footing, and both of them to slide across the leaves and slam into a tree. He recovered quickly, jumping to his feet, and landing on top of Leena. She struggled to get free, but Reed held her pinned in place. When she finished squirming, Reed sniffed her out for injuries, grateful to find none.

Below him, Leena's body started to shift. Her fur receded, giving way to skin, her bones popping and sliding underneath. As soon as he realized what she was doing, he moved off of her and began his own shift. The moment he was fully human, he found himself flipped onto his backside, staring up at the most beautiful dream he ever could have imagined.

Fully nude, Leena straddled his waist, pinning his shoulders to the dirt with her hands. The curtain of her hair blocked her body from his view, but the visual wasn't necessary for his body to react. If she noticed, she gave no indication of it. She just stared down at him with a look of pure joy on her face.

"Is it always like that?" she asked, awe evident in her tone.

"Just wait until the full moon," he responded. "It is so much more intense. The moon takes away all inhibition.

That's why I wanted to do this in the daytime, to ease you in to it. It's hard to explain, but you'll feel it soon enough. Everything is tied to the moon for us. We are bound to her—"

His words were cut off by her mouth on his, and all thought escaped him.

❧

Leena had barely registered the words that Reed had been saying. Her entire body hummed with the excitement of the morning. She hadn't known that running around on four legs would have been so...exhilarating. It had come as natural to her as riding a bike to dart through the trees at a speed no human could ever dream to match. To know that Reed was behind her, trying to catch her, had made the experience all the more invigorating.

The feel of the dirt giving way to her paws as she ran was like a drug coursing through her veins. The only thing that had come close to that feeling was being held down by Reed, and now having him trapped below her. She knew that he could escape if he wanted, and she was certain that he knew it too, but he let her win this round, and she rewarded him with a searing kiss.

He threaded his fingers in her hair and pulled her down to him, deepening the kiss, and bringing their bodies fully into contact. His skin was hot against hers, but she barely registered it as he thrust his tongue between her lips in a movement that seemed to reach all the way to her soul.

Her hips moved, unbidden, grinding her pelvis against his elongated shaft. He groaned into her mouth, and when she stopped moving, he gripped her hips and rocked them back and forth. The placement of his erection caused the most delicious friction between her folds, wrenching a cry of pleasure from her that bounced off of the trees and echoed through the woods.

Oh. My. God. She could have sworn that she would have seen heaven in that moment, if only she would have opened her eyes.

Around them, leaves swirled as if they were picked up in a twister, but the air around them was still. It was then that she realized that she had caused the whirlwind.

A crunching noise sounded from Leena's left, causing both of them to go completely still. The leaves fell to the ground and everything around them went silent. The only sound was that of the snapping twigs and rustling leaves that drew closer to them. The moment Reed registered what it was, he flipped Leena onto her back, covering her naked body with his.

"What are you folks doing out here?" a man's voice said, just before his boots came into view. "Ah, hell. You-all need to get out of here. Don't you know that these are hunting grounds? You could have been killed."

"We didn't know," Reed said, his voice hard and gruff. "We'll be on our way."

The man came closer, bending down to try to get a look at Leena's face. Reed shifted, keeping her from his view. "Ma'am, are you okay?" the hunter asked. Oh, how to answer? She could be the perfect smart ass and tell him that if he had waited about ten minutes before coming by, she would be floating on cloud nine, but she didn't think that she could get the words out. A part of her was completely embarrassed by the fact that a stranger had caught her fooling around in the woods, and it was that part of her that kept her mouth shut.

"She's fine," Reed answered, his ire rising. Leena guessed his irritation had something to do with the fact that his naked backside was presented to the man as a perfect target, and he had no means to defend himself if the need arose.

"If you don't mind, sir, I'd like to hear it from the lady."

So, the man had a death wish.

"I'm fine," she called out to him, adding a mumbled, "If you consider dying of embarrassment 'fine.'"

He must have heard her, because he let out a soft chuckle. "No need to be embarrassed by young love. Just be more careful of where you decide to pull over to have a romp."

He did not just say that…. If Reed didn't have her arms pinned to the ground she would have slapped her palm over her forehead.

She waited until the hunter's footsteps receded, before shoving Reed off of her. "So much for learning to hunt," she muttered.

Reed didn't respond; he just stood and looked around, getting his bearings. After a few moments, he marched off, leaving Leena to follow.

"Reed," she called after him. "Reed!"

He turned on his heel to face her, his face contorted with anger.

"What's wrong?" she asked. "If you're upset about what happened, I'm really sorry. I was so caught up in the feel of the shift, and the run, and I didn't stop to think."

"It's not you," was all he said before turning back and stomping away. She let him go, but this was far from over. When they weren't standing out in the open, completely nude, she was going to get him to tell her what had pissed him off so thoroughly.

Chapter Fourteen

Reed knew that Leena wasn't going to let this issue drop, but right now he couldn't worry about that. He had no desire to tell her what had upset him about what had happened in the woods. What was easily the best morning of his life had turned to *shite* in a matter of seconds. He should have sensed that hunter. He should have been able to protect her. Instead he put her in harm's way. The thought made him want to punch a hole through the nearest tree as he was walking back to his truck.

Leena wouldn't see it the same way that he had, he knew that, but his instincts to protect her railed at the fact that he was caught off guard. He was so engrossed by the feel of her body against his, that he hadn't sensed, or even heard, that hunter until he was too close. That man could have just as easily been Steven's men, sent to dispose of Reed and Leena, and Reed wouldn't have been able to do much to stop them.

So fecking stupid, he admonished for the umpteenth time.

He had dropped Leena off at one of the stores that she had needed to get a few things from, and every part of him wanted to follow her to make up for not being able to protect her earlier, but she had wanted to go alone. He had tried to fight her on it, but she had made it quite clear that she had no desire to have him stalk her through a few feminine stores, especially while he was brooding.

Brooding...pfft. She hadn't begun to see brooding. This was slightly discomfited if anything, and he had a damn good reason, even if he didn't care to share that reason with her.

It wasn't lost on him that he was more upset by her brooding comment than her stalking one. That was probably due to the fact that what she said was relatively accurate. He would have followed her around, unsure of what he should do, until she was ready to leave. It could also be because stalking was the way of a wolf.

He had tried to follow her anyway, determined not to leave her alone, but the death glare that she shot him when he killed the engine of the truck could have matched his da's in intensity. She was dead serious. She had gone from putty in his hands to pissed off as quickly as...well, as quickly as he had.

The entire drive, she sat silently next to him, her arms crossed over her chest. Briefly he wondered if she knew that doing so did wonders for her already amazing breasts, but the look on her face had deterred him from saying anything to that affect. He knew that her anger was his fault, but he couldn't ease her irritation without explaining why he was upset—which he didn't intend to do.

He just hoped that she believed him when he told her that it wasn't anything to do with her. How could she have believed that he was angry about her jumping him? He was rock hard the second she tackled him to the ground, and if that weren't indication enough that he was fully into what they were doing, then him digging his fingers into her hips as he rubbed her over his knob should have been.

He had been with a number of women over his lifetime, but nothing had ever matched what he felt in that moment. The thought did cross his mind that he probably shouldn't have been so ready to take her in the dirt, but if she had any reservations about their location, she hadn't shown them. If anything, she had spurred him on with her cries of pleasure.

It wasn't until after they were caught by the hunter that Reed had realized that her emotions hadn't consumed him in the slightest. In fact, the pleasure that *he* had felt with their contact was so strong that it overshadowed the emotion coming from her altogether. For once in his life his pleasure was all he had known. The damn hunter was lucky that Reed was pissed off at himself or he likely would have ripped the man's throat out for interrupting them.

Reed parked his truck down the street from Amy's house, and walked to the spot where he had determined the rogue had been watching her from. The rogue's scent was stronger this morning. At some point after they left last night, he had returned to watch Amy. He wondered if Reed's scent going into Amy's house affected the man at all. It was obvious that he had some form of attachment to Amy, whether she was the one that got away from him, or it was deeper than that, Reed didn't know. He did have a plan to goad the man in the hopes that he would try to find Reed instead of Reed having to look for him—preferably before he had to stand by and watch a bunch of men paw at Leena all night.

His hands balled into fists at the thought, but he refused to let the anger show on his face as he marched over to Amy's front door. Before he rang the doorbell, Reed ran his hands over the doorjamb, marking it with his scent.

A man answered the door, presumably Amy's husband if his arms crossed over his chest and his scowl were any indication. "May I help you?" he asked coolly.

"I'm here to see Amy," Reed said. The man's face flamed red and Reed could feel the fury coming off of him. "I'm a friend of Leena's," he added, and the tension that had grown between them dissipated instantly.

The man called for Amy, and reached his hand out. "Matt," he said.

Reed took his hand, something he would have preferred not to do, and shook it. "Reed."

Amy came down the steps just then, shocked to see Reed had come alone. "Where is Leena?" she asked.

"She had to run a few errands this afternoon. Do you mind if I come in?"

"Of course not. Come on in." He followed her inside to the kitchen, which he realized was their main gathering place. He sat on the stool at the island that Leena had occupied the night before. "Would you like something to drink?" Amy asked.

He accepted a glass of water before Amy sat down across from him. Her husband, Matt, sat next to her. It would have been easier for him to talk to her without Matt there, but no way was he going to ask the man to leave. If any man asked him to leave Leena's side to talk to her privately…that man would likely cease to exist. Not that he had the right to think that way. Leena wasn't his just yet; but it was his mission to make her so.

"I just came over to talk to you about two things," Reed started. "The animal that we're looking for was over this way again last night. I just need you to keep an eye out and let us know if you see it." Amy nodded, and Matt drew his eyebrows in confusion. He opened his mouth to speak, but Reed cut him off before he had the chance. "And I would also like your permission to court your sister. Normally I would ask Scott since he is the man of your family, but I don't intend to wait until we return to Pittsburgh."

After recovering, and pulling her jaw off of the granite countertop, a high-pitched squeal emanated from her. With Reed's enhanced hearing, the sound of it was akin to being stabbed in his eardrum. She jumped up from her stool, ran over to him, and threw her arms around his neck. He hugged her back, absorbing her elation and her gratefulness. What she had to be grateful for, he didn't know. If anything, he should be the one to be grateful to her and her family. He hadn't truly been living until the day that he pulled Leena from that marsh. Without her, he would still be living his empty, unfulfilling life. He hadn't known that anything was missing from his life until he found her, and he had no desire to lose it.

"I knew it!" Amy screeched into his ear, and he winced at the sound. "Leena didn't believe me, but I saw the way you looked at her. You better treat my sister right. Not like that douche-b, Jason. You got it?"

Reed grinned. "You have my word."

⋙⋘

Leena was surprised to find everything that she was looking for, and more. She had managed to locate both a hair and nail salon, and the women inside were buzzing with the chance to make her over. Several hours later, her hair was curled in tight waves, her fingers and toes were done into a French Mani/Pedi, and she had a bag of make-up to take with her.

No way would the rogue recognize her...she barely recognized herself.

She had called Reed at the number he gave her before he sped off down the road, letting him know that she was finished. She had contemplated calling in a taxi instead of calling him, but he was already angry, and she didn't want to push him into an enraged state. Besides, it would have taken just as long for a taxi driver to get to her as it would for Reed to. If not, then longer.

When he arrived, she climbed into the truck warily, but his mood seemed to be a bit more somber than it had when he dropped her off. The cab of the truck didn't crackle with the intensity of his rage, at least. She expected him to drive off the moment she was situated in the truck, so when they sat idling for a few minutes, she glanced over at him to see that he was openly staring at her.

"What?" she snapped at him.

The corner of his mouth quirked up. "Nothing at all. I just wanted to make sure that it was really you."

"Well, you've seen, now drive."

"I don't know," he said, leaning over toward her. "I think I need further proof."

Heat flared through her body, but she ignored it and his kissable lips that were inching closer and closer to her. She wasn't giving in to him that easily after what he put her through earlier.

"Just drive."

She turned away from him to stare out the window, but not before catching the look of surprise that crossed his face. He could feel her desire for him, she knew that, but just because she felt desire for him didn't mean that she would give in to those desires. He was sadly mistaken if he thought that it was that simple.

They drove in silence for the entire trip back to the hotel. Even with the uncomfortable quiet that hung between them, Reed didn't lose his chivalry. As Leena struggled to adjust the bags that she had in an attempt to make them easier to carry, Reed had taken them from her hands and preceded her to the hotel.

Once inside, she decided to give him another chance to talk to her. After he deposited her things onto the sofa in the sitting room she said, "Are you going to tell me what upset you this morning?"

His features became unreadable, and he stayed quiet for several long moments. She just started to think that he was never going to say anything, so she grabbed one of the bags and marched toward the bathroom.

Finally, when she was getting ready to close the door behind her, he called out, "I meant what I said." She reemerged, and waited for him to continue. "It wasn't you. I was angry with myself."

"For what?" she asked, genuinely puzzled. If anything, Reed should have been proud of the way that he had handled things. The moment the hunter approached, he had covered her body with his own. If the hunter had fired off a shot, Reed would have taken the bullet. On top of that, when she half expected Reed to jump up and pummel the man, he remained where he was, shaking with his fury.

"You wouldn't understand," he said.

"Try me." She crossed her arms over her chest and waited.

With a heavy sigh, he said, "I should have been more aware. I should have known that there were hunters about. And I should have heard, or sensed, that man approaching sooner than I had. My job is to protect, and I had a piss-poor go of it."

Leena noticed that as his ire rose, his brogue got even thicker.

Goodness, even his voice was swoon-inducing.

"Listen," she said, "I may not understand all of this werewolf business, but I do understand the need to protect people. Or have you forgotten the reason that we're here in the first place? You may not have kept that hunter from getting close to us, but you did use your body to shield mine well before he would have gotten a clean shot off. If that's not enough, think about what getting away from him would have entailed. If we had shifted into our wolves, those men would have been far more likely to shoot at us."

He cocked his head to the side, seeming to wrap his head around what she had said.

Before she could blink, Reed took three large strides toward her and pinned her to the wall next to the bathroom door. She twined her arms around his neck, and that was all the invitation that he needed. In the next instant his mouth was crushing hers. His tongue swept past her lips, forceful and demanding. He lifted her off of the ground, slamming her back against the wall after situating her ass in his hands.

The man had to know how lascivious he was. Never had her body reacted to a kiss like it did with Reed. Heat coursed through her, followed by a delicious tremor that seemed to originate from her center and spread out toward her fingers and toes. His touch was like a drug and she was finding that she just couldn't get enough of it. His body was flush against hers, and still she pulled him closer to her, willing their bodies to meld into one.

Now that she knew that he could endure her touch, she couldn't stop herself from running her hands over the taught muscles of his back, digging her nails into the cotton of his T-shirt. The material ripped underneath her fingers, but Reed never stopped devouring her mouth, he just answered her fervor by sliding his hands up the fabric of her shorts. Even as a pained groan escaped him, and a warm liquid trickled over her outer-thigh, he deepened their kiss.

It took Leena a few moments to comprehend what had happened, and when she did, she pushed him away. She pulled his hand from her thigh, and up to her line of sight. There on his palm was a deep gash, blood flowing freely from the wound. She hadn't even remembered strapping her dagger to her hip under her shorts.

"Oh my God!" she squealed, jumping out of his hold. "You're bleeding!" It wasn't until after the words left her mouth that she realized how ridiculous they sounded. *Thank you, Captain Obvious.*

Reed shrugged as if it didn't make a difference that the bone to his middle finger was visible. "It's just a scratch."

He leaned down to try to reclaim her mouth, but she swatted him away. She dragged him into the bathroom, knowing full well that he let her pull him. After holding his hand under the running faucet, Leena ripped a strip out of her already-ruined shorts and wrapped it around his hand. Any normal person would have had to make a trip to the hospital, but she knew that Reed would be healed by the time they left for the evening.

"I'm so sorry," Leena said as she tied the knot of the makeshift bandage.

Reed shrugged again. "Worth it," he said, and she couldn't help but grin. He looked down at her shorts that used to be a creamy khaki color, and now had a red stain spread over her hip and thigh. "I'm sorry about your shorts."

Lifting her shoulder, she said, "Worth it," mirroring his response to her. The corner of his mouth lifted into a smile that caused her stomach to do somersaults. God he was gorgeous. Even with his blood covering her, the heat that he had sparked in her hadn't been doused. He hovered over her, a dangerous look in his eyes, and it took all of her will power not to shove him down to the tile floor.

She cleared her throat and inched around him, picking up the bag that she didn't remember dropping, and then she laid the contents out on the counter. He quirked his eyebrow at her when she first pulled out a vial, but when he saw what it was his look of confusion turned to one of admiration. The plant extracts should act as a natural perfume, masking their scents and giving them new ones.

"I figured absorbing plant extracts would be the best way to alter our scents without smelling like chemicals. I got some for you as well, and I was hoping that you could be the guinea pig. That way, if it doesn't work, I can try something else on myself."

He nodded in answer. "How should it be applied?"

"Well, I was thinking that the best way would be to soak in the bathtub. The water should help to make it less potent, and make sure that it gets all over your body to hide your natural scent. You should probably also use the hotel shampoo to change the scent of your hair."

Reed took the vials that she proffered and looked them over. "Cedar wood, Spanish Sage, and Ginger." He uncorked each and held all three bottles under his nose. "Not bad."

The combination was nowhere near as appealing as his natural scent of sandalwood, peppermint, and the earthy undertone of werewolf, but it was the best that she could find. After instructing him how much to use, Leena left Reed in the bathroom and sat at her computer as she waited for Reed's verdict.

Reed could still smell the difference in himself as he sat waiting for Leena to finish getting ready. It wasn't unpleasant, just different. Leena assured him that the scent wasn't as strong as it seemed to him, and that it must be the fact that it was foreign to him that made the fragrance stand out. It made sense. Her new scent hadn't been overwhelming either, but he definitely preferred her natural jasmine and citrus scent to the roses and ylang-ylang that she now smelled of.

When she had told him why she chose those two plants, Reed had to literally bite down on his tongue to keep himself from telling her that she wasn't going to use them. Apparently her Nana knew a lot about herbs and the perfume that roses and ylang-ylang gave off were said to be aphrodisiacal. She planned to use the rogue's heightened sense of smell against him. If Reed weren't railing at the thought he would have admitted that it was a rather brilliant idea. As it were, he barely walked away without growling in frustration.

It wasn't bad enough that he had to stand by and watch other men paw at the woman that he planned to make his mate, but add in the fact that she pretty much smelled like sex and he was barely containing his rage.

Just then Leena emerged from the bedroom and all thought fled. He hoped that he recovered quickly enough for her to not have caught his jaw dropping to the floor, but if her shy grin was any indication, he hadn't been so lucky. Jaysus…she was absolutely breathtaking. She was sheathed in a golden ruffled dress that barely reached mid-thigh with gold glittering shoes that brought her closer to Reed's height. Her brown hair curled down just past her breasts, and her already beautiful face was made up with just enough color to change her appearance, but not enough for her to look as if she were even wearing any make-up if you hadn't known what she looked like beforehand. Every bone in Reed's body screamed for him to tear the dress from her, throw her onto the bed, and forget all about the rogue, but he knew that she wouldn't go for that. She wanted to capture this bastard even more than Reed did.

"Do you think he will recognize me?" Leena asked. She tugged at the hem of her dress nervously, belying the sex goddess image that she was portraying. She seemed almost shy about the way that she looked, which Reed didn't understand because she had admitted to wearing more revealing dresses for her dance competitions.

"I don't think he will," Reed said, after clearing his throat. Jaysus, he was a bumbling idiot around her. It wasn't as if he had never seen a beautiful woman before. *Quit your gawking arsewipe.* "The differences, though subtle, are vast enough that he would have a hard time placing you, even if you do look familiar to him."

She nodded and grabbed the second key card for the room off of the desk. Lifting the hem of her dress, she tucked the rectangle into the black strap at her thigh. It took Reed a moment to realize what it was, and when he did he couldn't help the smile that spread across his face. It was a sheath filled with silver throwing knives.

Leena looked up, catching Reed's grin and she frowned. "Is something funny?" she asked defensively.

"Not at all, I was just admiring your arsenal. I was wondering where you might have hid your dagger in that dress. I hadn't thought that you might have replaced it with smaller knives."

"I didn't replace it, I added to it," she said with a mischievous grin. "I found a metal smith while I was out and he let me use his machines to make these." She pulled one from the sheath and flipped it in her hand a few times before handing it to Reed.

He didn't know a lot about throwing knives, but this one was beautiful. Despite its small size, it was weighty enough that it would soar through the air with little force. It was sharp, its dual edge coming to a point at the tip, and the blade was long enough to imbed into a heart. What did it say for him that he was more turned on by the strap of blades around her thigh than when she had come out in her super revealing dress?

Reed handed the blade back to her and she slid it back into place. "Out of curiosity, where are you concealing the dagger?" Reed asked.

She bit down on her lip, and the action was sexy as hell. He almost missed her movements as he adjusted his too-tight jeans. She tucked her finger into the top of her dress and pulled it down to show her cleavage. Tucked in between her breasts was the hilt of the dagger. It was as if Reed had been punched in the gut. The air fled from him, and his jeans became even more uncomfortable as an image of a similarly shaped phallus replacing the dagger popped into his head.

They really needed to get the feck out of that hotel room before Reed tackled her to the floor and erased her pretty new scent with his own. Leena put her dress back into place, the dagger concealed in the most delectable valley of cleavage known to human and werewolf kind alike. Reed slid the key card into his pocket, and they were out the door.

The entire drive, Reed had to will himself to watch the road rather than Leena's bared thighs rubbing together as she shifted nervously in the seat next to him. In his long lifetime, Reed had suffered many injuries... He had been stabbed through with a sword, had the flesh flayed from his bones, and even had liquefied silver pumped through his veins. That car ride was absolute torture in comparison.

Gods help him to survive this night.

Chapter Fifteen

Leena didn't know why she was so nervous about using seduction to lure the rogue to his death. Sure, she'd never actually killed anyone before, never helped kill someone, or even legitimately thought about killing someone. That wasn't what was making her anxious though. Surprisingly enough, the thought of bringing this rogue to his death didn't faze her one iota. She wondered if the lack of human emotion towards killing another person was thanks to the wolf in her. It wouldn't be the first time that the wolf sought to protect Leena, and they had only been one for about a week now.

Of course, her nervousness could have had something to do with the way Reed had watched her since the moment she stepped out of the hotel's bedroom. She knew that this flawless immortal was attracted to her for reasons beyond her imagination, but the way his eyes devoured her every time he looked in her direction almost made her forget her purpose in South Carolina. Almost.

The need to dispatch this rogue was so overwhelming that it overshadowed even her growing need to have Reed pin her to the wall again, only this time they wouldn't be interrupted by her dagger slicing into his hand. The cut had healed up nicely. When he had offered her his hand to boost herself into his truck the only sign of the wound was an angry red line on his palm.

The fact that her attraction to Reed was strong enough to come so close to distracting her from her desire to bring this rogue down was a little frightening to her. She had never had such powerful feelings for anyone before, and the fact that he was almost a complete stranger was all the more confusing to her. She wasn't about to go there now, though. She had to keep her mind on stopping this rogue.

She wasn't even angry at the rogue for what he had done to her anymore. He had unintentionally given her a gift, and she couldn't hate him for that. He gave her the wolf, he gave her the ability to move objects telekinetically, and he gave her Reed. Not that she thought that Reed was hers, but the rogue was the reason that Reed had found her, and she would always be grateful for that. No, she was angry at the rogue for what he had done, and continued to do to her sister, and for the two women that he had killed. She had a responsibility to protect the women in the area from suffering the same fate as Megan and Heather.

Leena would never admit it to Declan and Reed, but she saw now why they thought that she would make a perfect fit for their alpha bitch. It wasn't lost on her that she felt an overwhelming need to keep an entire city of women as safe as possible. Women that she had never met, aside from her sister. The only thing that Leena knew was that there was a threat to them, and she had the means to stop it, and so she would.

With a renewed sense of determination, Leena straightened, put her stage face on and waited for Reed to join her on the pavement. This was just another dance performance, and confidence during your performance was crucial to winning in competition. She pulled every emotion that Reed had sparked in her that day and used it to add the sultry sway to her hips as she walked toward the door. She could do this. She had to do this.

∽⌒∾

As Reed approached Leena, the first thing that he noticed was how strong her emotions were. For the first time since he found her in that marsh her emotions were as potent as everyone else's. Then it registered in his brain what she was feeling and he couldn't stop his body from reacting. Arousal. The feel of it was so strong that it sparked his own interests. If they were anywhere else, Reed would have slammed her against the truck, ripped that pretty dress from her, and taken her right there in the parking lot. Audience or not, he didn't care.

The only thing that held him back was the knowledge that they were close to getting this bastard, and the moment they were rid of him, Reed could take Leena back to Pittsburgh and spend the next few days acquainting himself with her luscious body. He scrubbed his hand over his face to purge the delicious images that popped into his head, and then flourished his hand for her to precede him to the doors of the night club.

From the street Reed could feel the thump of the bass in the music blaring from within. He could tell before they even opened the door to enter that this club was going to play hell on his sensitive senses.

Once inside, he followed the narrow hallway which opened up to a large domed room. The dance floor was in the middle of the room set lower than the perimeter which contained the bars and tables. He stepped up next to Leena who stopped at the railing to overlook the crowd, amused to see the look of horror on her face.

"It's like a freaking mating ritual," she shouted over the music, just loud enough for him to hear.

Reed grinned as his gaze swept over the sea of gyrating bodies. "This is nothing like a mating ritual. If you want to see a mating ritual, I'll take you to one someday."

Her jaw dropped as she turned to him. "You actually have mating rituals?"

Reed didn't miss the edge of disgust in her voice and it made him wonder what she thought a mating ritual comprised of. "We do," he answered. "It's an actual ritual that binds two people together forever, something like a marriage, only far more permanent. They don't consummate the ritual — at least not in front of the guests." He said the last with a teasing smile and she laughed.

She took a deep breath, glancing back at the dance pit below. With a quick squeeze of his hand, she squared her shoulders and descended the staircase to the right of them to join the crowd. After she managed to get close to the middle of the dance floor she began to snake her body to the rhythm of the music and a grin slowly crept onto her face. Despite her reservations it was apparent that no matter the setting, dancing brought her joy.

Reed watched her for a few more moments, enthralled by her graceful movements. The second that she had started to move, it was as if a light had been sparked inside of her. It was a beacon that drew the attention of every man in the vicinity. It wasn't long before one of those men stalked through the crowd to get to her. He approached her from behind, running his hands down the sides of her body before locking onto her hips the moment he was close enough to touch her. Reed's hand balled into a fist next to him, but he didn't make a move.

Leena turned in the man's arms to face him. She wrapped her arms around his neck and moved her body in such a way that should be outlawed. The move brought her face close to the man's body, giving her the perfect chance to catch his scent untainted by those around her. Shortly after, she extricated herself from his arms and moved on, her next victim finding her moments after.

Forcing himself to look away, Reed opened his senses and slowly scanned the upper level of the room. Tracking by scent was going to be difficult, even though he had already committed the rogue's signature aroma to memory. The room was packed with hundreds of people, and getting close enough to sniff a bunch of other men would be suspicious. His best bet was going to be filtering through emotions to narrow down his prey, and then figuring out a way to get close to them.

It proved to be no easy task as Reed worked his way through the crowd of non-dancers, sifting through the myriad emotions trying to find ones that were out of place. After about twenty minutes, he had only suspected two men, and neither had carried the scent of a werewolf. He just hoped that Leena was having better luck than he was.

❧❧

Leena let the room around her fade to black as she closed her eyes and focused solely on the music. Every now and then a new man would approach her and she would find a new way to catch their scents without being obvious in what she was doing. So far none of the men had carried the musk of werewolf. She was just about to hunt down Reed and see if he wanted to move to one of the other clubs when another man grabbed a hold of her from behind.

She opened her eyes as she turned to face him, and the first thing that caught her attention was the feral look in his chocolate brown eyes. His gaze roamed over her body as she snaked it to the rhythm of the music. Instead of feeling heat where his gaze fell, like she did with Reed, she felt an icy chill.

Her heels put her at the perfect height to sniff his neck. All she had to do was wrap her arms around him and pull him closer to her. She brushed her pelvis against his to distract him from the deep pull of breath that she took to catch his scent. Finally, there it was…the hint of werewolf.

Leena stifled her sigh of relief as she released her hold on his neck and pulled away. With each pass of her body against his, she allowed the movements to become more and more suggestive. His grip tightened on her hips as his length brushed against her. Instead of allowing herself to recoil, she pushed on, chanting to herself that she almost had him, and that the women of the area, including her sister, would soon be safe.

As she pressed her body closer to his, she was able to see over his shoulder, and what she saw caused her to gasp. Reed was standing just behind the rogue, his fists balled and an intense fire in his eyes. He raised his fist, and just as it crossed Leena's mind that he intended to clock the rouge, he loosened his fingers and grabbed her arm instead.

"Come with me," he gritted out past clenched teeth.

Leena half-heartedly tugged her arm from his grasp, but his grip tightened and the flame in his eyes intensified, so she allowed him to pull her away from the rogue. If they thought that the rogue would let her walk away from him without a fight, they were sadly mistaken. He grabbed Reed by the front of his shirt and growled, "Release her."

Before that moment, Leena had thought that she had seen the extent of Reed's power, but she was dead wrong. His look of anger turned murderous, as the air around them seemed to disappear. It felt as if an invisible force was pushing on Leena from every direction and she gasped for breath. She didn't know whether she should be afraid of what Reed might do and flee, or if she should step between the two werewolves and try to talk some sense into Reed.

The pressure around her seemed to build, until the rogue released his grip on Reed's shirt. No more words were exchanged between them, but the rogue knew that it wasn't in his best interest to challenge Reed, and Leena could see why. His aura alone had practically immobilized her.

The weight of it disappeared as quickly as it had come.

Leena couldn't help but be impressed by his control, but her anger superseded her awe. As the rogue shoved through the crowd to get away from Reed, Leena turned a scowl in his direction. "What do you think you're doing? I had him! We need to go after him."

"That wasn't the rogue," he said, the ire in his voice causing his Irish accent to thicken.

Leena's heart fell into her stomach. Not him? Indignation caused her to stutter her response. "But...but...are you sure? He was a werewolf, I could smell it, and you should have seen the feral look in his eyes." She had been so certain that she had their rogue in her clutches. The way he looked at her was almost vicious in its approval, as if he couldn't decide which he would like more, ripping her clothes from her body, or her flesh.

"I'm certain," Reed answered, his teeth still gnashed. "And the reason he was looking at you so was due to your scent. You smell as if you're ready for sex just as much as your dance moves implied it, and I don't mean the aphrodisiacs that you used. I could pick up on your arousal from across the room."

The last he snapped at her, as if her arousal were the ultimate offense. And to think that this infuriating man had been the cause of said arousal was enough to send Leena into her own fit of rage. She thrust her finger into his chest, not allowing herself to admire the feel of his bulging muscle that flexed with each clench of his hands.

"Listen here. You don't concern yourself with my sexuality. You may be my superior when it comes to the whole werewolf thing, but you do not own me."

Without saying anything further on the matter, Leena turned on her heel and stormed away from him.

"Where are you going?" he shouted after her.

"Wherever you aren't!"

She glanced quickly around the room. Hanging above a steel door with a push bar latch-release was a glowing a red EXIT sign. Leena altered her course and made a beeline for the door. She suddenly needed to get some air.

Chapter Sixteen

A part of Reed saw the conversation with Leena as it played out and screamed at him to shut his damn mouth, but he had ignored it. That voice must have been his better judgment, because looking back he should have listened to it. He had watched as the light in her eyes had dimmed at her disappointment, and then flared back up with her anger.

As much as he preferred her arousal to her rage, she was still just as beautiful as ever while jamming her fingertip into his chest.

He still didn't know what had come over him, but the moment he saw Leena rubbing her body all over that other werewolf's, Reed had been a hairsbreadth away from ripping the guy's head from his body in front of everyone here, consequences be damned. He had never had such little self-control before, let alone over something so infinitesimal. Hell, he'd never even shown this much interest in a woman before that he would notice her arousal at all.

Raking his fingers through his hair, Reed tried to get a grip on himself. He knew that he should go after Leena and apologize, but that was as unlikely to happen as it was for her to turn on her heel and run back into his arms. She would cool off, and once she did they could get back to work finding the real rogue. For now he would leave her be.

He scanned the room trying to decide what to do in the interim.

An image sprang to mind of him dancing with several women as Leena returned to the dance floor, making her as jealous as she had caused him to be. He squashed that thought right away. Never mind the fact that he wouldn't last two seconds absorbing more than one woman's emotions, but even though he had no intentions of running after Leena to apologize, he did still intend for her to forgive his behavior, not hate him for the rest of their unnaturally long lives.

He could wade through the crowd again to try to pick up the rogue's trail. For some reason, even though that was the most productive option, it seemed to be the least appealing. His gaze fell on the bar. Reed didn't drink liquor often since werewolves took a long time, and a lot of alcohol, to get drunk he saw no point in it, but tonight he was in the mood to give it a shot. Or about a dozen of them.

The one thing that he was grateful for in this bar was the fact that it was so large that about seven bartenders were staffed. That gave him the opportunity to get several drinks from each one of them instead of sitting at the same stool looking like a drunken creep buying fifteen shots of whiskey and watching a bunch of women dance around him. As he tossed back number sixteen, he finally started to feel a little woozy.

Reed never truly understood how much of a natural filter he had against the myriad emotions of the people around him, but as his cognition slowly drained away, the floodgates opened up. He could no longer differentiate the emotions that he was feeling, let alone who they belonged to. Still, he called out to the bartender for another shot of Bushmills, stealing glances at the large metal door that Leena had stormed out of.

What was he doing? He wasn't even in a relationship and he was already buggering things up. Not to mention, even to himself, that he sounded like a whimpering *eejit*. What was happening to him? He was a fecking warrior for fecks sake. Apologizing to a woman that he hurt wouldn't take that away from him, sitting here pouting while he waited for her to get over it did.

He threw back the final shot of whiskey, slammed the glass down on the counter, and shoved his way through the crowd. He had a beautiful woman in a sexy golden dress to grovel to.

⋞⋟

Leena stepped out into the poorly lit alleyway behind the bar. Thankfully her eyes had adjusted quickly, but the darkness was the furthest thing from her mind. How could she have been so stupid? Just because that man carried the scent of a werewolf, Leena had been ready to condemn him. If it hadn't been for Reed, she would have been ready to take him out.

Not that she wasn't still totally pissed off at Reed for the way he had handled things. As if she didn't feel bad enough that she was entrapping an innocent man, to have Reed jump down her throat afterward had been more than she could handle.

She tilted her head up toward the sky and closed her eyes, taking in all of the smells and sounds. She needed to stop and reevaluate her situation. Here she was, standing in the alley behind a nightclub wearing the tightest dress known to man, in six inch heels, trying her damnedest to capture a rogue werewolf, regardless of the consequences...

Of course, catching this killer was important—it was probably one of the most important things that she had ever done—but she needed to be smarter about the way she was going about it.

Her mood turned sour, Leena glanced toward the door to the nightclub. A part of her wanted to get back in there and try to find this guy, while another part of her wanted to hail a cab and go to one of the other locations so that she wouldn't have to face Reed, and a third part of her wanted to head back to the hotel and call it a night. Without needing to think about it, Leena knew which part would win out. No matter her encounter with Reed, she knew full well that she was not ready to track down the rogue on her own. Even if she knew how to figure out who he was, she was under no disillusions that she could take him on her own.

She would just have to put her anger towards Reed behind her, she decided, and she turned back to the steel door. As she approached it, she noticed that there was no way to open the door from the alley without a key. Slapping her palm over her forehead, Leena chastised herself for her stupidity. Of course there wouldn't be a way to get back in from the alleyway. There isn't a business owner around that would make a back entrance to their establishment so easily accessible.

Glancing down to the mouth of the alley, Leena thought about going back around to the front door when a thought struck her. Perhaps she could open the door. She crouched down to examine the mechanics. Unfortunately the latch was covered by a thick steel guard plate, blocking her view of it. Blast. That just made this much harder than she expected. Still, she wouldn't be deterred so easily. She had this awesome power, and she was determined to learn how to use it.

Leena closed her eyes and pictured the door from the inside. The latch-release push bar was a faded-gold steel with the majority of it covered with worn vinyl. She focused on that latch release, imagining herself pushing it in. Nothing happened. She placed her palm on the door next to the steel guard and concentrated harder. *I can do this*, she chanted to herself. With a deep intake of breath, Leena put everything that she had into moving the release. After a few long seconds that felt like hours, Leena heard the mechanism give way.

A huge grin spread across her face as she grabbed the handle and pulled the door open a crack. *I did it!* With nothing more than her mind, Leena was able to open a door that was supposed to be nearly impenetrable from the outside.

In her excitement, Leena almost missed the sound of footsteps approaching from her left. By the time she registered it, a large hand came into her peripheral view and the handle was wrenched from her grasp. The sound of the latch clicking back into place reverberated through the alleyway.

"Running back to Prince Charming are we?"

The voice that spoke into Leena's ear raised the hairs on the back of her neck and sent a chill of trepidation down her spine. She turned around slowly, willing the hitch in her heartbeat to slow.

His eyes were the absolute darkest she had ever seen. The irises and pupils looked to be the same shade, giving an eerie effect. His dark hair curled in waves around his cheekbones, giving him an almost boyish look, if not for the craze in his eyes.

Putting on a face of false bravado, Leena cocked her hip to the side, resting her fist there to give it a slight attitude. "Excuse me?"

"You almost had me," he said, drawing closer to her. He lifted a strand of her hair from her chest, twirled it around his finger, before letting it fall back into place. "Your hypnotic dancing, your luscious scent, the hint of werewolf. It was all a perfect combination. Too bad that good-for-nothing *prince* gave you away."

He leaned in to sniff at her neck. While he was distracted, Leena reached for the hem of her dress and slid a knife into her palm.

"You smell...familiar," he said, closing his eyes to try to sift through all of the scents, "but then not at the same time." He pulled back slightly, perusing her face and body. Before his eyes ever landed on the knife in her hand Leena had already lashed out at him with it.

At the last moment, he deflected the blade and instead of embedding into his chest, it glanced off of his bicep, cutting into his shirt. When he looked down and saw the blood beading below the shredded fabric his face contorted in anger and he backhanded Leena across the face. She stumbled to the side from the force of the slap. *Son-of-a-bitch!*

That's it, now she was pissed!

She stuffed her hands between her breasts and withdrew the dagger that Reed had given her. It was longer than her knives, and it would do far more damage. Perfect. The rogue leered at her. "What else do you keep between those beauties? A tank?"

"Come and find out," Leena spat before lunging for him.

She tried to be unpredictable in her movements, but no matter where she tried to strike out at him, he was ready for her. She swiped at his chest, he deflected, she thrust toward his abdomen, he side-stepped, and when she went for his face, he kicked her in her sternum, causing her to lose her breath and stumble backward.

She couldn't move in this godforsaken dress. Switching her grip on the hilt, Leena drew the tip of the blade over each of her thighs, cutting slits into the dress. She kicked her heels off, and faced off with the rogue once more. Much better.

This time when she lunged for him, he wasn't fast enough to shield himself. She sliced a line across his cheek. Not quite as damaging as she'd hoped, but at least she got him. His fury shone through the blackness of his eyes as he threw his fist toward her face. She was able to dodge it just in time, and his stance left him open enough for her to bring her knee up to his stomach.

He grunted in pain, but the fact that she had hurt herself as well made her victory short-lived. These werewolf men were definitely built like tanks. A few more slices landed on the rogue's arms, just as a few more of his punches found their mark on Leena.

Leena thought back to her training with Reed and smiled internally. She was about to be a bona fide genius, or a complete moron.

She took a few steps away from the rogue. His lip twitched in a sneer, assuming that she was backing off. Instead she used the distance between them to gather a little momentum as she ran toward him. She jumped at him, wrapping her legs around his waist, and using her weight to knock him to the ground. Before he had a chance to shove her off of him, she slammed her dagger through his shoulder. She pulled the dagger back out, holding it over her head, ready to thrust it back into the rogue's chest, this time aiming for his heart.

The steel door to the nightclub slammed open, distracting Leena long enough for the rogue to toss her off of him and onto her ass. They both glanced at the door to see a drunken Reed standing in the doorway trying to process what he was seeing.

Rather than going for Reed while he was inebriated, the rogue took off down the alleyway toward the street, shedding his clothing as he ran. In a last-ditch effort, Leena withdrew another throwing knife and flung it in his direction. She hit him in the back of his thigh, but the wound wasn't enough to stop the rogue as he disappeared around the corner of the building.

"Reed! We need to go after him!"

∽ʘ∾

Reed took a moment to process what he just saw. He seemed to be moving in slow motion, as he watched a silver knife fly past his face and embed into a man's leg. *What?*

He made his way toward Leena, who was picking her shoes up off of the ground, when he walked into a scent that halted him in his tracks. The rogue. Then Leena's words registered. *We need to go after him.* As Leena drew nearer to him, he saw a cut on her cheek in the middle of what looked to be a bruise darkening her flawless skin. It was as if cold water had been tossed in his face. Instantly he sobered. He had struck her. That fecker was going to pay.

Reed grabbed the front of his shirt in each fist and ripped it from his chest. He roared out to the night's sky, as he called his wolf to him. The change came faster than any time previously, which was pretty damn impressive if he said so himself. His wolf was out for blood just as much as his human side was, and it was all too ready to take over.

When his transformation was complete, he gave one last look to Leena, and tore off in the direction that the rogue had gone. He could hear her footfalls behind him as she tried to keep up. At least if he was seen out at night in the city with a woman chasing after him, it would look as if her dog had gotten loose and she was trying to catch it.

The rogue's trail was easy to pick up, thanks to the wound that Leena had inflicted on him. She had handled herself well.

He had known that she would make a good addition to the *Lyca Laochra*, but he didn't think that she would have been able to take on a fully grown, male werewolf on her own. Reed had never been so happy to be wrong about anything before in his life.

The thought of her taking on a killer werewolf by herself caused his chest to tighten. *She's safe,* he assured himself. He didn't know what he would have done if she had been hurt worse than what she was, and he didn't want to know. Thankfully he didn't have to worry about that. She was strong.

Reed shook off the fear of what could have happened. He needed to stay focused on the task at hand.

The rogue's trail turned down a different alleyway, several blocks away from the one behind the nightclub. Reed slowed down slightly, allowing Leena to catch up to him.

About halfway down the alley, Reed came across a pile of clothes with the Rogue's scent all over them. He must have changed into his wolf.

The trail continued onto a nearby dumpster. Reed followed as Leena stayed behind and watched as he jumped from the dumpster to a nearby fire escape, to a stone wall. On the other side of the wall was a parking lot. The rogue had gone that way.

Instead of jumping down into the parking lot, Reed landed back in the alleyway where Leena waited for him. He glanced at the top of the wall, then to Leena, and back again. It was the first time he stopped to look at her after taking off after the rogue, and he noticed that she had been smart enough to grab his clothes for him.

She followed the movement, looking from the wall back to him. "What?" she said. "I can't get up there. Just leave me behind."

Reed shook his head back and forth vehemently. No way was he going to leave her on her own. The last time he let her go off on her own she ended up getting into a fight with a murdering lunatic. Not happening.

He walked closer to the wall and dropped his head, hoping that she would catch on to what he was trying to say. Again she looked back and forth between him and the top of the wall. After a few moments she finally said, "You want me to step on your back? Are you sure?" He nodded.

She considered it for a moment, before blowing out a puff of air. "Here goes nothing," she mumbled. With a running start, Leena leapt onto his back with her right foot, kicked off of the building next to them with her left, caught the edge of the wall, and hoisted herself over.

Without wasting any time, Reed made his way back over the wall himself and continued tracking the rogue. He wove between buildings, crossed numerous streets, and even went through a few marshlands. It was obvious that the rogue was trying to throw Reed off, but he wasn't about to give up that easily.

Reed just started to wonder if he would ever be able to catch up to the rogue when he noticed that the scent became more potent. He was gaining on him. He hunched closer to the ground and picked up the pace, hoping that Leena would be able to keep up. As it grew stronger and stronger, Reed became single-mindedly focused on the trail. So much so, that he barely heard Leena scream his name before he was knocked off of his feet with a searing pain in his shoulder.

Chapter Seventeen

Leena was having the hardest time keeping up with Reed. She was able to ignore the pain in her feet as they fell upon pavement, rocks, and even some glass — *Thank you dancer's feet* — but the burning in her lungs wasn't quite as easy to ignore. She didn't think that she was slowing down, even though her body wanted nothing more than to keel over completely, but just after the third marsh that they had run through the gap between her and Reed started to grow.

Come on, she urged herself, as she doubled over and pushed herself to run faster, clutching her sides as they threatened to burst.

Focused solely on trying to run at a pace that would put Olympic athletes to shame, Leena barely registered the flash of fur that streaked past her peripheral vision. Just as she managed to scream out Reed's name the wolf plowed into his side, latching onto Reed's shoulder with his muzzle.

As she drew closer to them she could smell the blood that the wolf had drawn as well as see it streaking down his dark fur.

From the coloring of the wolf, she could tell that it wasn't the rogue — this wolf was several shades darker than their rogue. That was the only thing that saved it from having her dagger plunged into its throat. Instead, she used the dagger to slice through the muscle of his right haunch. The wolf yelped, releasing Reed's shoulder from its teeth. In a movement too quick for Leena to track, even with her heightened senses, Reed had the other wolf flipped onto its back and pinned to the ground.

The wolf didn't bother to struggle. As soon as it realized that it was trapped, its fur began receding, bones snapping into human shape.

When Reed realized what the other wolf was doing, he too shifted back to his human form. He was so swift that he actually completed the change before the figure on the ground finished morphing into a man. An incredibly handsome man with dark, chin-length hair smoothed back out of his face, save for a single strand that fell forward into his eyes. His beard was neatly trimmed, giving his gentle features a masculine edge. His chest and abdomen were taught with muscles that would have made any woman swoon, and that was before Leena got a glimpse of the rest of him. What was it with these werewolf men and their delectable bodies?

Leena shook herself out of her reverie and returned her attention to the matter at hand.

If either man cared that the other was stark naked, they gave no indication of it. Reed knelt back down next to the other man and wrapped his hand around his throat, applying pressure. Not enough to choke him, or even to prevent him from speaking, but just enough to show that he had the upper hand.

"Who the feck are you, and why did you attack me? Choose your words carefully, else they may be your last."

"My name is Grayson, my lord. Steven assigned me to border protection, and I was told not to let any outsiders enter our territory tonight. I meant no disrespect."

"Which is it, Grayson? Am I your *lord* or are you one of Steven's shifters? As I'm sure you know, you cannot be both."

"I grew up under your father's rule, but my mate is a lynx shifter, and I joined Steven's ranks for her. I have always preferred your father to Steven, but my mate cares for him dearly."

Reed appeared to mull that information over for a moment, before releasing Grayson's neck. "The werewolf that passed through here before me, he is under Steven's rule as well?"

Grayson's face went blank for a moment as Reed and Leena stared at him expectantly. After a moment's hesitation, Grayson answered. "Yes, he is. He hasn't been around much lately, but it wasn't a shock to anyone. He just recently lost his fiancée."

"What is his name?" Reed asked.

"James," Grayson answered, "I don't know his last name."

"Well that's helpful," Leena mumbled under her breath.

"I'm sorry I couldn't be of more help," Grayson replied. "I've only been with Steven for a few months, and even before the accident James kept pretty well to himself."

Reed nodded and pushed himself to his feet, offering Grayson a hand to help him off of the ground. He took it, stumbling to his feet. It was then that Leena remembered that she had sliced a pretty big chunk out of the back of his thigh. Using the same dagger that made the cut in his leg, she cut a strip off of the hem of her dress and handed it to him to wrap his wound. She even managed to do so without scanning the length of his body even once. Okay, twice. She was a woman after all, and Grayson was definitely worth looking at.

"Can you walk?" Reed asked, once the strip of fabric was tied around Grayson's thigh.

Grayson shifted his weight from his left leg to his right, testing it, but it gave out immediately. "Not yet, my lord, but it shouldn't be long. I can feel the muscle knitting back together."

Reed gave a short nod. "Good." He looked around for a moment before his gaze fell onto a heap of fabric on the ground. His clothes. Leena hadn't even remembered dropping them. After donning his pants and shirt, leaving the front unbuttoned, he reached into his pocket and withdrew a card. Reed held it out to Grayson. "This is my number. Call me if you see James again and I'll forget about the flesh you tore from my shoulder."

Grayson took the card from him. "Yes sir," he replied.

Leena held her hand out to Grayson to shake his before Reed wrapped a possessive arm around her and led her down the road several paces. It wasn't until the other werewolf was out of sight when the weight of the day fell on Leena all at once. They lost him. She had been so close to the man that was after her sister and she failed to stop him. Because of her pride and arrogance she not only put her sister back in harm's way, but she managed to get Reed injured as well.

She took Reed's hand in her own and stopped walking, stilling him. He looked back at her with concern. "Reed," she started, unsure of how to force the rest of the words out. "I am so sorry. I shouldn't have stormed away from you when we were in the middle of trying to catch a killer. It was childish of me, and now you're hurt because of it. I hope that you can forgive me."

Reed took her cheeks in each of his hands and brought his face down to hers, close enough for their noses to brush against each other. "Kalina, this was not your fault, it was my own. I was so focused on catching this rogue that I didn't realize that I stepped into Steven's territory. As for you storming away from me, you had every right. I was being controlling and overbearing. If I wasn't completely mad with jealousy I could have told you more calmly that the man back in the club was not our guy. If anyone is to blame, it is me."

Leena took a step closer to him and rested her forehead on his chest. Snaking his arms around her waist, Reed held her tight. They stood in silence, enjoying the feel of one another's embrace, trying not to think about how each of them had mucked everything up. They would find a way to draw this asshole out if it was the last thing that Leena did.

Reed buried his face into her hair, glad that the perfume of the plant extracts had faded and given way to her natural scent. Holding her close like this made everything that had happened that night bearable. They hadn't caught their rogue, but she was safe, and she was in his arms.

Already he cared far more about her and her wellbeing than his duties to the *Lyca Laochra*. He would just have to figure out a new way to draw the rogue—James—to them. Besides, one good thing had come from that night…they now knew what James looked like, and they no longer needed to use Leena for bait. That was enough to make the tear in his shoulder well worth it.

They stood in each other's embrace for a while longer before making their way back to the hotel. A taxi had picked them up where they got caught at Steven's border, which meant that Corrick, and by extension his da, had known already that Reed had let James slip through his fingers. Reed had wondered what story Corrick had given the driver, because he didn't even blink at Reed's blood-streaked shoulder, or Leena's torn dress.

What little staff that was on duty at the hotel that late at night, however, had watched them warily as they trudged to the elevator and waited for it to carry them to their floor. Leena had grown quiet as exhaustion started to set in, but with the threat of the rogue currently out of their control, Reed had only one thing on his mind.

His gazed roved over her tanned skin, caught on the rise and fall of her breasts as she heaved a sigh, and landed on the exposed arsenal strapped to her luscious thigh. A normal man might have seen her set of knives and been put off, but Reed found it damn sexy. She was strong, and tough. She had handled herself when she faced off against James, but she hadn't been too headstrong as to chase after him on her own when he fled. She had let Reed take the lead, trusting him to keep her sister safe.

The fact that he hadn't actually kept her sister safe never seemed to register with her. She had blamed herself for them losing track of James, and for the bite Grayson had taken out of Reed's shoulder. She allowed herself to lean on Reed for help, but she didn't blame him when something went wrong.

She was so different from any other female he had ever met before in his life, and here and now he planned to make her his.

Leena pulled the key card from her sheath and slid it into the door, preceding him into the hotel room. After taking a few steps into the room, she lifted her right knee to her chest to remove her shoe, and did the same with her left. Before her left foot had a chance to hit the floor, Reed swept her up into his arms and carried her back into the bedroom. He grinned when she let out a squeak as he caught her off guard.

He had intended to take things slowly with her, but any chance of that happening fled when he set her back on her feet.

She turned in his arms, shoved him back against the wall and pulled his head down to hers. The kiss was bruising, but Reed wouldn't have had it any other way. He threaded his fingers through her hair and deepened the kiss even further.

Her movements were fervent as she clutched at his biceps, his waist, his neck; pulling every inch of him closer to her. His body responded to each one of her touches, sending jolts of pleasure to the base of his spine. With a roll of her hips against his, Reed let out a groan. *Feels so damn good.*

While Reed had no problem with Leena jumping him, he needed to take back control of the situation, or he was going to lose it. He broke off their kiss and turned Leena to face the wall, pinning each of her hands above her head. He trailed kisses down the side of her neck, and when he felt confident that she would leave her hands on the wall, he moved his own hand to the back of her dress and tugged on her zipper.

❧❦

Leena's entire body trembled with anticipation as Reed lowered the zipper to her dress ever so slowly. His breath fanning across her overheated skin sent a delicious shiver coursing through her. When her dress pooled at her feet, she made the attempt to move her hands from the wall so that she could reach for him, but a growl from Reed stilled her, causing another tremor of delight. His fingers brushed her skin lightly as his hot mouth moved across her shoulders.

Facing the wall, Leena had no way of knowing where Reed would kiss her next. The only thing that she could do was feel, and it made each press of his soft lips, and each brush of his tongue that much more erotic.

As she squirmed and writhed with each of his touches, she barely registered when her bra and both of the sheaths had been removed from her, leaving her standing in only her scant lace panties.

Now freed from the garments, Reed stepped up behind her, his clothed body pressed tightly against her bare skin. She wanted so badly to turn around and strip him, but when she moved her hands from the wall again, Reed held both of her wrists in place with one of his hands, placing his other hand on her belly and pulling her body even closer to his, nipping her ear with his teeth as her punishment for moving.

There was no way that the Reed that stood behind her now was the same man who had claimed to have little experience with women. With the slight touches of his lips and his fingertips, he had caused her blood to boil in a way that she had never experienced before. Each of his movements were sure and commanding, as if he had used each moment of his one hundred and ninety-two years between the sheets, familiarizing himself with a woman's wants and desires.

He fisted his hand in her hair and pulled her head back to capture her lips in a searing kiss. She opened to him immediately, his tongue pushing past her lips to brush against her own. Her vision swam and the room around them faded to hazy shapes leaving nothing in the world but him—them.

Finally he turned her back toward him, but when she made to reach for his shirt to rip it from his torso, he pinned her hands back against the wall, leaving her open to his perusal. Everywhere his gaze landed caused a delicious heat to course through her and to pool low in her abdomen. Lowering his head, he wrapped his mouth around her breast, nipping at the tender flesh, wrenching a scream from her.

He released his hold on her wrists replacing his mouth with his hands as he dipped his head lower to nip at her belly, just above the hem of her panties. Leena lost it. In the blink of an eye, she had the material of his shirt wrapped around each of her fists and she tore the godforsaken thing from him, football-spiking it to the floor with all of the ire that she could muster for it keeping her from roving her hands over his gorgeous muscles. Reed let out a low chuckle, the vibration of it coursing through her tender flesh, as she raked her fingernails over his back.

He stood, looming over her, his emerald eyes boring into hers, and she almost cried out from the loss of his touch. Through the fog in her mind, she barely registered the whir of a zipper, or the tear of fabric, until she felt his skin pressed against hers, unimpeded by a stitch of clothing.

His palms glided over her thighs, as her back was pressed into the wall. She had a split second to notice that the ground was ripped out from under her, before the length of him was pressed between her folds. He moved against her slowly, before hauling back and slamming into her. That was all it took for the world to explode around her with an audible shatter.

Reed didn't wait for the tremors coursing through her to die down before withdrawing and pounding into her again, and again. It wasn't long before she was writhing in his arms, the pressure within her once again building to the point where she would surely burst. His fingers dug into her thighs as he picked up his pace, relentlessly hammering into her until he slammed home one last time, bellowing with his release, and taking Leena with him. White flashed behind her eyes as she ruptured. Distantly she heard a crashing noise, and the sounds of splintering wood, but she couldn't seem to bring herself to care as she collapsed onto Reed, completely sated.

She had never known that sex could be so...delicious. A small part of her wanted to call Jason and thank him for cheating on her. If he hadn't, she would have never known what true pleasure could feel like. The other part of her, the larger part, just wanted to stay in Reed's arms forever, and never let him go.

Chapter Eighteen

Reed couldn't think of a time when he'd been happier. Not even when his mum had been alive. Here he stood, buried in the most beautiful woman he had ever seen, every inch of her skin touching his, and his ability was barely a whisper. He'd had to hone in on Leena to get a true reading on how she was feeling, and when he felt her happiness and satisfaction, his chest puffed up with pride.

Briefly he wondered if this was the way that sex was supposed to have been with other women all along, but a part of him knew that the reason it had been so amazing was because it was with Leena. She had tormented him since the moment he found her lying in that marsh, the life draining from her. She teased him when others would have given him space, she had faith in him gaining control over his ability, and in a few days she had seen him for who he was, when others had taken years.

She was kind, yet fierce. Loyal. A dominant female to a T, and yet, she had submitted to him without hesitation. She was everything that a woman should be, and now that he'd had her, he wanted more. He wanted all that she was, and all that she could give, for all of their days.

In fact, if he could hold her like this—her naked form wrapped around his—for the rest of his life, he would die a happy man.

As if she had read his mind, she wrapped her arms tighter around his shoulders and nuzzled his neck. He could have sworn that he heard her let out a contented purr, but figured it was his imagination.

Reed considered moving her to the bed so that she could finally rest, but when he looked in that direction he decided against it. The last thing he wanted to do was change her mood and he knew that if she saw the room, it would be like dousing a flame. He took a moment to try to figure out how to get her to the sitting room without her noticing their surroundings at all.

That plan was quickly foiled when a loud knock sounded from the next room. She shot her head up, and he knew that she saw what she had done when she gasped. The room was in shambles. The television had been thrown across the room, the cabinet that it had been housed in looked as if a sledgehammer had been taken to it. Every piece of furniture in the room, aside from the bed, had been utterly destroyed.

"What the..." she whispered in awe, too shocked to finish the exclamation. Shuddering, she asked, "Did I do all of this?"

Reed was saved from having to answer her when another loud knock sounded from the front room. With regret, he pulled out of her and set her onto her feet. Leaving her standing in shock as she assessed the room, Reed grabbed his pants, stabbed his legs into them and shut her in the bedroom as he answered the door, trying his damnedest not to snarl when he flung it open.

On the other side of the door was the manager to the hotel, according to his golden name-tag, with two rather large men in security uniforms standing behind him. The manager tried to glance past Reed into the room, but Reed held the door in such a way that he wouldn't be able to see much, if anything.

"Sir, we received a few calls from the other patrons that they could hear furniture crashing from this room accompanied by a woman's scream. I'm going to have to ask that you let us inside."

Reed hesitated for a moment but then stepped aside, allowing the men to step into the room, and closed the door before deciding to speak. With a smile that he hoped didn't make him look feral, he said, "I'm sorry for the ruckus sir, the missus and I got a wee bit overzealous." Reed made sure to thicken his brogue when he spoke, knowing that most people found it charming.

The security officer on the left grinned, catching Reed's implication. The manager, however, was not amused. "No offense, sir, but I'm going to have to see your wife for myself."

Reed didn't allow himself to dwell on the feeling of rightness that he got from the man's use of the word "wife." Instead, he nodded to the manager, saying, "Of course," before he went to the bedroom door, knocked, and said to Leena, "*Mo ghrá*, could you please come out here so that these gentlemen can see that you are unharmed."

Shuffling noises sounded from the next room followed by a curse that only he could hear before it went absolutely silent. Reed could feel her nervousness as she waited just on the other side of the door. He was just starting to wonder if she would actually come out when the knob turned and she emerged, clad in a tiny silk robe that displayed more than it concealed.

He scrubbed his hand over his face and tried to ignore the tightening in his body as she sashayed past him, glaring daggers his way, before donning a breathtaking smile and extending her hand out to greet the manager. The security officers barely concealed their admiring looks, and while the possessive part of Reed wanted to rip their eyes from their faces, he also couldn't blame them. The hem of the cream-colored material caressed her tanned thighs mere inches below what would be considered indecent. The top gaped open at the front, straining to cover her generous breasts, and allowing the most enticing view of cleavage to ever be seen.

Dumbstruck... that's what she made him. After one hundred and ninety-two years on this earth, this wisp of a woman was able to turn him into a bumbling idiot, who wanted nothing more than to throw her over his shoulder, return to the bedroom with her and never let her emerge again.

As she spoke to the manager, assuring him that she was perfectly fine, Reed imagined all the ways that he was going to get back at her and a slow smile spread over his face.

⋖⋗

Leena couldn't remember a time when she had been more embarrassed, as the gazes of three strange men perused her, completely aware that she and Reed had just had the most amazing sex of her entire life.

When she was beckoned to emerge from the bedroom, after hearing Reed's implication of their rough and wild go at each other, she figured that she may as well sell it.

She didn't know why she had packed the tiny robe in her suitcase, but now was the perfect time to don it. She took it as a good sign when she had opened the door and Reed's jaw had fallen open. Even now she felt his intense gaze on her back as she held her hand out to the manager for him to shake.

"Hi, Kalina A—McAndrews," she introduced herself, remembering to use Reed's last name, since the manager probably knew it, as it was on the room reservation. "I'm really sorry for the damage we caused, and we'll reimburse the hotel, but as you can see, I'm totally fine. As my husband said, we got a little...carried away."

Heat flamed up in her cheeks, with her embarrassment, and she used it to her advantage, adding a coy smile to her face as she glanced toward the floor.

The manager stared at her a long moment before he gave a stiff nod. "As long as you're sure that there's nothing wrong..." He let the sentence trail off, shooting glances between Reed and her.

"Actually," Reed said from behind her, "would you mind checking to see if you have another room available?" He held his hand out to the manager, and slipped a few bills into the man's hand. Leena couldn't see how much it was, but when the manager's eyes widened, she knew that they weren't singles. "We will try to leave the new one the way that we found it, but I won't make any promises." As he said the last, Reed placed his hand around Leena's waist and pulled her closer to him. She looked up just in time to see him waggle his eyebrows at the other men. Dead...he was a dead man.

"Yes sir," the man said, "we'll have one made ready for you right away."

"No need to rush, give us about an hour to pack our things back up."

The men filed out of the room, and when Reed closed the door behind them, Leena threw a punch into his chest. He rubbed the spot that she hit, but the grin never left his face.

"You're incorrigible. Now I see how you and Shaun are such close friends." When all he did was continue to grin at her, she asked, "Why did you tell him that we needed an hour to pack, anyway? Practically everything we brought is still packed away already."

Still he remained quiet, a mischievous spark in his eyes, until suddenly he pounced. She barely had time to register that he had moved when Reed scooped her up and threw her over his shoulder, fireman-style. Leena squealed, half-heartedly pounding against his back and yelling for him to put her down. Briefly, she thought that it was a good thing that the men were not still in the room, because she knew that her robe had ridden up and exposed her most private areas.

Before long, Leena was tossed onto the bed, with several wood splinters scattered around her. She didn't have long to dwell on that fact, because within seconds Reed was slinking up her body and tugging at the cord at her waist. He nuzzled the tender skin just under her navel, and a delicious tremor ran through her body. A distant part of her recognized that her vulnerable belly was exposed and under the teeth of a dominant werewolf, but even that part of her lost all train of thought when Reed kissed his way down her stomach, until he paused between her legs.

When his tongue darted out to lap at her still sensitive flesh, it was all she could do to throw her head back and try to muffle the scream the threatened to break from her. With a few passes of his tongue, Reed had her writhing and fisting his hair through her fingers, until she realized how hard she squeezed and moved her hands to the comforter. She heard the fabric tear, but couldn't bring herself to care, especially when his teeth grazed her most sensitive area and the room imploded around her.

Leena barely had a chance to recover before she was flipped onto her stomach, face down in the mattress, with Reed nipping his way up her body until he hovered over her. He tilted her hips up just enough for him to slam his way home. With his second thrust he tucked his arm under her torso, bringing her back flush against his chest without letting his extraordinary weight pin her down.

As he picked up the pace, his nips became more fervent, and with each pierce of his teeth on her skin Leena was brought back to the precipice. Reed slammed his hips against her, and with one final thrust his teeth latched onto her shoulder, puncturing through her flesh. Instead of the expected pain, intense pleasure ripped through her, and she knew that the scream that was wrenched from her with her release would be heard from every patron on their floor, even after turning her face into the mattress.

Leena tried to tuck her arms underneath herself to push herself up from the mattress, but her arms were inefficient. Her limbs felt as if they had been replaced by Jell-O. Even if Reed hadn't been sprawled across her back, she doubted she'd be able to move.

As if he read her mind, Reed rolled to his side, and with his arms still wrapped around her torso, he turned Leena with him. Leena closed her eyes, realizing for the first time since they had returned from hunting the rogue just how tired she really was. Distantly she felt Reed's tongue lap at her shoulder where he'd bitten her, and the trace of his fingertip on her tattoos before the darkness consumed her.

Reed held Leena in his arms for a while longer, until he heard the elevator ding outside their room. Gently he tucked Leena back into her robe, which fortunately was still underneath her, making it much easier on him. He slipped his slacks back on, and made it to the front door before the manager had the opportunity to knock and wake her. He accepted the new key cards from the manager, and placed a few more bills into the man's hand along with one of Reed's business cards, in case there was a problem with replacing the furniture in the room. Not that he anticipated a problem. Not only had he given the man a substantial amount of cash, but the room was under Reed's credit card which had no limit.

After the manager departed, Reed carried his and Leena's bags to the new room before coming back for her. He knew that she had been tired, but when he carried her to the elevator, up two floors, and down the hall without her stirring in the slightest he knew that he'd taken it too far with his second assault on her.

Seeing her limp form as he carried her through the hotel squeezed at his heart until an image of her tucked under him as he sheathed himself within her body came to him. If he had to carry her around for days, it would have been worth it. Already his body was recovered and ready for her.

It wasn't lost on him that over the past one hundred and ninety-two years he hadn't felt the urge to copulate more than once every few years, and in the matter of a few hours he had become addicted to sex, so long as it was with Leena.

When he thought on it, he did have several decades to make up time for, so she had better prepare herself.

With a huge grin on his face, he deposited his sleeping beauty onto their new hotel bed, relieving her of her robe before slipping her under the comforter. He relieved himself of his own clothing once more before joining her under the blanket, tucking her tightly against his body. As Reed drifted off to sleep, his mind offered up several different ways for him to wake Leena in the morning.

That night had been the best night's sleep that Reed had ever had.

Chapter Nineteen

When Leena had awoken the next morning, it was to the most amazing feeling in the world. Her leg had been draped over Reed's hip, and he was easing his way into her. After another bout of mind-blowing sex, Reed had drifted off to sleep again, leaving Leena wide awake and staring at the serene face of the most amazing man she had ever met.

Yes, Reed was gorgeous, any woman with eyes and half a brain could attest to that, but her attraction to him had grown deeper than that. He was so fierce and protective, and though he spent a large portion of his time with a scowl on his face, when he smiled he lit up a room. When he fought, he could be vicious and calculating—as she had seen the previous night—but with her he was thoughtful and tender, carrying her to their new suite so that she could continue to sleep.

Leena knew that Reed had always had a rough go at life, especially once his ability started to come in, but it never stopped him from showing compassion for someone else's suffrage and it never hindered him from trying to find his own happiness in the world. She loved that he continued to be optimistic after a century and a half, and she only hoped that she could continue to be a part of his happiness.

They hadn't known each other for very long, and truth be told they had gotten off to a rocky start, but when Leena thought on it now, she couldn't imagine going back to a life without Reed. He was quickly becoming the center of her world. When she looked into his beautiful green eyes, all of the hurt and anger that she should be feeling was non-existent. Jason's betrayal, James going after her family, being turned into a werewolf, it all brought her to this wonderful man.

In all her life, Leena never imagined that she could be so happy. She tried to remember that feeling now, as she sat on one of the sofas of the living area in their suite. It had been three days since she awoke in Reed's embrace, and while every morning since he seemed to find a new way to wake her, this afternoon had gone downhill swiftly.

They still hadn't been able to find James, and since the full moon was approaching, Reed had started to grow restless. Even though James hadn't killed anyone else over the last few days, Reed had a feeling that if the full moon came, they wouldn't be as lucky. For the first time ever, Reed had called his father to send in back-up. That alone had sent Reed's mood afoul, and it had only grown worse.

When the knock sounded on their suite door, Reed had been lost in thought. Leena opened the door to see a smiling Tresize beaming down at her. Before she could protest, the big man swept her up into a bear-hug, and planted a kiss directly on her lips. Any other man that would have tried something like that with Leena probably would have had her fist in their eye, but with Tresize, all she could manage was a yelp and a giggle when he twirled around in a circle with her still clutched in his embrace.

He set her on her feet so that he could pull Reed into a bruising hug as well, but Reed had looked less than thrilled to see his longtime friend. Leena knew that he adored the big man from the way that Reed spoke of him, so she hadn't understood why his appearance had caused Reed to shut himself off from the two of them.

Now, Reed and Tresize sat opposite each other, arguing over their next move, while Leena waited to get a word in.

She had caught on to the fact that the werewolf men in general were pigheaded and stubborn — not to mention possessive as hell — but the two in front of her were taking it to a whole new level. Neither would listen to the ideas the other had, insisting that they knew how best to approach the situation. Leena couldn't even stand to listen to it. It was like listening to two toddlers arguing over who got to be the good guy and who had to be the bad guy in a game of Cops and Robbers.

If she were being honest, she had started to tune the pair of them out until one idea was thrown out that she absolutely was not okay with.

"What if we use the sister as bait," Tresize had said.

"No!" Leena and Reed had answered in unison.

"Why not? If he's as obsessed with her as you have said, then if we moved her somewhere well away from Steven's territory, he would be sure to follow."

For the first time since they began talking, Reed actually stopped to mull over the possibility of one of Tresize's ideas.

"No," she said, even more firmly. "We are not using my sister as bait."

"It could work," Reed whispered to her, as if he thought saying the words quieter would lessen Leena's rage at the thought.

Instead of railing at him like she wanted to do, she thought of another tactic. "You could offer me up to Steven in exchange for his help."

"No!" both men snapped at her in unison.

"Well, I would walk into Steven's arms willingly before I would put my sister in harm's way."

Reed gave an exasperated sigh, but reluctantly nodded in agreement.

When the two fell back into their argument, Leena grabbed her handbag from the side table and retreated. All of this arguing had made her hungry, and she doubted that they'd even miss her while they beat on their chests and squabbled for dominance.

She knew that she was supposed to stay close to Reed, but she only planned on going to the buffet across the road. Besides, she was taking his advice. The wolf in her was growing restless from the combination of their bickering and her hunger. She was killing two birds with one stone, really, and Reed had impressed upon her the importance of not starving her wolf.

The moment Reed heard the door click shut behind Leena, he threw a punch at the man who had been one of his best friends for the better part of fifty years. "Why you?" he asked, knowing that he sounded like a whiny *arsehole*.

Of all of the people that Reed's da could have sent to help him and Leena find James, it had to be the one man that had been interested in pursuing Leena. Reed had felt Tresize's emotions when he was talking to Leena back at the house, and Reed was certain that his da would have known how the big man felt as well, since he was able to read his actual thoughts, not just his emotions.

Granted, Reed had never actually expressed his interest in Leena, but if anyone knew that he had craved her from the start it would have been his da. Was this Declan's way of telling Reed to step aside? Did his own father not think that Reed could control his ability so that he could have a physical relationship with Leena? What cut Reed deeply was that he knew that that was the precise reason that his da had sent Tresize.

Reed knew that his da was trying to protect him, but the fact that he had no faith in him was like a slap to the face. He couldn't fully blame the man considering he had been battling with getting his ability under control for over a hundred and fifty years, but it didn't stop the ache in his chest at the realization.

The one thing that his da's lack of faith had done for Reed, was to show him how much more he appreciated Leena. She had been so certain that Reed would be able to get control over the emotions that he was inundated with, and had even given him some tips on how to get control. Instead of putting distance between them, she had tested how much Reed could handle, asking him questions if she thought that he was approaching his limitations. She was the only person he had ever met that had confidence in him.

Tresize examined Reed's face, and instead of answering his question, he said, "You've fallen for her."

Reed knew that it wasn't a question but he answered it anyway. "Yes."

"I thought that I could smell you on each other, but I thought that it was from being put in a one-bedroom suite." Reed didn't respond, but Tresize didn't really need him to. The dawning was clear on his face. "Reed, you and I have been like brothers for a lifetime. You have never even spared a woman more than a second glance. If you are telling me that you have fallen in love, I would never even dream of interfering." He stood from the sofa and pulled Reed to his feet, wrapping his arms around him in a tight embrace.

"Ah, I smell it now," Tresize said as he pulled away from Reed with a devilish grin on his face. "How was it?"

Reed didn't bother pretending that he didn't know what Tresize meant. An image of Leena sprawled out on the mattress beneath him, her head thrown back in ecstasy, flashed into his brain and a slow grin tugged at his lips. The past few days with Leena, despite spending the majority of their days running around in a foreign city searching for a killer werewolf, had been the best days of Reed's life.

Tresize had used the word "love" to describe what Reed felt for Leena, and while the word hadn't come to him sooner, Reed also couldn't deny the feeling of rightness when he thought it now. She was everything he had ever been missing in his life. The light in the darkness that he been his bleak existence up to that point.

"My man, you've got it bad," Tresize said, clapping Reed on the back with a bark of laughter.

It was easy to fall into a banter with Tresize about Reed's relationship with Leena now. He spared Tresize the details, sufficing it to tell him of how he deals with his ability where Leena is concerned. He still didn't know what it was about Leena that muted her emotions, but even if they hadn't been, Reed would have found a way to make it work with her. She was worth it.

The mistake that Reed made was telling this to Tresize. While he enjoyed ribbing the others about their conquests, he had never been on the receiving end, and while it was highly annoying, it was actually rather enjoyable as well.

⊰⊱

Leena didn't know whoever thought of making an all-you-can-eat buffet with Chinese food, sushi, hibachi, and desserts, but if she ever had the chance to meet them, she would bow down at their feet. She had been fortunate enough to be seated in the far corner of the dining room, away from the prying eyes of the other patrons. It had been easy for her to pile several plates high with different foods without catching anyone's attention.

After her second plate of dessert, Leena finally felt full. She wondered if she should return to the hotel, but the thought of listening to Reed and Tresize bicker didn't appeal to her in the slightest.

Instead, she pulled a pencil and notepad from her handbag and began sketching a new dance costume. That was her plan anyway, but the only thing that would come to her mind were images of Reed. She didn't know how he had gotten under her skin in such a short time, but he had.

Two years Leena had spent with Jason and she never felt for him half of what she felt for Reed in less than a few short weeks. In fact, Leena vowed there and now to never even compare what she and Reed had to Jason ever again. The two of them weren't even in the same ballpark.

Leena glanced down at her notepad, and instead of seeing a crude sketch of a uniform, she saw a pair of eyes that even on paper, lined in graphite, bore straight into her soul. She traced one with her finger, noticing an ache in her chest as she longed to touch the real thing.

Slamming a few bills onto the table, she shoved her chair out and made to leave when the playing of violins sounded from her bag. Leena pulled out her cell phone, and swiped to answer when she saw her sister's face.

"Hey Aim, give me a minute to step outside, it's a bit loud in here." She sifted through the tables and stepped outside into the thick humidity that hadn't waned with the rising sun. "Okay, go ahead."

"Dining alone today?" a male voice asked on the other end. "Sick of Prince Charming already?"

Dawning hit at the use of the name Prince Charming. "James," she said breathlessly, as if she had been punched in the gut.

"You've learned my name," he said, "I'm flattered."

"Where is my sister?" she screamed into the phone, not caring that people walking along the sidewalk stopped to stare at her.

He snickered, a slimy, reptilian sound that caused the hairs to rise on Leena's arms. "Why, she's here of course."

Leena clutched her phone with both hands as if it were a lifesaver in a vast ocean. "Please," she whimpered, tears stinging her eyes, "don't hurt her. She has a baby that needs her."

"I will not harm her. Yet."

"What do you want?" Leena asked. He had to want something from her, this she knew. If he wanted Amy, and he wanted to turn her into a werewolf, he wouldn't have called Leena beforehand.

"You." He stated simply. "You can save your sister, if you come here and take her place."

Words escaped her. The last thing that she expected was for the werewolf that had tried to kill her a few days before wanted her to take the place of the woman that he had overlooked her for on the day that he turned her into one of his kind. On top of that, Leena thought of Reed. In her lifetime, she had never been a selfish woman, so she gave herself an allowance now as she actually considered whether or not she would be able to give Reed up.

Part of her wondered why she even questioned it. Amy was her sister. Her flesh and blood, and she had been there for Leena her entire life. The other part of her, however, recognized that after twenty-five years, Leena finally knew what she wanted in her life, and she wasn't prepared to let it go. She knew that she would, however. Leena could never live with herself if she let something happen to Amy. Not only was Amy one of the most important people in Leena's life, but she had to think about Aiden and Matt. How could she selfishly consider keeping Reed in her life, and allowing Matt to go on without Amy? And when she thought about the possibility of Aiden growing up without a mother, she knew that she would do anything in her power to keep that from happening.

"How do I know that you have my sister, and that she's still safe? You could have already tried to change her and failed."

A rustling sounded on the other end of the line before Amy's voice came through the receiver. "Lee, don't you come here. This was all my fault, don't you —" her words were cut off by a snarl that was neither human nor wolf.

"Satisfied?" James asked.

"Where do I go?" was all she said.

"Good girl. A Yellow Cab should be coming around the corner shortly to pick you up, so that you can't tip Prince Charming off as to where you're headed. If anyone follows you, I'll kill your sister faster than you can blink."

The call was ended, and Leena could do nothing but stare, unseeing at her phone, as her sister's picture lingered on the screen. Vaguely she noticed a car come to a halt in front of her, but she couldn't tear her gaze from the device in her hands. Her sister was in the hands of a murdering psychopath, and Leena couldn't even call in the cavalry to back her up with her rescue.

She had no guarantee that James would let Amy go once Leena got to him, but she had no choice. If there was even the slightest chance that she could get Amy away from James, she would do it.

Leena wasn't ready to lie down without a fight, however, as an idea came to her. As the cab driver emerged from the vehicle, Leena let her fingers fly across the screen, typing two text messages as swiftly as possible, deleting the first and moving on to the second before the cab driver stepped in front of her.

"Miss, are you ready to go?"

Briefly she wondered if the driver knew that he was working for a psychopathic lycanthrope, but decidedly didn't question it. Slipping her cell phone into her jeans pocket, instead of her handbag, Leena opened the door to the cab and slid across the seat.

As the driver pulled away from the curb, Leena spared a longing glance at the hotel, and dared to hope that she would see her Irish werewolf again soon.

Chapter Twenty

After Reed and Tresize's talk, they debated tracking down Leena and joining her for food, but decided against it. Reed hadn't needed his ability to notice Leena's growing irritation with the two of them as she sat on the sofa, thrumming her fingers against the arm. In the time that he'd known her, it had been the first time that Reed was able to feel her emotions without trying to. Her frustration had been that intense.

He could only imagine the heavy sigh that she would release upon seeing the two approach her in the dining room, and while it caused a grin to spread across his lips, he decided to spare her.

The empty room service cloches were scattered on the vacated sofa, as Reed and Tresize leaned over a map of the greater Charleston area, working together for the first time in devising a plan. More than once he thought that it would have been nice if he hadn't burned the bridge with Steven, but when he thought back to the way that Steven had looked at Leena, he wasn't sorry. Still, it would have made things a ton easier if he could, at the very least, enter the Charleston city limits.

"It was here that he crossed into Charleston?" Tresize asked, pointing to the spot on the map where Reed had been halted at the perimeter by Grayson.

"Indeed."

"And he was wounded?"

Reed nodded. "Leena threw a knife and imbedded it into his thigh. I wouldn't have believed it if I hadn't seen it for myself."

Tresize smiled, but never commented on the pride apparent in Reed's tone as he told him about Leena's knife skills. "If I had a knife thrown into my leg, I'd want to take as close to a direct path toward my house as possible." Tresize drew three parallel lines on the map, the first line connecting the starting point of the night club, to the point that Reed lost James, and continued on through Charleston and beyond. The other two lines he drew on either side of that line. "I wouldn't have gone outside of this path, knowing that running would cause the blood to flow more freely. If we're lucky, he actually lives on the other side of the city limits, and we can start there."

"It's as good a plan as any," Reed said.

He stood to get a notepad and pen from the nightstand in the bedroom so that he could write down the address. As he returned to the living area, the hotel phone rang. That was odd. Anyone who would have needed to call him would have used his cell phone number.

He threw the notepad to Tresize, and changed his course to the nearest phone. "Hello?"

"Is this Reed McAndrews?" a male voice questioned on the other end.

"It is," he answered hesitantly.

"Mr. McAndrews, My name is Rick Abrams, I work for the Pennsylvania State Police. My cousin, Kalina, asked me to give you a call at this number."

Reed knew that the dumfounded look on his face would have been comical to anyone who saw him, but he just couldn't comprehend why Leena would have had her cousin call him on their hotel phone. If she needed him, all she had to do was come back up the steps, or call him herself. He had given her his cell phone number when she had retrieved her own phone from her sister's house. "Why would she need you to call me?"

"She told me to tell you that she's sorry, but she had to let James take her, because he has Amy."

"WHAT?" he yelled into the phone. He knew that the other hotel patrons would have been able to hear his shout, but he couldn't bring himself to care.

It was a mistake, it had to be. Leena was just frustrated with him and Tresize for their petty bickering, and she decided to play a prank on them. James did not have Leena.

The denial came easily to Reed, and while a part of him wanted to believe that very thing, he also knew that Leena wouldn't go to such lengths to get back at them. She would have come up to the room, put the two of them in their places and stormed back down to the dining room, leaving them with their jaws hanging open in her wake. She would call them out on being master idiots, but she would not have brought her sister or her cousin into their tiff. That just wasn't her style.

Just after Reed processed that what Rick had told him was true, his chest tightened to a painful degree, and a howl was wrenched from him. It never even dawned on Reed that he was on the phone with a human male who knew nothing of werewolves, as the anguished cry slowly died off.

Werewolves had laws about discretion, and if Leena's cousin were to question what he heard, it could cause a large amount of trouble for their kind, whom Reed was sworn to protect with his life. For once, he couldn't bring himself to worry about the wellbeing of his people. The one woman that he had ever cared about had been taken from him. What was worse is that she didn't even call Reed to come and protect her, instead she called her cousin, a man that Reed hadn't even known existed, to have him break this news to Reed.

"Mr. McAndrews?" Rick said tentatively. Reed didn't respond, but Rick must have figured that Reed was still listening, because he continued. "Leena doesn't have much time. Her text came in about twenty minutes ago. Per her message, I tracked her cell phone's location until it stopped moving. Every bone in my body screams for me to get the police involved, but Leena's message said to give you this address and no one else."

The pain in Reed's chest lessened at his words, but it didn't recede completely. Leena was still missing. The fact that she had known that Reed would come for her was the only thing that kept Reed from tearing their room apart in a fit of rage.

"Where?" he snarled into the phone.

Rick gave him an address for a warehouse on Cainhoy Road. "And Reed?" he said just before Reed hung up the phone. "Those girls are like sisters to me; please bring them home safely."

"I will, or I'll die trying," Reed answered before dropping the receiver back onto the base.

Reed looked to Tresize and a malicious grin spread over his long-time friend's face as he cracked his knuckles. "Please tell me that we're going to kill this bastard."

"His own mother won't recognize him when we're done."

"Perfect."

In the time that they had known each other, Reed had only ever seen Tresize look fit to kill a handful of times. He was practically an oversized teddy bear, kind and nurturing to all who deserved it — and he always knew who deserved it — but the man had a particular soft spot for women and children. He was a skilled fighter on any given day, but with two women in danger, and one of them being his pack's alpha female, Tresize would be ferocious.

Initially, Reed had been upset to see the big man. Now he couldn't think of anyone else that he'd rather have by his side as he set out to find Leena and bring her home.

❦❦

Leena stood in a vacant parking lot, staring at the warehouse building in front of her. She had barely had the chance to close the door to the taxi before the driver sped off leaving her stranded. There was no turning back now, even if it had been an option before. She checked the time stamp on her phone noting that it took about twenty minutes for them to arrive at the warehouse. She just had to stall James for about thirty. Even if she couldn't deal with him on her own, she knew that Reed and Tresize could take down this lunatic, and that as soon as they got her message they would be on their way here.

She knew that it was dangerous to bring her cousin Ricky into this mess, but not knowing where she was headed meant that she couldn't risk contacting Reed on her own. That had been James' intention, after all. What he hadn't counted on was Leena's cousin working for the police. She knew that Ricky would be able to track her cell phone and give Reed her location. She just hoped that James wasn't smart enough to move them by the time Reed could catch up to her.

Stepping up toward the entrance, Leena tried to see beyond the glass door, but the interior was too dark for her to make anything out. With a deep breath, she pulled the handle, bracing herself for a possible attack. None came. She entered the small office and waited for her eyes to adjust to the dark before proceeding to the only other door in the room.

This time when she wrenched the door open, a figure stood on the other side, waiting for her. She threw a punch, but the stronger man caught her fist in his hand and squeezed. With his free hand, James plucked Leena's cell phone from her grasp, and she watched as he scrolled through her call log, and her messaging log.

"Who is Chloe?" he snarled.

"She's my assistant," Leena answered, her chin jutting forward stubbornly. "I have a dance studio, and if you're insisting on me being here with you, I needed to let her know that she needs to cancel my classes."

He stared into her face a long moment before giving a short nod and releasing her fist. Her phone, however, he did not return to her. Instead he dropped it onto the cement floor and smashed it with his foot. "Hey!" she screamed at him. "I just got that damn thing back!"

Without responding to her, James turned and walked away from her, to the far corner of the warehouse. Leena had no choice but to follow him, taking in her surroundings as she went. It wasn't until she was almost at the other end of the warehouse that she saw her sister lying on the ground.

Leena moved to run to Amy's side, but James held her back.

"Let me go," she snapped.

James growled at her, but Leena didn't back down. She wrenched her arm from his grasp and ran, dropping to her knees next to her sister.

"Amy," she whispered, lightly smacking her cheeks to rouse her. She looked up to James who had followed her. "What have you done to her? You knew that I was on my way here to take her place!"

A sneer crossed his face. "Did you honestly think that I would let her leave? She is my insurance."

Leena didn't respond to him. She just turned back to Amy's prone body and continued to slap her cheeks. "Amy! Wake up!" Tears stung at her eyes, as Leena searched frantically for a pulse at her sister's wrist, and then neck. It was there, thank goodness. It was faint, but steady.

"Calm yourself, woman. She's merely drugged."

"You gave her way too much! She's just a human. Is that how you get your pleasures? By torturing and killing human women?"

"They were never meant to die!" he roared, knocking a stack of shelves to the ground in a fit of rage.

"Oh, that was convincing," she said, letting the sarcasm drip from her words. "Please, continue to tell me how you didn't intend to hurt those women as you throw a tantrum and my sister lays unconscious on the ground with enough drugs to put down an elephant."

Blinded by his anger, James wrapped his fist in the front of Leena's shirt and pulled her up from the ground. She was nose to nose with the maniacal werewolf as he snarled in her face. "They were meant to live! I had intended to change them, not kill them!"

Leena let herself mull that over for a second before responding. Just because he hadn't intended to kill those women, didn't change the fact that that's what happened. "Why try to change them? There aren't enough werewolves in the world for you?"

Slowly James lowered Leena back down to her feet, turning away from her so that she couldn't see his face as he spoke.

"You couldn't possibly understand what it's like to live for hundreds of years with no one by your side. No mate, no children. Every day is lonelier than the previous. I've tried going after werewolf women, but there are few under Steven's rule, and even fewer that are available to court."

Leena never expected James to be so forthright with his explanation, and even less had she expected him to seem almost normal with his response. She thought that James would have been a raving lunatic, but as he spoke, she could see that he was sound of mind…mostly.

He spoke of his loneliness, and with each word Leena could hear the hollowness in his voice. However, it didn't stop her from goading him, as she expelled a breath between her teeth. "Pfft, you think that's an excuse to take a woman's life?" He whipped back in her direction with a glare that would have told anyone else to shut their mouth, but Leena continued. "Why did it have to be a werewolf woman? There are other Shifters, not to mention that you could have dated a human woman. Besides, you didn't even know those women! What if you had been successful in changing them, and decided that you didn't *want* to live with them for the rest of your life? Had you thought of that?"

"The thought has recently crossed my mind," he said pointedly.

It was intended as an insult, Leena knew, but she didn't let it bother her. This idiot may not care for her, or her big mouth, but she had someone that did. She just had to hold out a bit longer for him to come for her.

"So, that's your plan," she said sardonically. "To force me to live with you for the rest of our lives, bear your children, and have us hate each other for the next few hundred years, all because I was the one woman who survived being changed by you?" By the look in his eye, Leena knew that was exactly what he had planned. "What would you do to keep me with you? Hold my sister hostage for a few decades? Keep her away from her son so that you can have your own children? Did you think about anyone besides yourself when you devised this harebrained scheme of yours?"

"Enough!" He barely had the word out when the back of his hand connected with Leena's cheek. The slap of his skin against hers reverberated through the empty warehouse, muffling the sound of her cheekbone cracking.

The sting brought tears to Leena's eyes, but she refused to let them fall. She wouldn't give him the satisfaction. Instead, she blinked them back, and glared daggers at the asshole in front of her. She had started to feel slightly sorry for James, understanding how lonely he must have felt all these years, even if she hadn't agreed with the way he had handled it. Now, the only thing she felt for him was hatred. He would die today, she would see to it.

"Have I struck a nerve? What was it, that you hadn't considered anyone but yourself, or that you're planning to keep me with you for the rest of my life when you haven't even been able to get through the past ten minutes?"

James swung at her again, but this time she was ready for it and ducked, throwing her own punch into his gut. He doubled-over in pain, but recovered quickly, the look in his eyes showing her that he wanted her dead as much as she did him.

It hadn't been her intention to start this fight with him. She had been trying to stall him for as long as possible in order to give Reed time to arrive, but now that it had started, there was no backing down. Leena only wished that she had taken her dagger with her when she had gone to eat earlier.

Slowly, methodically, James began to circle her. She joined him in his deadly dance, not wanting to give him an opportunity to take her by surprise. After several moments, he lunged at her, and Leena spun to the side to dodge him. When he came after her again, Leena made a mistake and paid for it dearly. A punch landed at the base of her sternum, knocking the wind out of her. It took her a moment to catch her breath, and in that short amount of time, James had flipped her flat on her back glaring up at him before she could finish inhaling.

The smug look on his face told Leena that he thought that he had her in a precarious position, but when he took a step closer to her, Leena swept her leg under his, knocking him off of his feet. His stumble gave her just enough time to jump back to her feet before he was on her again.

Punch after punch, kick after kick, they fought. Leena tried her damnedest to tire him out, but the man was resilient.

When finally the exhaustion started to show on Leena's face, James sneered at her. "You know, I think I'll change your sister after all; and with no need for you any longer, I think that I'll enjoy tearing the skin from your bones and watching you try to regenerate it."

As he threw another punch, Leena blocked, her reactions slowing. She sent out a silent prayer that the cavalry would come crashing in already, because she didn't think that she could hold him off much longer.

⊰ঔৈ⊱

"Reed, slow the fuck down!" Tresize called out from the seat next to him. "We will be of no use to Leena if you kill us in a crash."

"We likely wouldn't die, just break several bones."

"Breaks that would take time to heal. Would you rather have to sit still waiting for a few bones to stitch back together, or would you rather slow this truck down to only twenty miles over the speed limit?"

Reed actually had to stop and think about it before he slowed the truck by five miles per hour. From the corner of his eye, he could see Tresize shake his head at him, but there was nothing more that he could do to placate the man. The reasonable side of him knew that he needed to take more care with his driving, but the side of him that could see reason was far overshadowed by his need to protect his mate.

Even when he told himself that Leena wasn't his mate, the cloying need to get to her and keep her safe did not subside.

In his lifetime, Reed never thought that he would actually find a woman that he wanted to share every moment of the rest of his life with. He had hoped, but deep down he always thought that it was futile. Often he had wondered if the gods had a sick sense of humor, but now he knew that he had just needed to wait for her to come into his life.

It sounded like a cheesy line pulled from one of those romance movies, and he knew that if he had verbalized it to any one of his friends they would tease him mercilessly, but with every fiber within his soul he felt that it was true.

Now that Leena had come into Reed's life, he couldn't believe that the gods would be cruel enough to take her from him now. He briefly tried to imagine going back to his former existence, and he knew without a doubt that he would not be able to. Without regard for Tresize's previous warnings, Reed pressed his foot back down on the accelerator and passed a Buick in the opposite lane of traffic. The Buick and the Charger that was coming in the opposite direction both blared on their horns as Reed swiftly cut back over in front of the Buick.

Reed could feel the anxiety coming from Tresize, but decided to ignore it. If they made it through this, he would get over it.

They drove another few streets at speeds that would have gotten Reed arrested if he had passed a cop. Although, if he would have been thinking about it sooner he would have noticed that not only had he not come across any police officers, but every traffic light that he approached seemed to change from red to green before he got to the intersections. He briefly wondered if Leena's cousin had something to do with that small mercy.

When they pulled into the parking lot of the warehouse that Leena's GPS had last shown her, Reed slammed his foot on the brake, and jumped out of the truck, not bothering to concern himself with turning the truck off. If someone wanted it, they could have it.

He ran to the door of the warehouse ready to tear the flesh from James if he had harmed one hair on Leena's head. When he wrenched the door open, the door fell from its hinges and Reed dropped it to the ground, not bothering to care that the shattering glass probably tipped James off to their presence — if they were still inside.

Another door stood before him, and Reed had that one torn from the frame as well, despite it being made of steel. When he stormed through the gaping hole in the wall, his vision turned to red when he saw Leena and Amy lying face down on the concrete floor, both seeming to be unconscious as James loomed over Leena's body.

Reed let out a wolfish howl before tearing his shirt from his body and calling his wolf to him. He knew that the change was risky with James so close to him, but his wolf would not be denied this kill. He had just enough clarity left in him to see Leena turn her head toward him and whisper his name before her eyes closed again.

Chapter Twenty-One

Leena didn't know how long she had been unconscious — the last blow that James had hit her with had knocked her off of her feet. The only thing that she knew was that she was stirred by the sound of a wolfish howl echoing through the barren warehouse. She turned her head toward the source of the howl and was greeted by an image of a shirtless Reed. At first she thought that her brain was offering up beautiful images to help her cope with the pain.

When she whispered his name, his face contorted, and the look of pure rage turned to one slightly more calculating before his bones started snapping and his flesh shifted to accommodate his new frame.

No way would her brain offer up such a gruesome image to placate her. He was really here. She closed her eyes and let out a breath of relief before reaching for her sister's hand. He came for her. She knew that he would come.

Leena forced her eyes to reopen just in time to see a black wolf soaring through the air toward James. Leena struggled to keep consciousness as she watched the wolf fight James in his human form. They circled each other, Reed darting closer to tear strips out of James' flesh and scurrying away faster than her addled brain could follow.

One thing that she had been able to comprehend was the loss of her sister's hand in hers as Tresize lifted Amy into his arms as if she weighed no more than child. He bent down next to Leena with Amy still in his arms, but after her reassurances that she was fine, the big man followed her orders to leave her on the concrete floor and take her sister away from the warehouse.

When Leena was able to bring her attention back to the battle going on around her, she had a hard time focusing on anything but the amount of blood that was spattered all over the floor, not to mention on both James and Reed. She couldn't tell who had been more severely injured, she could only pray that it wasn't Reed as she watched him sink his teeth into James once more.

Darkness overtook her once more, and when she opened her eyes again it was to a familiar sight. She was scooped up off of the concrete floor and pressed against a bared chest. She took a deep breath, taking in the scent of the man that had saved her life once before in this manner. She wrapped her arms around his neck and nuzzled in closer before she allowed herself to be taken completely by the darkness.

❧☙

If Reed could have resurrected James just to have the satisfaction of tearing his head from his body once more, he would have. He deposited Leena on the front seat of his truck and examined her injuries. A few broken bones, several cuts, and more bruises than he could count. The only thing that kept Reed from going absolutely crazed with fury was the knowledge that all of those injuries would be healed by the morning. Her sister, on the other hand needed a hospital. James had pumped her full of enough tranquilizer to put down a fully grown male werewolf. It said something for the strength of the Abrams women that Amy was still breathing, however faintly.

He left Leena in the truck to rest, as he rejoined Tresize back in the warehouse. As he entered the room, Reed saw the big man fishing through the pockets of the prone figure on the floor until he pulled out a set of keys.

"I was going to take his car to get Amy to the hospital," Tresize said.

Reed nodded. "Yes, do that. I will clean up here and when Leena wakes, we will meet you there."

With a quick pat on Reed's back, Tresize left the warehouse without another word. Reed took a quick glance around, his gaze landing on the severed limbs of the man who had attempted to take everything from him. Any other rogue wolf, and Reed would have said that the removal of his arms and legs as well as his head may have been overkill. As he looked at James' body, he wished that the man had another limb that he could rip from his body.

After finding a tarp, Reed put James' remains onto the plastic before going outside. He shifted back into his wolf form and used his claws to dig a hole between the trees. As the dirt gave way beneath his claws, he thought more than once how much easier this would be if he possessed Leena's ability.

Even without Leena's gift, he was able to make relatively short work of disposing James' body. With a bit of bleach that he found in a storage closet, the warehouse was cleared of all evidence of what had occurred there that day. The doors on the other hand, were irreparable. Still, Reed propped the steel slabs against what remained of the door jambs.

When he returned to his truck, Leena had finally come to, her bruises already reduced to a pale green. When he opened the door, she slid across the seat to him, grasping his face between her hands. He was hit with her overwhelming relief before she claimed his mouth in a possessive kiss. She was safe, her sister would be safe, and James was no more. Everything was falling into place, and they could finally go home and get started with their lives.

Four moons had passed since that day at the warehouse, and those months had been everything that Reed could have ever hoped for and more. There had been a few things to overcome, such as the challenges from a few of their females that Leena was presented with. She had been able to dispose of Annabelle's clique as quickly as, and even more efficiently than she had with Annabelle herself. It had been weeks since she had been approached for a fight. It was in those weeks of peace that he was finally able to get her to agree to this.

He stood in the courtyard of stone, outside of his father's home, surrounded by his closest friends and family. He had made Leena a promise that day in the night club, and he meant to keep it. She walked toward him, arm-in-arm with her sister, Amy. Amy had recovered from the tranquilizers that James had pumped through her system and had flown to town on the pack's private jet for the occasion.

The two sisters stopped in front of Reed and his brother Corrick. They smiled at each other before Amy brushed a kiss on Leena's cheek and placed her hand in Reed's. He had promised he would take her to a mating ritual, but at that moment he had never imagined that it would be theirs. As the sun set, the slightest wisp of the moon could be seen through the clearing in the trees. The two of them knelt on the stone and called their wolves to the fore. As his da chanted a few words in ancient Gaelic, Reed sunk his teeth into the shoulder of the light brown wolf in front of him. She followed his lead, sinking her teeth into his own flesh. There should have been pain, but there was none. There was only joy as the realization that the one thing that he had waited one-hundred-and-ninety-wo years to find was finally his. His mate. He howled his delight to the waxing moon, practically oblivious to the guests around them shedding their human sides and preparing for the night under the full moon. The only thing that he registered were her sapphire eyes staring into his own.

Made in the USA
Columbia, SC
03 December 2017